TUDOR DAWN

The Tudor Saga Series
Book One

David Field

SAPERE
BOOKS

TUDOR DAWN

Published by Sapere Books.

20 Windermere Drive, Leeds, England, LS17 7UZ,
United Kingdom

saperebooks.com

ISBN: 978-1-913028-39-8

'The king was in his counting house, counting out his money,
The queen was in the parlour, eating bread and honey'

Extract from the children's nursery rhyme 'Sing a Song of Sixpence', popularly believed to be a reference to Henry VII and his queen, Elizabeth of York

PART I

I

Twelve-year-old Henry, Second Earl of Richmond, sat hunched in front of the roaring fire in the Great Hall of Pembroke Castle, shivering uncontrollably despite the heavy cloaks that the grooms kept piling onto his shoulders and the mulled herbs that servant girls would periodically bring up from the kitchen, on strict orders from the physician. Henry was suffering another of his agues and he knew from sorry experience that in spite of all the excessive solicitations being fawned upon him, it would last at least another two days.

The door burst open and 'Black William' Herbert stamped in with his usual lack of grace. Throwing himself onto the bench beside Henry, he removed his boots and hurled them towards a corner of the fireplace, stretching his stockinged feet towards the blaze.

'God's tits, it's a cold one out there,' he complained.

Henry wrinkled his nose, partly against the blasphemy of the man and partly against the rank smell of his stockinged feet, which had no doubt been imprisoned in riding boots since sunrise. William enjoyed his hunting and it was to be doubted whether any wild boar still existed within a fifty league radius of Pembroke; however, in their absence William was not above driving an elderly or weak peasant into the undergrowth, though very few of the castle's retinue could be persuaded to join him on his forays of butchery.

'How goes your ague?' Herbert enquired, as if he cared.

Henry sniffled in response and wiped his running nose on yet another kitchen cloth before hurling it into the open fire. 'It will be gone ere the banquet,' he assured his questioner. 'When does my mother come from Woking?'

'Three days hence, before nightfall, according to the Steward,' Herbert replied. 'Sir Henry must first attend to a matter at Court, then they ride west, breaking their journey first at the castle at Kenilworth. It seems they are held in high regard by the Earl of Warwick.'

Henry's mother, Margaret Beaufort, had given birth to Henry — with considerable difficulty, as she was wont to remind him — at the age of thirteen. His father Edmund's untimely death of the Plague whilst being held a prisoner in Carmarthen Castle by William Herbert — the same William Herbert who now held the young Henry a virtual captive in Pembroke — had left his mother a widow at fourteen. Not only had Herbert been indirectly responsible for Henry's father's death, but he had also been granted his Uncle Jasper's lands and title when he fled into exile, leaving Henry at the mercy of Edward IV, and his mother a homeless widow.

Sir Henry Stafford, a staunch Yorkist, had married his mother when she had been a widow barely a year and the boy had seen little of her since. He had grown up more familiar with the professional embraces of a succession of nurses than the more natural ones of his birth mother, who was, with her new husband, now regularly at the Court of Edward IV.

Mother and stepfather were due to visit Pembroke for only the fifth time in as many years. Henry, for his part, had little regard for the man who had replaced his father in his mother's bed and only wished for the return from self-imposed exile of his uncle, Jasper, who had been more like a father to him for several years, before being obliged to flee the country when Henry VI was deposed by Warwick and Jasper was attainted for treason for his support for the former Lancastrian King. It was through Jasper that Henry had been made aware of a more romantic side to his ancestry. He could trace his Tudor bloodlines all the way back to the legendry Cadwaladr of Anglesey, who the Welsh regarded as the last of the ancient Celtic Kings. It had also been whispered to him that Welsh folklore foretold the return of a hero called 'The Son of Prophecy' by the bardish poets, who would pick up the mantle laid down by the likes of Owain Glyndwr and, before him, the magical Arthur Pendragon himself and lead the people of Wales to a new freedom.

'Will they be tarrying long?' Henry asked Herbert hopefully.

The older man inclined his head both ways, in a gesture of uncertainty. 'That will depend upon how matters go at Court, and whether the King has other duties for your stepfather.'

'Other duties?' Henry echoed.

'Duties other than keeping a hawk's eye on me,' Herbert replied with a sneer.

'Why does King Edward wish to keep an eye on you?' Henry asked, more out of politeness than anything.

Herbert narrowed his eyes as he turned fully to confront Henry on the bench where they both sat. 'Because *I* keep an eye on *you*,' Herbert told him. 'Your family's loyalty to the cause of Lancaster is an open secret and you are its most obvious pawn in the game, should the witless Henry not regain his reason.'

'Do they then keep such an eye on my mother?' Henry countered. 'If so, then it must be a kindly eye, for her letters are full of the fine compliments she receives from the royal couple.'

'From the Woodville whore, you mean,' Herbert sneered back. 'They say she bewitched young Edward, as she has no doubt bewitched your mother. As for why your mother is received so regularly at Court, there is an old saying that you must keep your enemies closer to hand than your friends.'

'Is that why you keep me so closely confined?' Henry challenged him.

'You would do well to keep a civil tongue in your head,' Herbert warned him. 'Those who have crossed me in the past have not lived long enough to reflect on their error. Now, I must leave you to contemplate the faces in the fire, ere I contract your contagion.' Herbert stood up, retrieved his boots from the side of the fireplace and shuffled to the door in his stockinged feet. He dropped the boots in the hallway outside and bellowed for one of the grooms to collect and clean them, before slamming the door behind him.

Henry sighed despondently and stood up. His legs felt weak and he persuaded himself that he must exercise them, before he lost all power of motion. It was a large hall, with many tapestries with which Henry had become over-familiar during his enforced leisure, while seeking excuses to put down the scholarly works that his tutor insisted that he study. He was an indifferent scholar and had no calling for the French, Latin and Greek that he was forced to consume twice daily. Nor was he interested in more manly pursuits, which was perhaps as well, since he was rarely allowed outdoors, and even then only with a heavily armed escort of surly-looking retainers who were clearly not employed by William Herbert for either their natural charm or their powers of conversation.

But he found relief, and pleasure of sorts, in the neatly-woven tapestries that kept the howling coastal wind from blowing out the candles that were lit daily to lighten the gloom of a Welsh winter. They were wool on linen and as Henry examined the fine weft carefully he mused over how long each one would have taken to work. His favourite was at the far end, on the wall behind the Steward's post. It was a full-length depiction of St. George, surrounded by saintly figures wearing surcoats on which were emblazoned the dragon of Wales; St. George himself, while wearing the more familiar red cross on the front of his surcoat, displayed the portcullis emblem of Henry's mother's Beaufort family underneath. The tapestry had been designed by Jasper and worked by nuns in a nearby convent. In happier days, little Henry had been carried on the pommel of his uncle's saddle to watch the holy women at work and they had each placed a hand on his head and called down a blessing on his soul. 'See how they revere you?' his uncle had said, 'and they being brides of Christ, sworn only to worship God. See that you do not betray their faith in *you* also.'

II

Three evenings later, Henry was looking down anxiously from his chamber window into the courtyard, as the retinue began to dismount and hand their bridles to the grooms. His mother was lifted from her side saddle by the still youthful Henry Stafford and as her feet found the solid ground she was seen to reach up for a kiss from him. Henry turned away in embarrassment and shame — his own mother, in the forecourt of the castle in which she had obtained sanctuary through her brother-in-law, the castle that housed her only son by a man who had fought for what he believed to be right and had not simply twisted and turned with the vagaries of the Court wind.

It was too much to hope that she would visit his sick chamber and within the hour a page knocked quietly and entered with the message that 'the Countess' wished to see him in her chambers. Henry changed into his favourite blue surcoat, checked his brown hose for flaws, smoothed his thin hair down under his bonnet and walked down the upper hallway to where his mother and Stafford were being accommodated in the guest quarters. He knocked on the heavily studded door. A groom pulled it open and Henry caught sight of his stepfather stepping swiftly into an adjoining chamber before his mother strode forward to meet him, stopping sharply a few feet from his dutifully outstretched arms.

'They tell me you were sick with the ague. Has it left you?'

'Yes, Mother,' Henry smiled indulgently. 'It is safe — as ever — to embrace me.'

She hugged him warmly to her, before whispering, 'Have a care of what we speak — I trust not Sir Henry's loyalty.'

'Yet you sleep with him?' Henry whispered back, before his mother cut in more loudly.

'My darling boy — how you have grown! This Welsh air obviously favours your natural humour.'

'It must therefore be a humour of driving rain and endless sea fog,' Henry quipped back. 'Had I the constitution of a frog it would suit me well. As it is, it gives me nothing but shivers that would unseat a cathedral statue and a nose that runs more freely than the Severn at high tide.'

A few minutes later, a page entered with a tray on which sat a flagon of Rhenish wine and two goblets. The colour rose briefly in Margaret's face before she controlled her irritation and asked the page, 'Were you not informed that Sir Henry is with us, boy? Why are there only two goblets?'

The page dropped his glance to the floor and spoke with the heavily accented Welsh form of English that Henry had learned to interpret. 'Sir Henry is below, isn't it, Countess.'

'Where exactly below?'

'In the Master's Chambers, where I served them both wine lastly before coming up here.'

'Set the wine down on that side table and both of you may leave us.'

As the boys backed out into the corridor, closing the door deferentially behind them, Margaret slipped silently to the door of the adjoining chamber and peered in. Nodding with satisfaction, she beckoned Henry to the double seat in the window from where she could keep an eye on the adjoining chamber whose door she had left wide open.

'We do not have long to talk, but there will shortly be a challenge to the throne.'

'Another one? After the last, my uncle was forced to flee to France — will I lose *you* as well this time?'

'Hush child, and listen. It is not I who will be at risk this time, but yourself.'

'How can this be, while I am condemned to sit behind these dripping walls and listen to the rain and wind as they conspire to batter the sea birds into mere bundles of wet feathers?'

'Because of who you are, and who I am.'

'We are both mortal and we are both at the whim of the Yorkist usurper. Was it ever any different?'

Margaret pressed her fingers to his lips in a sign for him to remain silent, then lowered her voice. 'It is talk such as that as will lead to your downfall. Once the uprising takes hold they will be seeking sacrifices and will search every nook and cranny of the nation until they find someone to blame and execute. You — and to some extent I — have the most to gain should Henry be restored to his rightful throne.

'Warwick has fallen out badly with King Edward, because of his marriage to Elizabeth Woodville, which has led to the ascendency at court of the Woodville family, some of whom have been granted positions of great office. The Woodvilles are also inclined towards the house of Lancaster and Warwick seeks to promote his own cause further by replacing Edward on the throne with his brother Clarence. He aspires to marry his own daughter Isabella to Clarence, so that she may become Queen, but Edward opposes that marriage as well.'

'Is there anything that Warwick does that is *not* opposed by the King?'

'Warwick is by far the most powerful noble in the land and the King would do well to appreciate that, if he wishes to retain his throne.' She lowered her voice as she continued to explain. 'I have of late been allowed access to the former King

Henry, who languishes in the Tower. He was a great friend to your late father and his queen Margaret and I were once on intimate terms. His wits are much restored and in return for my visits — that were made possible through the Constable of the Tower, who is secretly also in the pay of Warwick — I was instructed to pass letters between Henry and Margaret, who is currently in France, amassing her own army. These letters were entrusted to one of Warwick's men, who I dare not name since he is close to the throne, but he in turn conveyed the letters via Yorkshire, where another trusted Warwick captain is raising his own force. It is all designed to restore King Henry to his rightful throne.'

Henry shook his head and smiled. 'Dearest mother, this is obviously something close to your heart, but my head spins with all this detail. As I understand it, there is to be a rebellion based in Yorkshire and yet the King is himself a Yorkist, is he not? Why would Yorkist supporters seek to restore a Lancastrian monarch to his throne?'

Margaret sighed. 'You have much to learn about statecraft. The House of York is divided in many ways and no less so since King Edward took up with the Woodvilles. If Edward is deposed, Clarence becomes the next in line and he is thick with Warwick.'

'But none of these would seek to restore the Lancastrian Henry to his rightful throne, surely?'

'The restored Henry would owe everything to Warwick, who seeks only to continue wielding a power greater than the King. When the wind so directs him, Warwick may well choose to restore a Yorkist, if it suits his purpose. No doubt, when the time is right, he will depose Henry again and replace him with Clarence.'

'And what thinks this powerful Warwick of we followers of Lancaster?'

'A poison that must be swallowed, it would seem, if his ambitions are to be satisfied. But should aught go wrong, do not doubt that he will seek to blame everything on the Lancaster cause and those who are known to be loyal to it will be imperilled. Hence my warning you to be circumspect in your dealings and wary of who you contact.'

Henry laughed ironically. 'My only "contacts", as you call them, are with the Steward of Pembroke Castle, my tutor, and a few scrofulous local children who pass for pages and serving girls. But if we are discussing dangerous contacts, do you not share a marriage bed with a man loyal to King Edward?'

Margaret blushed briefly, but was determined to get her point across. 'There is no accounting for love and I dearly love Sir Henry. But, as you rightly say, he is closely bound to the King, particularly after he graciously gave dispensation for our marriage. Should there be a general call to arms against any uprising in the north, be assured that my husband will loyally perform the knight service in return for which he holds his lands. There is also much personal warmth between him and King Edward, who but two years ago graced us with his presence on our estate at Woking.'

'So you really came here to warn *me*, while going behind your husband's back?' Henry pointed out. 'And I fondly imagined that for once you had remembered my birthday — it was some six weeks ago, on the twentieth-eighth of January, in case you *had* forgotten. It is now March.'

Margaret slapped Henry playfully across the head, pulled him towards her and kissed his cheek. 'You were ever an impudent, disrespectful boy. There was a horse in our train loaded solely with gifts. Who shall I give them to *now*, I wonder?'

Henry laughed lightly and pulled away from her, standing up to his full height, which for a boy of twelve was not great. 'I thank you for the presents and for your motherly concern. I must now give *you* fair warning — the castle cook is a hopeless soak and her food is more of a threat to my continued health than any Earl of Warwick.'

Henry spent an uncomfortable hour or two at the banquet, seated at the head table with only his mother between himself and Stafford and William Herbert on his right, drunk as usual. Stafford was his typical nervous self, attempting to establish some sort of relationship with his stepson, but clearly anxious not to give anyone cause to accuse him of being too close with a Lancaster. In a perverse way, Henry felt sorry for him, although he resented his mother's obvious affection for the man who wasn't his father.

Herbert was as boorish as ever, snarling at the serving boys and fondling the bottom of the poor girl who was kept busy filling his wine goblet from a jug that seemed almost as heavy as she was. At one point Herbert spat out a piece of mutton fat and turned to Henry. 'Does your tutor teach you mathematick?'

'Numbers, certainly,' Henry replied guardedly, as he chewed nauseously on a piece of chicken that had been stuffed with God knew what and tried to swill away its taste with a mouthful of small beer. 'I have no gift for anything else, I am told, and certainly not what my tutor calls the geometry of Euclid, whatever that may be.'

'Numbers will be sufficient,' Herbert conceded. 'The Steward's eyes are failing him and of late his management of the estate accounts has been careless. Perhaps you might earn your keep by assisting him — it will also help to fill those hours in which you seem to dream idly around the place.'

Two days later, Henry was introduced to the intriguing world of estate accounts and found that his aptitude for numbers was greater than his doubting tutor had given him credit for. It was simply a matter of ensuring that the totals in the right-hand column, which recorded all the estate outlays, did not exceed those on the left, which represented the sums of money with which the Steward was periodically, if grudgingly, entrusted by Herbert. Sometimes there was some left over at the end of a week and the Steward showed Henry how it could be 'carried over' to the next page and set off against future expenditure.

While Henry sat happily learning how to balance an account book, affairs of State were taking another violent turn in the north. His first inkling that his mother's predictions might be coming true was in late June. He looked up from where he was seated at the table in the Steward's pantry, assisting with the weekly balance, when the door was flung open and there stood William Herbert, dressed for a lengthy journey. By his side was a facially-scarred, shifty-looking man with weapons of various descriptions hanging from the belt of his stained tunic.

'This is Thomas Gwynne,' Herbert announced. 'I have to leave urgently on the King's business and in my absence Thomas has instructions to ensure that you do not venture beyond the castle walls. Should you do so, he has orders direct from the Earl of Warwick to slit your throat.'

For the next two months, Henry took care not to venture beyond the castle gates, content to take the summer air in the main entrance yard, while always aware of a malevolent pair of eyes glaring down at him from an upper floor whichever way he turned. On one occasion he gave Gwynne a cheeky wave, but the grimace he received in return made him unwilling to repeat the experience.

Henry learned from a letter from his mother that his regular jailor, William Herbert, had journeyed north to meet up with the King at Nottingham, ahead of marching out to confront the rebels led by Sir William Conyers. King Edward had been falsely advised by Warwick that the rebels lacked numbers and had therefore taken only a small force with him; by the time that he learned his mistake, Warwick had taken advantage of his absence from London to raise his own army, which marched north to annihilate the royal army at Edgecote Moor in Oxfordshire. At the first sight of the livery on the battle armour of Warwick's forces, Edward's troops fled from the field and William Herbert was captured and beheaded the following day.

Warwick had marched triumphantly back to London and ordered that Henry VI be released from the Tower and replaced on his throne, while his messengers were sent across the Channel to advise Queen Margaret that it was safe to come home. The opportunity was also taken to blame the Woodvilles for what had happened and a month later the head of the family, Earl Rivers, father of the now deposed Queen Elizabeth, and her brother John, were beheaded for treason at Kenilworth, after a trial that contained more show than evidence. Elizabeth herself fled to the sanctuary of Westminster Abbey with the royal children, while her husband — the deposed King Edward — was fleeing across the Channel.

Henry was pacing the castle yard one day in August when a troop of mounted knights in full armour clattered in and formed a circle around him. Believing that he had somehow strayed too far in his daily exercise, he looked fearfully up at the windows of the Great Hall, but the menacing visage of Thomas Gwynne had disappeared from sight. Several of the armed knights dismounted and disappeared into the castle, from which shouts and screams suddenly erupted. One of the knights reappeared carrying a gory bundle by its hair; Henry recognised the face of Thomas Gwynne on the severed and still dripping head, and all but fainted.

As he slid towards the ground he was grabbed by the arm and a welcome and familiar face grinned down at him.

'Now then, boy — you need a stronger stomach than that if you are to fulfil your family's destiny.'

Henry flung his arms around the man and yelled out in sheer pleasure, 'Uncle Jasper! Where did *you* come from?'

'France, most recently,' his uncle replied. 'But it is now a matter of where we are *both* going. Prepare your trunks for travel, my boy — you are to be presented at Court.'

III

Henry shuffled and squirmed in his new boots, while his mother fussily brushed the shoulders of his new blue cote-hardie to remove the dry scalp flakes from his thin light auburn hair. His uncle Jasper smiled and nodded to the courtiers gathered at the entrance door to the Painted Chamber, awaiting the summons to enter. It was late November and roaring fires had been lit in the antechamber, where lords and ladies either sweated in their finery or sought sanctuary from the heat in the far corners, while listening intently for the doors to be opened.

'Remember, when we enter, to bow the knee no less than five paces from the throne, keep your eyes on the floor and speak not until you are addressed. Even then, your head must remain down,' his mother advised Henry for the fifth time.

'The boy will acquit himself well, as befits a Tudor,' Jasper assured her. 'And the King will be more concerned for his loyalty than his Courtly manners.'

'Even so,' Margaret countered, 'there will be those who seek to portray him as a Welsh country oaf with no nobility of breeding.'

'His father was as clumsy as an ox that pulls the plough,' Jasper reminded her, 'yet King Henry loved him well enough, for his constant heart and undoubted courage. This is the court of Henry of Lancaster, not some simpering perfumed boudoir of the Dauphin.'

While they had been discussing him like some prize heifer in a county show, Henry had been gazing, awe-stricken, at the splendid crowd that filled the antechamber. Henry VI had been back in residence for several months, but held few audiences at this time, being more concerned to take up the reins of government and enjoy time with the family with which he had only lately been reunited. As far as Henry's gaze extended, the antechamber was a riot of fashionable colours and styles, the men in scarlet, silver and blue, their womenfolk in silk, damask and satin gowns in pastel shades of green, yellow and orange. Henry had never before seen women with their hair covered by such elaborate headgear; they called them 'hennins' and the long conical shapes allowed the women to hide their locks completely within them, giving a deep look to their foreheads accentuated by the severely plucked eyebrows that were also in fashion. Many of the Court ladies had a colourful veil hanging down the back of the hennin in a rich fabric that either matched or set off the flowing gowns that they accompanied.

As Henry's gaze swept the company, he became aware of a younger man who, he realised with a start, looked like an older version of himself. He was around twenty years of age and he was dressed all in black. He appeared to be slouching where he stood, across the antechamber from Henry, and fixing him with a scowl. But it was his face that fascinated Henry; it was aquiline, like his own, and somewhat sallow of skin. The hair that showed beneath his bonnet was darker than Henry's, but it was thin and almost lifeless. The eyes appeared to be as 'beady' as Henry's own and the overall effect was like looking at a portrait of how he himself would look when he reached manhood.

He tugged at his uncle's elbow. 'That man across from the main fireplace — the one dressed all in black — who is he?'

Jasper looked in the direction indicated and frowned. 'That is Dickon of York — the younger brother of the recently deposed Edward, and also brother of Clarence, who even now is in the presence, along with Warwick as usual.'

'He was scowling at me, as if I had done him a disservice.'

Jasper chuckled. 'You did him your greatest disservice by not dying at birth. Should Edward return, then die young, leaving no heir alive, it is only Clarence that stands between Dickon and the throne. But should Henry of Lancaster and his queen remain in power and have no further issue, as now seems likely, then after the young Prince of Wales you would be the strongest claimant to the Lancaster inheritance.'

'That is surely a great number of "ifs",' Henry pointed out.

'We live in marvellous times,' Jasper reminded him. 'Who would have expected Henry to be returned to power? And he would not have been, had not Edward fallen foul of Warwick. Be in no doubt that England is ruled by neither York nor Lancaster, but by Richard Neville in all but name. When we go into the presence, be sure to cause him no offence.'

'But surely my obeisance is due to His Majesty?'

'Your mother was correct,' Jasper replied. 'You have much to learn about affairs of State.'

The doors to the Painted Chamber swung open and the crowd in the antechamber fell silent as a herald in royal livery called out, 'Henry, Earl of Richmond, the Dowager Countess of Richmond and the Earl of Pembroke.'

The room they were shown into was long and thin, decorated like none Henry had ever seen in his life before. The ceiling was a bright blue, giving the impression that the entire room was open to the sky, except that it was embossed at precise intervals with royal shields. The left-hand wall was one huge mural depicting an ancient castle in its own grounds, while the window arches to the right were resplendent with richly-painted images of former monarchs. The floor was a blue and gold mosaic under Henry's boots as they walked slowly but firmly towards the small throne at the far end. It was high-backed, but not raised on a dais as Henry had expected. The King sat, slightly slumped, his right leg slightly in advance of his left, dressed in a velvet robe of rich purple with fur trimmings. On his head sat the crown of State and in his hand a vellum scroll that he was examining closely as the party approached.

Standing to his right and slightly ahead of him was a tall man with a stern face and a fierce black beard that was in need of a barber. Henry took him to be the all-powerful Earl of Warwick. Henry was so busily engaged in ensuring that he did not approach too closely to the King before kneeling that he hardly noticed the pale young man seated on a bench before the final window on the right, who must — he realised with hindsight — have been the Duke of Clarence.

Henry knelt as previously instructed and there was a soft chuckle from the somewhat fleshy face of the man on the throne.

'When a Tudor kneels to pay homage the nation must indeed be secure. Since I have met the Earl of Pembroke many times in the past I may safely conclude that you, young man, are Henry of Richmond.'

'Yes, your Highness,' Henry replied to the floor, wishing that his voice were naturally stronger.

'You may raise your head, young Richmond, and be proud of who your father was, and how he loyally served the cause of Lancaster before the storms of family dissent descended upon this realm.'

Henry looked up into a pair of kindly-looking, if slightly vacant, eyes. The King was smiling, so that must surely be a good sign. Then he looked slightly behind Henry and spoke again.

'Margaret Beaufort, Margaret Tudor, and now Margaret Stafford, you may all take a seat.'

Henry couldn't help a chuckle escaping his lips, then looked back up in horror in case the King had taken offence at his appreciation of the royal wit. But the King smiled back reassuringly and told him, 'During those sad days when my Queen and I were parted, the Dowager Countess of Richmond was a constant comfort to Margaret of Anjou. Welcome back to Court, Countess.'

'Your Highness does me great honour by allowing me to present my son,' Margaret replied quietly but firmly. 'As for her Highness the Queen, it was both a privilege and a pleasure to know her friendship, which we may hopefully resume without further interruption.'

Henry winced, in the belief that his mother might have gone too far to say such in the presence of the very man who had kept them apart. The Earl of Warwick had clearly picked up the same insinuation and looked across haughtily at where she had taken a seat, as invited, on one of the empty padded benches in a window arch.

'Those interruptions were due in large part to her Highness's choice to travel so widely out of the kingdom,' Warwick explained unctuously, 'but I, too, rejoice to see such kindred souls reunited in the flesh. Yet how shall we best employ the young earl, your Highness?'

The King looked puzzled for a moment, then transferred his gaze from Henry's mother to Henry himself.

'What say you, young Tudor? You look too puny of frame to be employed in my armies. Are you perhaps a lawyer, or a scholar, who may be employed for the benefit of the realm?'

Henry swallowed hard. 'In truth, your Highness, I am no scholar, and your Highness is correct to doubt that my weak arm could be usefully employed in wielding a sword. I have one ability of which I am aware and that is in the calculation of figures, particularly those that are financial.'

'Excellent!' the King enthused. 'My lord of Warwick, could you see to it that the Earl of Richmond is allocated a post in the Treasury?'

'It shall be done, Highness,' Warwick assured him, with a slight sneer in Henry's direction.

'And what of you, Earl Pembroke?' the King asked Jasper. 'Seek you a position at Court, like all those who form such a long line outside?'

'I seek nothing but that which your Highness has need of me for,' Jasper replied diplomatically, 'but unlike my nephew, I would be of no use in the Treasury. The Chancery, perhaps, since I have recently returned from France, where I might be of value to the nation in diplomatic discourse with King Louis.'

'We have emissaries enough,' Warwick chimed in, 'however, we may soon have need of a new Constable of the Tower. Our current one has of late been lax in matters regarding communications between prisoners and those that would conspire towards their escape.'

Henry felt a chill run up his spine at this veiled reference to his mother's recent communications between the previously imprisoned King and his exiled wife. Warwick had been the man behind the entire business and was now seeking the downfall of the man who had made it all possible whilst in his pay. He was indeed the most treacherous of devils, Henry realised, and not even the King had the courage to point out that the Constable whose downfall Warwick was seeking was the very man who had been instrumental in his restoration.

'I have no desire to be a gaoler, your Highness,' Henry heard his uncle reply from somewhere behind him, 'and perhaps I might be better employed ensuring that your western borders are free from those who would threaten our new-found peace.'

Henry saw Warwick's face freeze in a cold smile as the King agreed that he was happy to have a Tudor earl keeping down any rebellious Welshmen and hinted that Jasper might also be of future service in the northern counties. Then they were excused and returned to the antechamber, where Jasper congratulated Henry on his performance in his very first audience and muttered darkly about the treacherous duplicity of which Warwick was clearly capable. He was joined in this by Henry's mother, who seemed paler in the face than she had been before the audience.

'That poor man was too terrified of Warwick not to accept his money. By this means did he help to organise the restoration of Henry to his throne and now the helpless wretch is to be dismissed for a betrayal of his office that Warwick himself brought about. There are rats feeding on the corpses of the dead that have more conscience than that dreadful abomination of a human being.'

They left the Palace together and as Jasper and his mother continued to mutter between themselves, Henry was conscious of the piercing dark eyes of Richard of York following him out.

28

IV

Henry sat at his desk in the room assigned to the Under-Secretary to the Lord High Treasurer, wondering why he could not make the figures balance. He rubbed his eyes, which had grown blurred in the flickering candlelight as he sought to reconcile the numbers that had begun dancing on the vellum before him. As he squinted to clear his vision, he finally realised where the discrepancy lay between the sums collected and the sums sent to the vault. A licence fee had been entered into the accounts but not transferred to the King's vaults.

Henry sat deep in thought before rolling up the vellum and taking it to the Treasurer, Henry Bouchier, Earl of Essex, in his spacious suite of rooms in Westminster Palace.

The Earl seemed unmoved by what Henry had to tell him.

'Where is the error or the malignancy, if the sums due be properly accounted for to his Highness?'

'My point entirely,' Henry argued. 'The sum due in licence fee was not committed to the vault.'

'But it remains accounted for.'

'Where? Should the roll continue to show that his Highness has been underpaid by some two hundred pounds, those responsible for the roll may be accused of treason by way of dishonesty in the nation's accounts.'

'You may rest assured, Richmond, that no-one will report the loss to his Highness, since the cause to which it has gone is a more powerful one even than the maintenance of the crown.'

'There is no power higher than that of the sovereign,' Henry began to protest, before a horrible suspicion began to form in his mind. 'Unless, perhaps... '

Essex fixed him with a stern look. 'You would be as well not to complete what you were about to allege. Simply initial the roll and let us hear no more about it.'

'But if I initial the roll, I become the person who has kept two hundred pounds which were due to the royal vault. And if I am taken up on a count of treason, the only person who I can name in my innocence occupies such a high position of influence in this nation that it is almost treason in itself to besmirch his name.'

Essex smiled unpleasantly. 'You are rapidly learning the *real* business of the Treasury. Now, good day to you.'

Henry, for various reasons, never returned to the Treasury. For the first week, he pleaded illness and hid himself away in the house at Mortlake. Then he felt safer retreating further into the countryside and delighted his mother by turning up at Woking unannounced, claiming that he had been granted leave by the Treasurer to visit family. When his so-called leave exceeded two weeks, his mother grew suspicious and made enquiries when she was next at Court.

'Little wonder that you avoid London,' she said to Henry, upon her return. 'The King has let it be known that he wishes you to answer to various accusations made regarding your handling of accounts of State.'

Henry explained to her how Warwick was diverting royal revenue to himself and that even if Henry could give his honest account of the treachery he had discovered, Warwick would either talk the King into an attainder, or have him quietly murdered.

'I will speak to Queen Margaret personally,' his mother offered, although the look of alarm on her face belied the promise in her voice.

'Best that you say nought of your knowledge of the matter,' Henry told her, 'otherwise the Tudors will lose two of their number instead of just one.'

'But surely the Queen can be persuaded that no-one of our family would stoop so low?'

'The Queen perhaps,' Henry conceded, 'but can she sway the King? And can either of them stem the poison that flows from Warwick's mouth? Even if they believe him not, they are so overawed by the power that he wields that they will think it little price to sacrifice a mere boy who has no military force to command.'

They had been arguing backwards and forwards in this fashion for some minutes when there was a commotion to the rear of the main house and they could hear the raised voice of Jasper Tudor as he raced down the garden path yelling for them each in turn. He found them in the plant house and stood breathlessly in the doorway.

'Warwick has over-reached himself this time, by God! He has pledged English forces to assist Louis of France against Charles of Burgundy. I have but today returned from Calais, where the best accounts are that Burgundy has taken so ill to the news that he is offering support to Edward of York to regain his throne. I go immediately to Westminster to advise his Highness and Warwick that we must prepare to defend the nation, although it sits ill with me to be assisting Warwick in anything.'

'Warwick has been laying false charges of treason on young Henry,' Margaret told him.

'Another reason why we might all be best advised to leave this realm while we can,' Jasper replied. 'After all, if God has deserted England, may we not be permitted to do so also?'

V

The threatened invasion came just two weeks later, when Edward, together with his youngest brother, Richard of York, and an army of mercenaries supplied by his brother-in-law Charles of Burgundy, landed in a deserted rocky cove in Northumberland and headed for London. Picking up loyal Yorkists on the way, they reached Coventry, where they laid siege to Warwick's hastily-convened forces as he awaited reinforcements under the command of the remaining Yorkist royal brother Clarence, his son-in-law. The feeble Clarence was easily persuaded back over the fence in secret talks with Edward and attempted to persuade his mentor Warwick to surrender. When Warwick would not even receive Clarence's emissaries, Edward and his invading force marched on to London, which was supposed to be held for the Lancastrians by the Duke of Somerset.

At the first sight of Edward's growing force, Somerset and his troops melted away, leaving Londoners to cheer Edward's return as his weary soldiers marched back into the city without a blow being struck. While Edward was deciding what to do with Henry VI, who seemed content to offer himself up for another period in the Tower, Warwick's army pursued Edward south and made camp in Barnet, on the northern outskirts of London. Edward marched his army back north out of London, taking Clarence with him, in case his inconstant brother decided on another change of side, and bringing along the Lancastrian Henry VI, partly as a showpiece and partly in order to prevent the Londoners rallying behind him while Edward's back was turned. The Battle of Barnet that followed early the next morning was fought in a thick April fog, during which the confronting armies almost missed each other. Two hours and ten thousand armoured corpses later, it was all over. The Yorkists had won the day, and Warwick himself was dead, even though Edward had issued instructions that he be taken alive.

In the meantime, Margaret of Anjou had been raising troops in France, willingly supplied by Burgundy's enemy. She landed at Weymouth and immediately marched her mercenaries towards Wales in the belief that the traditional Lancastrian heartland would again answer the call to arms. Edward's army headed her off at Tewkesbury, where, on 4th May 1471, the Lancastrian side in the Wars of the Roses suffered its last defeat. Among the dead was the Lancastrian heir to the throne, Edward Prince of Wales. There were no Lancastrian claimants left three weeks later, after Henry VI died in the Tower.

The Battle of Barnet was to claim another victim in due course. Heavily wounded while fighting for Edward, Sir Henry Stafford was not among the victorious Yorkists who clattered back into London. He was helped off the battlefield with serious wounds and laid for his comfort in a neighbouring house, from which his wife Margaret had him carried back to Woking. He lay, groaning, as Henry nervously slipped to his bedside, mainly to comfort his mother who was crying pitifully. The wounded man turned his head to look at his young stepson.

'Take care of your mother, young Richmond. And stay out of affairs of State, else you will leave this world in the same manner as I am destined to do shortly. Tell your uncle to take you out of England while he can, since I know it is his dearest wish, and it would be best for you if you wish to live a long life. And now leave me, that you may not hear my cries when they change the dressings, as they must do if I am not to die of poisoned blood.'

Henry slipped quickly from the bedchamber and winced as he heard the battle-hardened man's shrieks of agony and his mother's wails of grief and sympathy. In the hallway stood his uncle Jasper with a stern countenance.

'I should rejoice to hear a Yorkist suffer so, yet I have not the heart. Nor shall I have a head if I remain much longer here in England. I am to be attainted for treason simply because I served the true king, Henry. You may come with me, or wait for further devilry that will lay your head also on the block. Which is it to be?'

'Where shall we go?' Henry asked.

'Wherever God and the prevailing wind shall decree. Anywhere but this benighted land that the Fates have cursed so roundly.'

VI

'Why are we heading west?' Henry asked breathlessly, as they thundered through Reading at dead of night, accompanied only by two of Jasper's armed Welsh henchmen.

'Because the Channel ports will be watched by Edward's men,' Jasper yelled back, 'and you are probably the person in England he most wishes to see in the Tower.'

'Why me?'

His uncle laughed out loud. 'You really have learned nothing of your destiny, have you?' he responded. 'Think yourself lucky that you have a mother and uncle to guard your interests, else the Tower ravens would have had your eyes long ere you reached your thirteenth year.'

'Where are we headed?'

'Where else? Pembroke Castle, where a vessel awaits us, moored in the river. Now please be silent — or if you cannot, then at least say loud prayers that we may continue to elude our pursuers.'

Those pursuers had almost caught them in Woking, but had been distracted by Margaret, who had berated the armed soldiers sent by Edward to secure the persons of Henry and his Tudor uncle for causing such a disturbance while her husband — the loyal warrior Sir Henry Stafford, who had given his all in the Yorkist cause — lay dying in an upper chamber. Fortunately, Henry and Jasper had already made their farewells and had been saddling up in the stables as the King's troops clattered past them in the courtyard.

By daybreak they had cleared Newbury and by sunset on the third day they were safely across the Severn and into Tudor country. Jasper had a chain of sentinels across the whole south of the country and by sending fast messengers ahead they were able to change their second horses, which were almost dead with exhaustion, and refresh themselves at wayside inns whose landlords not only refused payment, but insisted on sending their own retainers out with them as additional bodyguards for the man who, to them, was a local hero who had so often defended their interests against marauding Marcher lords. When they learned that the youth with him was none other than Henry Tudor, some of them even knelt and called him 'Majesty', to Henry's acute embarrassment.

In the early light of the fifth day, having arisen at cock-crow from their pallets at the final inn on their long journey west, Henry and Jasper sat on a hill looking down at Pembroke Castle. Any memories, happy or otherwise, that might have flooded back for either man were suppressed by the sight of hundreds of armed men in royal livery laying siege to Henry's birthplace and Jasper's traditional stronghold. Jasper's seneschal must have chosen to defy the siege in the hope that the King's men would believe that the men they were seeking were within the castle walls.

Jasper turned in the saddle. 'Quickly,' he urged. 'Back the way we came, this time to Tenby. It will not be long ere they discover that their quarry has flown and the mayor of the town will aid us.'

Before they had time to leave the brow of the hill, a shout rose up from the besieging troops and a group of men broke away to gallop up the hill towards them. Henry and Jasper had a half mile start on them and the advantage of fresh horses and a lack of heavy armour; they raced to the mayor's house in Tenby and hammered furiously on the door. Mayor Thomas White was surprised, but delighted, to see Jasper again and he led them through a series of natural caves down to the harbour, where he persuaded a local captain to take the two escapees on board his fishing vessel and out to sea. All that they had was either on their backs or in their pockets, since even the few meagre possessions they had managed to leave Woking with were still in the panniers of the abandoned horses, but as the shoreline faded from view and soldiers in York livery could be seen from a distance, running in and out of houses on the harbour-side, they heaved sighs of relief and sank back against the gunnels of the boat.

An hour later, Henry was facing the other way, heaving his stomach contents over the side as their transport bounced up and down in a swell that it had never been designed to withstand. It was meant to be a coastal fishing barque, not an ocean-going transport, and its captain was hard put to prevent it being blown out into mid-Atlantic by the strong easterly gale that was not unheard of in August, but was destined to drive them miles off the course that Jasper had originally intended.

As his uncle conducted a conversation in Welsh with the captain, yelling to be heard above the wind, Henry began to pray hard. He had rarely been on water before and if this was what foreign travel was all about, he wanted none of it. The waves crashing over the bulwarks had soaked him to the skin within minutes of their leaving harbour and by the time they had crossed the mouth of the Bristol Channel he was shivering and coughing, in between fits of dry-retching with nothing left inside his stomach.

'It seems that you are as fit a sailor as you are a soldier.' Jasper grinned as he sank down beside Henry and handed him a hunk of dry bread. Henry closed his eyes and shook his head, only to find that his uncle was trying to force-feed him.

'I have felt like you many times in the past,' Jasper assured him, 'and nothing is worse than puking when you have nothing left to puke. This may only be dry bread, but it will be nothing lost when you heave it over the side later. Would you like some wine from my gourd? I filled it from the landlord's supply in Carmarthen, so it is probably the quality of cow's piss, but it will settle your stomach.'

Henry shook his head again. 'Where in God's name are you taking me?' he croaked.

'France, I had hoped,' Jasper replied. 'It is over there somewhere, beyond these mountainous waves. I had intended that we should follow the French coast back up the Channel until we made Calais, or perhaps only Honfleur, but our captain assures me that we could reach it only as kindling, if this gale continues. But France is very large and we both believe that if we maintain our present course, we may make land somewhere on its north-west coast. After that, who knows?'

'The captain is both brave and generous,' Henry replied. 'Have you coin with which to pay him?'

Jasper smiled. 'You remember those at the inn at Carmarthen, who knelt before you?'

'Yes.'

'Those men were the first of many who will one day kneel before you, if God keeps faith with the worthy and the deserving. The captain is similarly persuaded and holds it great privilege to be providing sanctuary to the future King of Wales.'

'England, surely?'

'To them it is Wales. But either way, he refuses payment.'

For the next three days Henry divided his time between praying, when awake, and dreaming of a watery Hell when asleep. His stomach had somehow settled to the constant but unpredictable bucking and lurching of their seemingly frail boat as it was tossed this way and that, while the captain — who seemed never to require any sleep — kept the rudder tightly gripped in his rough red hands while swearing profusely in Welsh. On the fourth day the wind — but not the sea — dropped away and Henry awoke from a half slumber to hear the captain shout in Welsh to Jasper, who scrambled to his feet and gave a cheer as he looked over the bow of their vessel.

'St. Michael and all the angels know where we are, but at least it is land, and hopefully French land at that.'

Henry rose to stand uncertainly beside him, but all he could see was what looked like a chain of rocky islands, against which the waves were crashing in mountains of spray. 'Can we land on *those?*' he asked disbelievingly.

'Not unless we are seabirds,' Jasper replied, grinning. 'But if our good captain follows the shoreline, as the wind seems to insist that he must, we may find safe anchorage somewhere along here.'

Two hours and a good deal of Celtic cursing later, the captain steered the boat into some sort of estuary, where the swell dropped most noticeably once they passed the rocky outcrops on either side of the entrance. On the right hand side of the channel there appeared to be a township of some sort and the captain unfastened a set of oars from the inside of the boat and steered the vessel towards it. As the bow clunked up against the stone jetty of what looked like a small harbour, Jasper leapt up onto dry land. Once Henry had lurched unsteadily onto the quayside, Jasper looked around him and spotted an inn further down the greensward.

'I assume that your lessons in French were as useful as tits on a bull, so yet again it shall be Uncle Jasper to the rescue. If anyone manages to engage you in conversation, remember that you are the unjustly exiled King of England.'

'That would be a wicked falsehood,' Henry objected.

Jasper sighed. 'So would it be were I to pretend that we had money with which to pay our way.'

'I cannot lie so glibly,' Henry objected with a grin.

'But I can — and in French, even more miraculously. Follow me, your Highness.'

'When I am King, you shall be my Treasurer.' Henry told Jasper between mouthfuls of what tasted like mutton and what he hoped was not some sort of mountain goat.

'And when I am,' Jasper grimaced back, 'I shall order better wine than this pig's piss. It is thinner than one of Warwick's smiles and I fear it may have been strained through the landlord's hose. How good *is* your French, may I enquire?'

Henry frowned. 'According to my tutor, it was better than my Latin, about as good as my Greek, and infinitely worse than my English — why?'

'Because we are in a land in which they insist on speaking French and you must learn it if you are to survive without me.'

A look of alarm crossed Henry's face as he put down his paring knife. 'You would not abandon me in this foreign land? Not now that you have brought me to it?'

Jasper smiled and shook his head. 'Not of my own choice, no. Your mother would have my entrails. But who knows what will happen soon? You are, after all, a king and I a mere servant of the Privy Chamber.'

'Is that what you told these people? That you are merely my servant?'

'Indeed — how else to explain why I have no coin? I have told them that we were wickedly cast adrift by those in Edward's Court who had been ordered to kill you, but who took pity on the man they regard as their rightful sovereign. I have also advised them of an ancient custom — which, I am proud to say, I have just invented — whereby one sovereign lord assumes the care of another in times of adversity. I have asked that word be sent to their ruler that just such a sovereign is now seeking to invoke that ancient custom.'

'Do you think the French King will be so disposed?'

'The French King most likely, since he supported the most recent Lancastrian Queen, Margaret of Anjou, when her throne was usurped by the return of Edward of York. It was King Louis' soldiers, in the main, who fell at Tewkesbury. But since he and Margaret were distant cousins, and since Edward was a supporter of the rebel Duke of Burgundy, he had little choice. Likewise, he will no doubt support your cause, since you are related through your common grandmother, Catherine of Valois. However, we are not, as yet, in France.'

'But...' Henry began to object, before Jasper silenced him with a wave of his hand.

'We are certainly on the north coast of Europe and once this place was ruled by the English Crown. But now it is a separate principality called Brittany, with its own Duke who has no love for the King of France. This township in which we sit is called Le Conquet and many miles inland is a town called Nantes, wherein resides Duke Francis, who will shortly send soldiers to arrest us for living so well at his expense, since I have instructed the landlord that the reckoning should be sent to the ducal palace. Now finish your meal and let us retire. If I am still not awake in three days time, you have my leave to kick me for signs of continued life.'

It was in fact just over a week before half a dozen heavily armed soldiers arrived in order to arrest Henry and Jasper and take them to the Duke's palace at Nantes. They had at least paid them the courtesy of bringing spare horses and as they plodded through dense woodland just north of Pont-de-Buis late on the second day, Henry gave voice to his thoughts.

'I have been giving our immediate future some serious attention. Assuming, for the moment, that this Duke Francis does not have us hung upside down for prevailing upon his hospitality and if, as you say, he is at odds with the French King, who you assure me is our friend, then will the Duke not simply hold us hostage for his own ends?'

Jasper smiled. 'God be praised, you at last begin to display signs of statecraft! You are correct that you have just become an important bargaining counter in a dispute that is not of your making and even less to your interest, but if, as you say, the Duke is aware of your importance to the King of France, why would he have you killed immediately? More sensible, as you say, to hold you hostage. This is what I am hopeful will happen — if and when it does, be mindful to impress upon him the importance to you of having your own servant to attend you.'

Two days later, their small procession wound its way into Nantes, where they were escorted roughly into the presence of Duke Francis II, an elegant, feminine-looking man in his late thirties, who regarded them with a scowl as they knelt before him. He said something curtly to Henry, but it was Jasper who answered. A short conversation then ensued, following which Jasper turned to Henry.

'He wishes to know why, if you are a king, you kneel to a mere duke.'

'Tell him that I bow out of respect for his royal house, as a fellow royal.'

The Duke smiled and addressed Henry in his broken English. 'You are a man *trés diplomatique*. Why travel you to my country?'

'I am cruelly cast out from my own,' Henry replied, 'and I thank you for addressing me in English. Your English is better than my French. I would learn more of your language.'

'It is possible,' the Duke replied, 'since you will be my — my — *invitées*?' He looked enquiringly at Jasper.

'Guests,' Jasper supplied.

'*Oui*,' the Duke replied with a thin smile. 'Your servant has better French than you,' he observed to Henry, raising his hand in a signal for them both to rise to their feet. Then he turned and addressed a richly-dressed man to his left, who nodded and left the chamber. The Duke smiled at them. 'I have given instruction that you shall come with us while we return to Vannes. Then we shall see where it is you are to be my guests. You are also, of course, my prisoners and should you seek to leave, my men will remove your heads from your bodies.'

VII

Almost a year after they had scrambled ashore at Le Conquet, Henry and Jasper were the guests of honour at the Chateau de Suscino, on the Atlantic coast south of Vannes. It was a castle in the old style, set in its own rural pastures in which Henry learned to hunt, as well as to fish in the nearby ocean. He learned to swim in a lake that lay beyond the ancient moat, but retained his fear of the ocean. There were endless banquets, since the ducal family used the chateau as a retreat from the dust and murk of the town and the combination of good food and healthy exercise resulted in a rapid height gain by the young Henry, who was now past sixteen, a handsome, slender youth, earning the admiring glances of the ladies-in-waiting who were forever in attendance on the Duchess Margaret.

Not only had Henry's physique improved, so had his French, under the tutelage of a local clergyman who spoke excellent English himself and began to guide Henry through the finer points of his own native language. These lessons were far more enjoyable to Henry than the attempts by Jasper to pass on his skills with sword and battle-axe. The young King-in-waiting was well aware that someday he might be called upon to lead an army into battle in order to win the crown to which, he was slowly being convinced by Jasper, he was entitled, but he shrank from the thought of hacking limbs from a fellow man, or smashing in his head with an axe. Not only that, but violent exercise or sudden excitement seemed to bring on attacks of breathlessness that he had experienced since childhood. His chest was his weakest part, he knew, and it seemed to be his lungs that attracted the slightest infection, or refused to perform their function when he was under stress. He tried to explain this to Jasper, who shook his head in faint disbelief and reminded him that 'it is traditional for every monarch to lead his men into battle.'

One day, as Henry was lunging half-heartedly at a target that had been set up in the meadow beyond the chateau walls, Jasper strolled over with a parchment in his hand. He had, once they had some sort of permanent accommodation, begun a course of correspondence with England and it was not unusual for him to keep Henry abreast of developments at home outside the hearing of any chateau spies who might have sufficient grasp of English to pass information back to the Duke.

'Your mother has remarried, it would seem,' he told Henry.

'Another Yorkist?' Henry asked.

'What other kind of noble does England possess? And yet there may be hope. Your latest stepfather is Thomas Stanley, the Earl of Derby. He is one of the most powerful men in the realm, being descended in his own right from Edward I and also, by marriage, from Henry III. His first wife was Warwick's sister, yet he holds vast estates in Lancashire and Cheshire and may well be well disposed towards the Lancastrian cause.'

'If he is not already, my mother will make him so.' Henry grinned.

'Indeed, and your mother advises me that she is, by this marriage, invited back to Court, where she is once again close with the Queen Elizabeth.'

'Is there aught else I have not been told?' Henry enquired, 'or is the future King of England dependent for his knowledge on his mother and his uncle?'

Jasper clapped his hands in sheer delight. 'He calls himself "the future King of England"! May God be praised for giving the boy — at long last — a full realisation of his true destiny!'

'A slip of the tongue merely.' Henry blushed. 'But since it would seem that all that you and my mother desire of me is to sit on the throne, I must, it would appear, meekly comply.'

'Do nothing "meekly", nephew, if you aspire to be King.'

'Does this latest letter from my mother ask aught about her son? Such as his welfare, or his happiness?' Henry demanded peevishly.

'She asks if you have yet shown interest in those of the fair sex.'

'And why might that be? Has she chosen me a bride also? A queen-in-waiting, to join me here in exile?'

'If so, she says nothing of it,' Jasper replied with a thoughtful stare across at the ocean. 'But if I judge my brother's widow correctly, she wishes me to add something to your education.'

Several days later, there was yet another banquet, on the feast day of some local saint who Henry had never heard of. The Duchess was there, with her full retinue of ladies-in-waiting in their brightly-coloured gowns and matching hairpieces, and Henry sat in his usual place of honour two places away from the Duke, with the Duchess to his left and Jasper on his right. Below them, on the lesser tables, sat the cream of the ducal Court, while jugglers and mummers moved between them, seeking to build up the party atmosphere before they moved to the top table in search of gifts of coin.

'Just look at that one in blue,' Jasper whispered as he ogled the Ladies of the Court below them. 'If she leans forward any further, her duckies will be in the soup.'

'I think that the one in green is more comely,' Henry responded over the top of his trencher. 'The one with the long dark hair and the piercing green eyes.'

'Each to their own,' Jasper replied, not taking his eyes off the scene below them, 'but the one you admire is almost certainly of pure Celtic stock. Mind me to dance with her and enquire.'

After the meal, the minstrels left their gallery and moved into the main hall for the dancing. Henry was a reluctant — and therefore a poor — dancer, but he could now manage a somewhat wooden *quadrille*, after considerable tuition from the chateau's *valet de dance*, a post which, so far as Henry was aware, did not exist in English noble houses. He very gallantly partnered the Duchess in several such expeditions to the dance floor once the lower tables had been cleared by the pages. However, his habitual shortage of breath got the better of him in the end, unlike Jasper, who never seemed to miss an opportunity to lay hands on the waist of an elegant lady of the Court. During one dance Henry noticed Jasper with the girl in green that Henry had admired earlier and as they both looked in his direction the girl smiled and nodded, while Jasper nuzzled her neck.

Two hours later, Henry was lying in his bed when the chamber door opened and the girl in green slipped into the room, closing the door daintily behind her. She tiptoed to Henry's bed and untied the cord that held her gown together in a bow around her neck, letting it slip to the floor. She was completely naked underneath and she smiled seductively down at Henry.

When there was no response from Henry, she pulled back the sheets and slipped into bed with him. She rolled on top of him and began rocking backwards and forwards as she straddled him.

'Thank you, Uncle Jasper,' Henry gasped to himself. 'But don't tell Mother this time!'

There were regular visits from Henry's girl-in-green, who introduced herself as Eloise and one day Henry plucked up the courage to broach the subject with Jasper, who grinned.

'It was ever part of the duties of a servant of the bedchamber to supply whores for the royal apartments.'

'She's not a whore, surely?' Henry protested.

'Think you that you were her first?' Jasper smirked. 'Her family presented her at the Duke's court when she was a mere thirteen years old, since when she has, shall we say, been of much service to visiting dignitaries, whom she has serviced with considerable enthusiasm. I know because I made discreet enquiry before she came to you to ensure that she was not infected with the pox.'

'You obviously know her well,' said Henry suspiciously. 'Have you also been one that she has "serviced", as you put it?'

'You forget that I am merely a servant of the royal household and therefore I must content myself with wenches from the kitchens and scullery, of which, I may say, there is a copious and pleasing supply. May I now inform your mother that you are aware of those of the opposite sex?'

'Yes, but do not tell her *how*! What news is there from England?'

Jasper snorted. 'It lies under a blanket of uneasy calm, although it may be that the royal brothers will come to blows ere long. Clarence had thought to wed the Warwick heiress, the Lady Anne Neville, but young Dickon whisked her away to a nunnery, from where he married her in July of last year, one hopes before she could take vows of chastity, since she is already with child.'

'And the other York? King Edward?'

'He grows fat, or so your mother says. He has also taken mistresses, to your mother's disdain and to his queen's considerable distress. You should also know that he has petitioned the King of France for your return to England. I have that from our host.'

'And what else says he?'

Jasper sighed. 'He is first and foremost a strategist and a diplomat. He cannot afford the arrival of French troops in Brittany, but even less can he contemplate the arrival of English warships on his coast. Both sovereigns are campaigning hard for your enforced company and King Louis of France has the stronger claim, since I am his cousin through the House of Valois, which makes you his second cousin. It is his argument that he has the stronger claim to the guardianship of his kinsman.'

'Will he prevail, think you? And if he does, what will Louis do with us?'

'With *you*, is the more apt question. There was a time when he would have supplied you with an army, in order that you might reclaim your throne, as he did with Margaret in the cause of the late King Henry. But that was only because Warwick and Edward threatened his ambitions over Burgundy. That threat no longer exists and Louis may feel safer leaving England as it is, rather than risk another hundred years of English knights trampling down his crops in Normandy.'

'By the same token, if Edward threatens to invade Brittany in order to regain my person, might Duke Francis not be placed in a position in which it is easier simply to hand me over? And if he does, then what?'

Jasper looked sideways at his nephew with admiration in his eyes. 'Your diplomatic senses have indeed sharpened while we have been enjoying this peaceful sojourn. I have advised Duke Francis that we are so content with his hospitality that we would fain enjoy it longer and that when you regain your throne, English troops will be available to aid the Breton cause.'

'Since it is my throne that you have pledged and my troops that you have committed, perhaps it might have been more loyal had you consulted me first.'

Jasper chuckled. 'By God, you are learning, boy! I see that I must look to my manners, else the first head you remove after your accession may well be mine.'

'Uncle Jasper,' Henry assured him, 'I would fain cut off my own head before yours. I would not have survived from one year to the next without you, of this I remind myself daily, and when I regain my throne you shall enjoy the highest honour in the land. Below mine, of course.'

Two months later, Duke Francis settled for a compromise that resulted in Henry and Jasper being more closely confined, and officially categorised as prisoners. This seemed to satisfy both monarchs who were calling for their handing over, since King Edward of England could not openly admit that he only wanted Henry back for long enough to have him executed, while it suited King Louis of France to pretend that he had direct influence over the security of the Welsh upstart rather than have English forces cross the Channel to improve it. Francis, for his part, was enjoying his possession of someone who Louis wanted and who he could use as a piece on the chequer board should circumstances demand it.

So Henry and Jasper were not handed over, but neither did they remain together. Jasper was transported miles inland, behind the impregnable walls of the Chateau de Josselin, well beyond the possibility of any escape. He was kept in what amounted to little more than a luxurious prison cell and while there were strict orders issued that he was not to be mistreated in any way, he was not to be allowed the same freedom he had enjoyed in Suscino.

As for Henry, he was hidden deep in woodland in the Chateau de Largoet, near the town of Elven, midway between Suscino and Josselin, north-east of Vannes. His gaoler this time was Jean, the lord of Rieux, whose grandfather had fought alongside Henry's ancestor Owain Glyndwr in his rebellion against the English and though Henry's prison chamber was in the massive *Tour d'Elven*, the highest dungeon in the nation at some one hundred and fifty feet above ground level, it had wonderful sea views. He was well treated and felt safe in his new accommodation high in the sky, until Duke Francis finally buckled under the pressure.

In the summer of 1476, the English envoys who had been besieging Francis with requests for the release of Henry into English custody, accompanied by increasingly large offers of bribes, all of which Francis had dismissed, finally adopted another ploy. The Duke's honoured prisoner was not sought in England for a beheading, they assured the Duke, but in order that he might be restored to his rightful earldom, reunited with his mother who was now highly regarded at the English Court, and married to a Yorkist princess, in order that the two warring houses of Plantagenet might live in perpetual harmony. Even Henry's mother, the Dowager Countess of Richmond, and more recently the Countess Stanley, believed what was being urged upon the Breton ruler who had Henry in safe custody.

Henry was escorted from the Chateau de Largoet to Vannes, where he was handed over to a group of English emissaries with a serious military escort and taken across country to the

Channel port of St. Malo, with a view to being shipped back across the water.

It was here that Henry's constitutional chest weakness came to his rescue — that and his morbid fear of the ocean following his stormy crossing from Tenby five years earlier. As he gazed, horrified, at the heaving seas beyond the harbour entrance, Henry suffered a seizure that rendered it difficult to breathe. He fell to the ground, clutching at his throat and rasping hoarsely for breath, while those attending him called for a physician. The physician confirmed that this was no pretence, but a genuine malady, and the nonplussed envoys had Henry put to bed in an inn, where he slowly began to recover. By the time he did so, Duke Francis's senior diplomat and adviser, Pierre Landais, had finally convinced his ruler that he had made a serious error of judgment, and had raced to St Malo with the sickening belief that he was too late.

But he was not. Henry was still in St. Malo, and in blooming health, and while an angry argument was raging in the street outside between Landais's men and the English who had so nearly acquired the most valuable hostage in Europe, the object of their dispute slipped out of the inn and sought sanctuary in the local cathedral. He was rescued by the Breton party and taken back to Vannes, and a profuse apology from Duke Francis, who took special care to ensure that when Henry retired to one of the guest chambers, Eloise de Arradon was sent in shortly afterwards, to reinforce the apology in the way she was most able.

VIII

While Henry had been demonstrating his morbid fear of the ocean, and the fact that his system did not react well to sudden stress, his mother had been busily engaged in holding open the back door to communication with the court of Edward IV. Her new husband, Thomas Stanley, was related to Edward by birth, in the line commenced by Edward I. He had also been a brother-in-law of the late Earl of Warwick, and probably owned more estates than any man in England other than the monarch himself.

Ever mindful of the need to keep powerful men close about him, Edward had appointed him Steward of the King's Household, a position that glued him to the Court on an almost perpetual basis, and Margaret was not one to miss any opportunity to attend Court with him and continue her friendship with Queen Elizabeth. Elizabeth, for her part, needed all the friends she could get as the hostility towards the Woodville faction was fed further by the ominously shadowy presence of Edward's youngest brother, Richard of Gloucester. The middle brother, Clarence, had been officially attainted after his support for Warwick, and his immediate future hung in the balance, leaving Thomas Stanley, Earl of Derby, and Richard, Duke of Gloucester, as the voices most influential in the royal ear.

As a result Elizabeth's natural friendship with Margaret flourished. Margaret, keen to have her son returned to court, and with a match in mind between him and her goddaughter, Elizabeth's eldest, the Princess Elizabeth, despatched her priest, Christopher Urswick to guide Henry on the path back to England.

Urswick found Henry seated in the ornamental garden to the rear of the Chateau L'Hermine in Vannes, closely studying a book on heraldic design that he had found in the collection of Duke Francis, who was still so remorseful for almost yielding his noble guest over to his enemies that he had rehoused him in the second grandest building in the dukedom's traditional capital, where Henry had been reunited with his uncle. Security was loose to non-existent, and Henry was making up for his somewhat austere childhood by indulging himself in art of all descriptions, most notably paintings and statuary.

Henry looked up as the priest stopped before him.

'Good afternoon, my lord. I am your mother's confessor.'

Henry laughed pleasantly. 'That must be the easiest office in the entire Church. Are you so deprived of hearing of mortal sins that my mother has sent you here to keep you more gainfully occupied?'

The priest smiled back gently. 'I will indeed hear any confession that you may wish to make before God, but I come also with your mother's urging that you return to England. She misses you, and would see you safely back where you truly belong.'

'Where I truly belong, or so my Uncle Pembroke assures me, is on the throne of England. Has it recently become vacant?'

'No, nor does it seem that it will become soon. King Edward enjoys rude health — rather *too* rude, I would imagine. Were I his confessor, I doubt I would have been so free to travel so far, even with such a simple request.'

At that moment Jasper Tudor appeared at the top of the garden, eating an apple. He waved cheerily at the two men, then stood uncertainly at the side of an ornamental yew hedge. Henry waved him over.

'Uncle Jasper,' he said as his uncle joined them, 'here is a priest sent by my mother to hear your confession. Unfortunately, he is only here for a week, so he may need to leave you only partly shriven.'

The priest explained his true business, and Jasper's face clouded.

'Does Gloucester now prey upon my brother's widow? Or has he poured his poison into his brother's ear, that he may secure your return to your death through the gentle urging of your mother?'

'Why Gloucester?' Henry asked.

'I too have my sources of information,' Jasper replied guardedly. 'They say he covets the crown, and is seeking ways of persuading the Council that Edward is illegitimate. He also means no good towards the middle brother Clarence.'

'Yet all the advice I have is that the King would have me return on honourable terms,' Henry argued. 'He even offers his daughter in marriage, mark you. Would a man wish his eldest child to be wed to one whose head was shortly to be removed?'

Jasper sighed. 'It is not Edward you must fear, but those who plot against his throne. I have no doubt that the King's intentions toward you are honourable, and that your mother may bring sufficient influence to bear upon him through her husband Stanley that no ill will befall you unless the throne becomes vacant. But when — and if, for whatever cause — it becomes so, then what price the head of the remaining Lancastrian claimant?'

Urswick had been standing politely to the side, listening to this exchange. He bowed his head and looked back up at the two men.

'I have delivered my message, and must now return with your answer.'

'Tell my dear mother,' Henry advised him, 'that I send my deepest love, and the heartfelt respect that will always be due to her. Tell her that I am well, and that my dearest wish is to be back in England with her. But tell her also that Tudor blood flows through my veins, and that I may not easily be bought by the promises of others which they may be in no position to honour. Either I return to England as its assured monarch, or I remain here in Brittany.'

'I will so inform her, my lord,' the priest replied with a sad bow of the head. 'Should either of you need confession, I shall be in the chapel until nightfall, ere I leave for England in the morning.'

'If you would care to stay for the remainder of the week,' Jasper advised him with a smirk, 'I could promise you such confession from me as would cause the string around your simple robe to dance in sheer excitement.'

'Excitement is for mortal sinners. Good day to you, my lords.'

As they watched the priest make his humble way back up the path, Henry turned to Jasper. 'Must I remain here for ever?'

'No,' Jasper replied, 'you may, should you so choose, return to England and place your head upon the block.'

'May I not raise an army over here and invade?'

Jasper stared thoughtfully into the distance.

'Best let an army come to you.'

IX

Three years later, that army began to assemble. In April of 1483, King Edward IV died suddenly, officially of a fever, but rumours spread that it was poison.

Realising that he was about to die while his heir was still in infancy, the late King Edward had appointed his brother Richard as Lord Protector until Edward V should come of age. Orders were issued for the two royal princes to be brought to London, and Richard of Gloucester then had the young Edward's family retinue arrested, and took responsibility himself for the safe removal of Edward to the Tower of London, the traditional residence of monarchs awaiting their coronation.

Then Richard broke sanctuary in order to remove the young Duke Richard to the Tower, allegedly as company for his older brother who was pining for him. At the end of June, Richard intimidated a clergyman to preach in St. Paul's Cathedral that the late King Edward IV had been the illegitimate offspring of an archer in his father's army who had bedded Edward's mother.

The people of London, fearing that anarchy had returned, were appeased by Richard's assurance that he was only seizing power in order to ensure that there was no uprising by the Woodvilles, who had long cast covetous eyes on the English throne, and had set their comely prospect Elizabeth, the now Queen Dowager, to ensnare Edward by witchcraft that she had been taught by her mother, but rumours began to circulate in June of 1483 that the young princes had been murdered on Richard's orders.

The proposal to marry the Princess Elizabeth to Henry Tudor was renewed and strengthened by the promise that this would coincide with the Woodvilles, and the remaining Yorkists loyal to the memory of Edward, rising up to place Henry on the throne. A conspiracy slowly began to form, as Margaret used her most valuable and trustworthy contacts, while her husband Stanley, the Earl of Derby, continued in the loyal service of Richard as the ongoing Steward of the Household.

He was also among those who urged Richard to assume the crown, after Edward's heirs were declared by Parliament to have been illegitimate, given that the late King, prior to being seduced into marriage by Elizabeth Woodville, had been pre-contracted in marriage with Lady Eleanor Butler. On 6th July 1483, less than two months after his older brother's death, Richard of Gloucester became King Richard III of England.

While King Richard embarked on a ceremonial progress of the nation, pausing at York Minster to have his young son Edward created Prince of Wales, Margaret was busily fuelling the fires of unease that followed the disappearance of the royal princes. Margaret had no shortage of recruits for an organised rebellion against Richard, but it was a dangerous game, and few could doubt that anyone caught plotting against the newly self-appointed King would not retain their head for long. It required careful and discreet intrigue among people who could be trusted, and Margaret was fortunate to have spent her life collecting trusted allies.

In Brittany, Henry and Jasper received visits from several envoys travelling in secret from the rebel ranks. They were carrying letters from his mother, urging Henry to take this golden opportunity to seize his destiny, and from Buckingham, promising to support Henry if he invaded. Margaret also sent a considerable sum of money that she had raised by way of loan in London without, it would later be claimed, the knowledge of her husband Stanley, and this was intended to pay for an armed force raised in Brittany.

Henry, Jasper and Duke Francis sat discussing the proposal in mid-October 1483, around the upper dining table in the Chateau L'Hermine, at which the servers had laid out wine, cheeses, fruit and wafers.

'I know,' the Duke assured them, 'that many men would go with you, for the gold and for the love they have for you. For myself, although you have become like a son to me, I would not stop in the way of your becoming King of England, and ask only that, if successful, you will come to the aid of Brittany against the King of France, should we call upon you.'

'You may rest assured of that,' Henry replied without consulting Jasper, as had become his usual practice in the past year or so. 'If you had not shown me such hospitality when I first landed all those years ago, I would now be dead, or hiding my true identity while working as a page in some noble Breton house.'

'How many men can you spare?' Jasper enquired.

'As many as you can pay,' the Duke replied. 'My land is currently quiet, and there is no threat from France, since the old King Louis grows frail.'

'We will also need ships,' Jasper reminded him, 'and the more men and horses we take over, the more ships we will need.'

'Of course,' the Duke replied. 'Our only threat comes across our eastern border inland, and we need ships only for fishing.'

There was an uncomfortable silence, then Henry asked, 'If you were in my place, would you answer this call?'

The Duke smiled. 'I have seen you grow from a rather frightened young boy to a strong man who no longer requires either my advice or my protection. *Bon chance*, and may God go with you.'

'We may need Him at least to cross the Channel,' Henry shuddered, as his mind returned to the aspect of the entire enterprise that he most dreaded.

Henry was right. Ten days of remorseless rain led to him clutching the side of the vessel transporting him to England, trying not to faint in sheer terror as his ship, and one other, became all that was left of the fleet of some thirty or so ships that had left St. Malo a few days previously.

They finally limped into Plymouth Harbour, a week late, and unaware that Buckingham had already been publicly beheaded on a specially constructed block in Salisbury Market Place on All Saints' Day. There were soldiers lining the quayside, waving and inviting Henry to come ashore. He might well have done, had Jasper's eagle eye not spotted a baggage wagon left carelessly at the side of an inn door. He squinted through the still pouring rain, and yelled down the side of the ship to Henry, who was waving back to the soldiers on the quayside.

'Before you get too friendly, make timely use of your love of heraldry. Whose heraldic device is a white boar?'

'Richard of Gloucester,' Henry replied, his eyebrows raised in question.

'Yet again Uncle Jasper has been your salvation,' came the response. 'Order the captain to turn this vessel back to Brittany — those are the King's men, waiting to place your head firmly on English soil at the same time as your feet.'

Richard's rage upon discovering that his quarry had evaded him was terrible to behold, and there was much work for royal headsmen to perform in the ensuing weeks. Within a year, there was not a noble house — or indeed a tradesman's house — that was not playing host to a guest of Duke Francis, who had turned against the English King.

Jasper reckoned their number to be in excess of five hundred, and among them were notables such as John Morton, the Marquess of Dorset, and Sir Richard Willoughby. Whether they were inspired in Henry's cause, or anxious to escape the block back in England, it made no difference. They were in Henry's camp, and could only return to England wielding a sword. During this period, Henry and Jasper were obliged to rely, yet again, on the generosity of the elderly Duke, who seemed to regard Henry as the son he had never had.

Back in England, Margaret was under increasing threat. Richard passed an Act of Parliament that divested her of all her lands, which he then gave to Stanley, with a stern demand that he keep his troublemaking wife at home, where he could maintain a close watch on her. He also had a further statute passed, entitled 'Titulus Regius' that confirmed both the bastardisation of all the children of his late brother and Richard's valid claim to the throne.

But Richard had seriously underestimated the deviousness of which Margaret was capable, and the fervour with which she pursued her ambition to place her son on the throne of England. Messengers went backwards and forwards between her place of home detention in the north and Henry's place of exile in Brittany, and barely a fortnight would pass without the young Earl of Richmond being brought up to date with events at the English Court. Many of those bearing messages declined to make the return journey to a nation that was now being ruled largely by fear. Richard was also mistaken to rely on his memory of the nervous looking boy at whom he had scowled in the antechamber of Henry VI fourteen years previously. The boy had become a man, and a man who was above average height, pleasing to the eye and affable to the ear. He offered hope to those who rallied to his cause across the Channel, and all he needed was the manpower, the finance, and the support of those back in England who cowered under Richard's yoke.

Jasper had finally persuaded Henry that he had only one way forward, and that way lay to the north of the Breton coastline. He could either spend the rest of his days as the honoured, if somewhat embarrassed, prisoner guest of the Duke of Brittany, or he could do what everyone else seemed to think him capable of, namely claim the throne of England. At Vannes Cathedral, a few months after his hurried return from the failed first invasion, Henry was persuaded by Jasper to put his support to the test. He stood before his loyal English and Breton supporters and swore an oath to each and every man present that he would lead them back across the Channel and claim his rightful throne in England, where they could all live their lives under his benevolent rule, and reap the rich rewards that flow from loyalty to their monarch. The rousing cheers with which this oath was greeted not only threatened to dislodge some of the loose coping from the roof of the ancient cathedral, but it committed Henry to a course of action from which he could not retreat.

It was soon rumoured that King Richard sought to unite all the remaining York factions under one roof by marrying Princess Elizabeth once his own Queen died, which she conveniently did in March of the following year. Horrified when she learned of these rumours, Princess Elizabeth herself arranged for a letter to be smuggled to Henry, assuring him that she was still available for marriage, and enclosing a ring as a sign of her continuing fidelity to the pledge that their respective mothers had made some years previously.

Richard sent Elizabeth north, to his stronghold at Sheriff Hutton, where she might be safe from any Lancastrian intrigue, but the damage was already done. The exiled Richmond supporters were finally convinced that the best hope for England lay in the uniting of York and Lancaster in a marriage between Henry of Richmond and the young Princess Elizabeth, and on Christmas Day 1483, at St. Pierre's Cathedral in Rennes, during a Mass conducted by the personal priest of the young heiress Anne of Brittany, Henry had risen to his feet and sworn a solemn vow to sail to England and claim both his crown and his bride. He was now committed beyond recall, and the cheers that raised the roof in Rennes were echoed more quietly in secret corners of England that were being prepared for such a return.

The first step required Henry and Jasper to slip out of Brittany unnoticed, which they did in September of 1484, separately. Both, however, employed the same ploy of travelling out of Vannes on a pretended short visit to a friend; in Henry's case, once he was a few miles down the road he slipped into nearby woodland, where he changed into a page's clothing and continued, in disguise, the journey across the French border to be reunited with Jasper.

By February 1485, they were being welcomed to the court of Charles VIII, which was in reality under the financial control of his older sister, who found Henry attractive, and his plan to overthrow the ever-threatening English monarch who had sided with her opponents even more so. Any apprehension Henry might have felt regarding Duke Francis regarding him as an ungrateful surrogate son who had sneakily transferred his allegiance to Brittany's traditional enemies was dispelled when the ailing Duke allowed Henry's supporters free exit from his territories, and by the spring of 1485 the French capital was awash with English nobles and their retinues eager to return home behind a new king. Not only did Charles and his sister give Henry and his followers sanctuary and hospitality, they also financed a further contingent of hardened French soldiers to swell the numbers.

On 1st August 1485, Henry's provisional, under-sized, army of Yorkist deserters, lifelong Lancastrian supporters and French mercenaries set sail from Honfleur in Normandy. For once, Henry Tudor's presence in the Channel did not provoke a storm, and six days later they slid up the muddy beach at Mill Bay in Pembrokeshire, just as the sun was beginning to set on the traditional Tudor heartland. Heaving a sigh of relief, Henry knelt on the home ground he had left as a frightened boy of fourteen, and as a man of twenty-eight he called upon God to 'Judge me, Lord, and fight my cause.' Then he stood up, turned to face the men scrambling ashore behind him and issued his first battle order.

'Follow me, in the name of God and St. George!'

X

After reaching the English shore, Henry was passed a piece of cloth which he unfurled in the evening breeze. It was a red dragon on a field of green and white, and Jasper's mouth opened in a smile of recognition.

'The ancient banner of Cadwalladr!' he shouted.

'Indeed,' Henry replied. 'It was made up by a seamstress in Paris on my instruction. I hope that my memory served me correctly, since it could not be found in any book of heraldry to which I had resort.'

Jasper studied it more carefully. 'Your memory did not play you false, nephew. And you even had the wench cut the eyelets, which leaves us only to find a flagpole on which to fly it, and a man to bear it aloft, since that is not a task befitting the heir to the throne.'

Henry surveyed the now silent ranks of men on the beach, and fixed his gaze on the tallest one he could see. He beckoned him forward. 'Your name, good sir?'

'Sir William Brandon, sire. I serve the Earl of Oxford.'

'You now serve a king in all but name,' Henry smiled back at him. 'Should your arm be as brawny as it appears, you shall be my standard bearer.'

'It shall be an honour, sire, and I shall preserve it with my life.'

'Pray God it does not come to that,' Henry replied, before looking back at Jasper. 'It is some years since we were last in this part of the world, as I recall, and the circumstances were such that I did not have opportunity to note the details. Where are we, in truth?'

'By my reckoning, we are somewhat south of Haverfordwest, in my own country of Pembroke,' Jasper replied. 'It has a castle on which once sat my pennant, and it will serve as both a place to rest the men and horses, and a means of acquiring a suitable pole for our new battle standard. Might I also suggest that we carry a second standard, that of St. George?'

'I would deem it an honour to carry that,' John de Vere shouted out.

Henry smiled. 'Since a man who serves the Earl of Oxford carries the one, it is meet that the second be carried by his liege lord. The honour shall be yours, my lord.'

It was dark by the time the invasion party of less than a thousand had fully assembled on the greens surrounding Haverfordwest Castle, whose gates were opened at the first sign of the Richmond host's approach. Grooms were sent out immediately to local merchants to acquire the necessary food and drink, and the Castle Steward ordered out such canvas tenting as was available to shield Henry's men against the showers of rain that occasionally spattered down. The horses were pegged on long halter ropes, and by the following morning they had reduced the castle greensward to brown earth.

Two days later, they were still awaiting the men expected to rally to the call. Henry sat despondently by a window in the ancient keep tower, looking gloomily down.

'This is your territory, Uncle — where are they all?'

'It *was* my territory,' Jasper reminded him, 'but as you may recall, I have been absent from it for some time. Even Pembroke has passed to others who are in favour with the usurper Gloucester. Our arrival has been long anticipated, and Richard has let it be known that it will be deemed treason even to fart in our direction. But at the same time, the men in this area remain loyal to the memory of the noble Tudor who was their friend, and your father. As a result, while they will not hinder us in any way, neither can they be seen to actively assist.'

'If they will not come to our cause,' Henry asked, 'why should we not simply return to France?'

'Because,' Jasper explained patiently, 'in the mountains to the north are men who have no love for any English King, Yorkist or Lancastrian. They are as wild as the sheep they tend, but they may be persuaded by coin to slit throats with great eagerness, particularly if they are English throats.'

'You propose that we take on the armed might of Gloucester with a few shepherds?' Henry asked in disbelief.

Jasper grinned. 'When you were a child, and the snow fell in the forecourt of Pembroke Castle, did you ever make balls from it that you could throw?'

'What in God's name is your point?' Henry demanded testily.

'Simply this, that if one takes one of these balls made from snow, and pursues it along the ground, it grows larger by the minute, until it is almost beyond moving. By the same token, once we have what looks like a sizeable army, shepherds or not, men will be more encouraged to join it, in the belief that there is safety in numbers.'

'Men are not snow,' Henry grumbled, 'even if they be as white in the hair as he who rides into the courtyard with two heavily armed henchmen.'

Jasper looked over Henry's shoulder through the window and smiled.

'It has been many years since I last saw him, but unless my eyes grow false as my years advance, that is Rhys ap Thomas. I wrote to him from Brittany, and he has promised to aid our cause.'

'Send word to the Steward to have him admitted,' Henry instructed.

Jasper chuckled. 'If he be half the man he once was, he will admit himself.'

Less than five minutes later, their visitor stood before them, looking uncomfortable. Jasper read the look, and frowned. 'You come to break your word, by my guess.'

'Rhys ap Thomas breaks his word to no man,' the older man replied, 'but therein lies the dilemma.'

'You have pledged yourself to Richard of Gloucester?' Henry enquired.

'It is worse even than that,' the Welshman admitted. 'I swore a solemn oath before God that I would defend these lands in the name of the rightful King. As you know, I am Richard's lieutenant for the whole of south-west Wales, and I am duty bound to advise him of your landing.'

'He will learn of that ere long anyway,' Jasper observed, 'so it may best come from you. As for your oath, this young man beside me is the rightful King.'

Rhys said something in Welsh, and looked enquiringly at Henry, who shrugged his shoulders.

'You speak no Welsh, yet you fly the pennant of Cadwalladr from your battlement, and you expect me to support your claim to the Welsh crown?'

Henry's eyes blazed with defiance. 'According to my uncle, you once fought with Lancaster, as did your ancestors for many generations. I am the last of the Lancasters, and the lawful King of both England and Wales. I am also a Tudor, with bloodlines to Owen Glyndwr. Wales would be safer under my crown than that of any Yorkist.'

Rhys smiled thinly. 'Forgive me if I offended. There is obviously the old Tudor fire in your belly, and would that I could bring my men to your battle colours. But the oath I took was before God, and I would perjure my immortal soul were I to break it.'

'If it is a matter of keeping your peace with God,' Jasper suggested, 'you might wish to speak with the Bishop of Ely, who is somewhere in our train. If you are satisfied that this young man is the rightful King of England, then you keep true to the strict words of your oath by lending him your sword arm, and you break your oath if you do not.'

Rhys looked undecided. 'Leave the salvation of my own soul to me,' he eventually replied. 'In the meantime, go in peace through my lands, though Richard would have my head were he to learn of it.'

'His own head will be unsteady on his shoulders, when we are victorious,' Jasper replied, 'but we shall not forget your courtesy to us when that day comes.'

Rhys bowed slightly as he left, and Jasper moved back to the window to watch his departure.

'We shall see him again,' he said as he turned back to Henry, 'and when we do he will fight under the banner of Cadwalladr. If not, he would have ordered it to be lowered ere he departed.'

The next day they began a slow march through central Wales, and men came to their standards in increasing numbers. First across the peninsula to the coast at Cardigan, then along the rugged shoreline that headed north, after which they planned to turn inland for Shrewsbury. Late in the afternoon of 14th August, almost two weeks after their landing, a large group of wild-looking savages stood ahead of them, at the side of the road. Each of them was armed with either a sword or a large knife, and in one case an axe of doubtful serviceability, and they cheered as Sir William rode past them with the dragon standard, ahead of Henry and Jasper who were riding together a few yards to his rear. Jasper spoke to them in Welsh, and they cheered again, and ran back towards the rear of the column, clearly intent on joining it. They were the fifth such group to join them in the past three days, and Jasper turned smugly to Henry.

'Did I not promise that these men would follow me?'

'You did. There must be some two thousand armed men to our rear.'

Jasper turned to look at Henry with proud eyes. 'I have watched my brother's boy become the man his father was, and more. Do not allow yourself to forget that these men have pledged their lives in your cause. Do not waste those lives by recklessly giving battle when the time is not meet. We must take London without taking to the field, while Richard is hopefully still in Yorkshire, tending to his stately gardens and patting his weakling son on the head.'

The next morning, as Henry and Jasper rode out from Machynlleth, there was a small party of armed men waiting in the roadway ahead of them. Henry ordered his standard bearer to let them past and leaned down in his saddle to greet the one who moved his horse slowly forward to come alongside his.

'You are Henry Tudor,' the man said.

'This I already know,' Henry replied jokingly, 'but if yours was a question, then it is indeed true. I am he. And now we have that established, who might you be?'

'Rowland Warburton. I serve Sir William Stanley, whose domains you are about to enter. Shed not a drop of blood, or it will go the worse for you.'

Jasper leaned across from his saddle. 'Allow me, sire,' he said to Henry as he looked haughtily at Warburton. 'You speak to the rightful King of England as if he were a peasant poaching your deer. You serve Sir William, you say?'

'That is correct,' the man replied, far from subdued by Jasper's tone.

'And he is the brother of Earl Stanley?'

'That is also correct.'

'Then know you not that the man to whom you are denying lawful progress is your master's nephew by marriage?'

'This I knew also,' Warburton replied, 'which is why I am charged to guide you as far as the English border, and ensure that your men do nothing that will require my master to protect his own.'

'Mind me not to employ you as a foreign ambassador,' Henry said dismissively to Jasper as he treated Warburton to a reassuring smile. 'Your master — and my uncle — does us much courtesy. Rest assured that we will shed no blood until we spy the white boar of Gloucester. In the meantime, your kindly offer to escort us to the border is much appreciated. Pray ride alongside us while we admire the beautiful countryside of which your master must be greatly fond.'

As they approached the gates of Shrewsbury, they found them closed against them. Henry sent a messenger to the north gate, and watched impatiently as he saw the man admitted, then waited some thirty minutes before he re-emerged, looking red in the face. He walked up to where Henry sat waiting on horseback, with Jasper to one side of him and Rowland Warburton on the other.

'Well?' Henry demanded as the messenger stared down at his own feet in the roadway.

'I spoke with a man who claimed to be the Bailiff of Shrewsbury, sire. He told me to inform you that you will ride through his town over his belly.'

Henry snorted, while Jasper instinctively gripped his sword hilt.

Warburton addressed the messenger. 'There are two bailiffs of Shrewsbury. Spoke you with Roger Knight or Thomas Mitton?'

'The man with whom I spoke gave his name as Mitton, as best as I can recall.'

Warburton turned to Henry. 'If you would permit me, I will deal with this matter as befits the envoy of the man sworn to maintain peace in this county, if I have your word that your men will pass peacefully through this town.'

'You have that word,' Henry assured him. 'We will await your return.'

Warburton disappeared behind the still locked gate, and returned almost an hour later. 'The Earl may pass through first, with two armed men to guard against any treachery. You will find the Bailiff in the main street, by the church door. Once the Earl has passed through, the others will be free to follow.'

Henry set off at a slow trot, with Jasper on one side and the Earl of Oxford on the other. Halfway through the town, as they approached the old cathedral, a large man was lying flat on his back in the roadway. Henry walked his horse up to him, and looked down. The man looked back up at him with a shamefaced grin.

'I am Thomas Mitton. If I am to discharge my oath, you must step across my belly. But I would be much obliged if you would do me the courtesy of dismounting first.'

'Gladly,' Henry chuckled, as he jumped from his horse, and stepped over the ample gut with some difficulty. The horse was led round the side of the prostrate form by Jasper, still on his own mount, and as Henry climbed back into the saddle, he looked back down at Thomas Mitton. 'My thanks. When I am King, Shrewsbury shall have a charter to reward this day's courtesy. May my men now progress through the town?'

'They may indeed, sire,' Mitton replied. 'And God speed your enterprise.'

They had just cleared Shrewsbury, on the road to Stafford, when standard bearer William Brandon raised his hand for them all to stop, and pointed towards a wooded hill up to their right.

'A large body of armed men approaches, sire,' he warned them. 'Do we stand and fight?'

'No,' replied Jasper with a shout of delight, 'we stand and cheer. Those are the battle colours of Rhys ap Thomas!'

Their army had all but doubled overnight, and was now slightly short of five thousand. It was a mixed assembly of lifelong Lancastrians, disaffected Yorkists, wild Welsh hillsmen, fulltime soldiers from the hastily re-summoned army of the returned Earl of Oxford, the armed retinue of Rhys ap Thomas, and hired French mercenaries. They filled Stafford to overflowing, and it was decided to halt the progress for a day or so, in order to rest the men and horses. They had no way of knowing when — or if — they would encounter the royal forces on their way to London, and it was important that they be fresh for battle, should that be demanded of them.

They awoke the following morning to discover that Warburton had left their company at the inn that they had established as their temporary base. Fearing that they were about to be betrayed, Henry ordered that a watch be mounted on the town walls, and shortly after an indifferent breakfast of cold meats washed down with small beer, he heard a challenge from the north postern, as Warburton clattered back into town with a tall man riding alongside him. Henry turned to see Jasper at his elbow, gnawing on a chicken leg, his eyebrows raised in surprise.

'Prepare to meet another uncle,' he told Henry as he stepped back deferentially into the shadow of the inn doorway.

The tall man dismounted and walked up to Henry.

'My man tells me that you are Henry Tudor, but I would have known that from your likeness to your mother, my sister-in-law. I am Sir William Stanley.'

Henry bowed slightly. 'My uncle, I salute you. I also thank you for safe passage through your lands, and for the good offices of your man Warburton, who is well worth whatever you pay him.'

'Where lies your brother?' came Jasper's voice from the shadows, 'and does he ride for Tudor or for Gloucester?'

Henry winced visibly, and began to apologise for his uncle's abruptness, but Sir William waved his words aside.

'You, sir, must be the other uncle, the one who has seen Henry through so many hazards, and who is little short of a living saint, according to your sister-in-law. I was forewarned that you might be lacking in Courtly manners.'

'We are also lacking in fighting men,' Jasper reminded him, 'and I see none in your company. I can only ask again whether the good name of Stanley is to be added to this noble cause that we pursue.'

Sir William frowned, and addressed Henry. 'The matter is a delicate one. Richard is now in Nottingham, on his way south. He has learned of your unhindered progress through Wales, and believes that you intend to march direct on London. Somewhere between here and there, he will intercept you with an army somewhat larger than yours appears to be. But already

74

he demands to know how — and why — you have been allowed to progress so far without challenge from either myself or my older brother, the Earl Stanley. As you may know, I am the Chamberlain of Chester and North Wales, and it is through my forbearance that you have made it thus far. My brother is encamped with his army at Lichfield, from where he may march either to Nottingham to join the King, as he is commanded to do, or await your further progress south, and join with you at Atherstone.'

'Tell my stepfather that were he to join his force with mine, we should be assured of victory,' Henry urged him.

Sir William shook his head. 'Mind, I said that the matter was a delicate one. Richard holds my nephew George, Lord Strange, my brother's natural son, as hostage to his loyalty, and has him in his retinue, chained inside a bullock cart wherever he progresses, in order that he may have him instantly executed, as he has sworn to do if my brother does not join him without further delay. I am, however, instructed to advise you that because of the natural love and affection that my brother has for your mother, he will not take any step against your life.'

Jasper stepped forward, red in the face. 'Means he to act the part of a marshal at a tourney, judging who is the winner, and then feigning that he was on their side all along?'

'Softly, Uncle,' Henry counselled him, his hand raised in the air. 'Were you in the Earl's place, and were I in Gloucester's bullock cart threatened with instant death, what would *you* deem the best course to take?'

This was enough to reduce Jasper to soft muttering as he stepped back into the shadow of the doorway, and Henry turned back to Sir William.

'Give my stepfather my best regards, and tell him that I owe him much thanks for not ending our expedition ere it had chance to begin. I will respect his position regarding his son, and would ask only that he does not join his forces with those of Richard of Gloucester, the pretended King. If we are successful, and if his son remains alive, he will be released by us without harm, whether the Earl joins battle for us or no. If we are defeated, then the worst accusation against him would be that of cowardice, which may yet prove to be less than treason.'

'You have clearly never experienced Richard's rage when he smells disloyalty,' Sir William answered. 'But I shall convey your message without delay.'

XI

After the enforced rest at Stafford, Jasper persuaded Henry that they must move south without any further delay, if London was to be taken without interception by Richard's army, wherever it might now be. Henry agreed with some reluctance, and ordered Sir William Brandon, together with two heavily armed escorts, to ride at least five leagues ahead of the main army, at the head of which was the Earl of Oxford carrying the banner of St George to Henry's left, Jasper on his right, and Henry in the centre of the front rank of the horse-born knights who wore their various liveries. Henry had finally been coaxed into a suit of heavy armour that Jasper had ordered from a smith in Stafford, and over the top of it he wore a tunic with a simple red rose, the age-old symbol of the House of Lancaster.

They were marching down the old Roman road through Warwickshire when one of his men spotted a flash of armour to their north, and raced ahead to warn the leaders. Henry halted the procession and turned to Jasper.

'That must surely be Richard's army, marching to cross us. Should we remain here, they may attack our rear; should we not turn and stand for battle?'

'Begging your pardon, sire,' the man interrupted, 'but north lies Lichfield, and it is spoken through the ranks that Earl Stanley is camped there, and means to grant us safe passage.'

'Go you north,' Henry commanded him, 'and return with better tidings of who might be camped there. If it indeed be the Earl, ask him if he will join with us. We will continue our march until the next township, where you may rejoin us.'

The next township they came to was Atherstone. Henry called another halt, in order that men who so wished might attend divine service; in the meantime he sent scouts further south for signs of Richard's army ahead of them. Well before noon on Sunday 21st August, one of them raced back into Atherstone, leaped from his horse and knelt breathlessly before Henry where he sat polishing his armour.

'Sire, not ten leagues south of here, on a hill to the left, I saw tents being raised, and standards bearing the white boar being hammered into the ground.'

'On a hill, you say?' Jasper interrupted him. 'What like is the ground before this hill, say you?'

'A flat meadow, my lord, although it is somewhat boggy in parts, as best I could make out. There is a stream of sorts on the right, as you look up towards the hill.'

Jasper looked sideways at Henry. 'You will soon have need of that armour that you seem determined to rub into nothing. We cannot let them attack our flank as we march, so we must make camp in this meadow of which the man speaks, and give battle. Your destiny awaits you — sire.'

Henry grimaced. 'Would that I had attended divine service myself. Have John Morton attend me, that he may prepare my soul for what lies ahead. Break camp and set up in the meadow of which this man speaks. We meet Gloucester on the morrow.'

In the river meadow, the following day, the Earl of Oxford, commanding Henry's army, stood surveying the scene with a frown.

'Thank God we do not rely on cavalry,' he said as he spat on the ground. 'But it is an ill wind, as the saying goes. Ahead of our right flank is a treacherous bog in which horses would flounder. Any cavalry of Gloucester's must come at us head on, and we have bowmen to bring them down. Once they fall, they will form a barrier against those who follow.'

'Must we take our stand here?' Henry enquired. 'Might we not continue south, leaving Richard to raise his camp in order to follow a day's march behind us?'

Oxford opened his mouth to say something, then closed it again tactfully and looked meaningfully at Jasper, who put his hand on Henry's shoulder.

'Dearest Nephew, we shall strike a bargain. I shall not seek to rule the nation when you are King, and in return you must allow me, with Oxford here, to organise your battles. If we were to flee south, not only would we encourage Gloucester's men, who would deem us cowards, but they would be able to attack our rear flank once they caught up with us. I for one would not strike a handsome pose with a Yorkist arrow up my arse.'

Henry sighed. 'I must of course be guided by you, Uncle, and by the faithful Oxford here. But does not Gloucester have the advantage, being on the hill?'

'Indeed he does, sire,' Oxford replied, much relieved, 'but so did Harold's forces at Hastings, yet they were coaxed down onto the plain, where they were slaughtered.'

'I had no idea you were so old,' Henry grinned back at him. 'But it shall be as you say. Thank God that Stanley stands off a good few leagues to the north, and would seem to be true to his word that he will not enter the field against us.'

'If he does, we are carrion meat,' Oxford observed grimly. 'But were he to join his ranks with ours, a thousand hills would not give victory to Richard.'

Late that night, listening to the murmurings of men laying on the ground talking softly to each other in the nervous way of all soldiers who may be facing death, Henry was trying to divert his thoughts by sharpening a sword he was praying he would not be required to wield against a knight with real battle experience. Stuffed sacks hanging from trees were one thing, but desperate men fighting for their own lives were another, and Henry doubted that he had sufficient aggression in his soul to be the first to strike. He became aware of a whispered conversation in front of his tent, and looked up as one of his sentries opened the flap and peered in.

'An envoy from Earl Stanley, sire.'

He stepped back, and a tall, elegantly armoured, middle-aged man with a flowing white beard stepped into the tent and looked intently at Henry, who stared back at him suspiciously.

'Earl Stanley must be well served, if he has men as elevated as yourself to act as his messenger.'

'Earl Stanley conveys his own messages,' the man replied. 'I am he, and you must be my stepson. It is an ill time for us to become acquainted, but your mother bade me give you this.'

He stepped forward with an outstretched hand, in which was a small item of jewellery wrapped carefully in a rich cloth. Henry took the item from him, and peeled back the cloth to reveal a gold pendant. It was a long chain, and it supported a square looking cross of some description that looked vaguely familiar.

'It is the cross of St David,' Stanley said. 'It was your father's and he always wore it around his neck on the field of battle. Your mother asks that you wear it on the morrow, and pray to your father and the patron saint he so deeply revered.'

Henry felt a lump come to his throat. 'Is my mother close at hand?'

'No,' Stanley replied. 'This is no place for a woman, even one with the strength and determination of your mother. She rests at Lathom, my country estate, and is forbidden by Gloucester to venture beyond its gardens. She bid me convey to you her love, her best wishes for your triumph on the morrow, and her insistence that you acquit yourself as befits a Tudor.'

Henry smiled as he imagined the stern voice in which his mother would have given those instructions to the most powerful magnate in the land below the King. Then he looked back up at Stanley. 'Will you take wine, my lord?'

'No. I thank you, but I must supervise the positioning of my men on the field out there.'

Henry's heart missed a beat, as he asked, 'Mean you to fight for Gloucester?'

'And risk your mother's lashing tongue? I would rather place my head on a block at Richard's feet. But my son is his prisoner, and neither can I be seen to enter the melee for Lancaster. I shall array my forces to the side, but since I am sworn to preserve your life, you may rest assured that I will not allow a single arrow to assail you from where we will be pitched. I am here tonight not only to pass your father's keepsake into your hand, but to ensure that your men do not attack mine when they take up their positions during the night. To do so, it will be necessary for them to progress along this road behind you, by which you came from Atherstone. You will know that we were camped at Lichfield, since the scout you sent was less than skilled in concealment.'

They made their farewells, and Henry gave the order that Stanley's men were to be allowed safe passage through their lines. Then he lay down on his pallet, clutching his father's pendant in his hand, and finally fell asleep halfway through a fervent prayer.

XII

At dawn the next morning, the hesitant sun revealed the most extraordinary battle formations that England had ever witnessed. On the hill sat Richard's combined forces, with the Duke of Norfolk commanding the vanguard, Richard with his personal bodyguard in the centre, and Northumberland's troops shuffling uneasily in the rear, their commander fuming with the insult of being placed effectively on the left, in front of a bog that denied direct progress to his men. On Henry's left was what appeared to be the sole wing of the Tudor host, commanded by the Earl of Oxford, and tightly packed. To either side, on natural rises in the land, sat the armies of Earl Stanley, to Henry's right, and Sir William Stanley to his left. They looked for all the world like silent spectators as Henry stepped out of his tent, to be confronted by Jasper, accompanied by the largest man Henry had ever seen.

'This is John Cheyne,' Jasper advised him. 'He was the biggest man I could find.'

'He looks like the biggest man in England,' Henry replied as he gazed, awe-stricken, at a man almost seven feet in height, weighing as much as a small warhorse, and clad from head to foot in somewhat rusting armour. 'What did you find him *for*, pray?'

'He will be your personal bodyguard,' Jasper advised him. 'For the last time as your uncle, rather than as the faithful subject I shall become when this day's work is done, I am giving you an instruction which, since this is shortly to become a field of battle, is also an order. You are to remain in the rear, with your standard bearer ahead of you, and this man by your side.'

Henry looked again at the fearsome bulk of John Cheyne.

'But put him on a horse in *front* of me, rather than to the side, and no army could get past him. Thank God he fights *for* us, rather than against us. It shall be as you say, since I am as handy with a sword as you would probably be with a lute. But what means Earl Stanley?'

Jasper sneered up at the hundreds of men seated silently on horseback on the slopes to either side of them, like ladies at a royal hunt.

'It is as I predicted. He will wait until one or other gains the upper hand, then join the victorious side as a late entry onto the field.'

'Who leads us in the vanguard?'

'I do, sire,' said the Earl of Oxford, as he appeared from nowhere wielding a huge battle-axe. 'I have the Welshman's archers at my front, and my foot soldiers to follow behind them once they have mown a path through the enemy. Such cavalry as we have will form your bodyguard, along with this man-mountain your uncle has selected. Now, with your leave, I go to balance a ledger on behalf of those of my family that this Gloucester cur put to their unjust deaths.'

He turned on his heel and yelled a command. His forces moved forward across the meadow to be met with a barrage of cannon fire from the hill. Within a minute, the air was thick with arrows whistling in both directions, and here and there men began to fall.

Down below, as predicted, Richard's men were tumbling over the bodies of their fallen front ranks as they attempted to descend the hill through the narrow defile available if they were to avoid the bog to their left. Oxford's men were slowly gaining the upper hand, and beginning to work their way up the now blood-drenched grassy slope. Henry opted to make one last attempt to persuade Earl Stanley to come to his assistance, and rode, with his moderate mounted bodyguard, towards the slight slope to his right. Richard galloped down the hill, leaping over his own dead and dying as he thundered towards Henry and his retinue, and leapt from his horse, wielding a battle-axe high above his head like a man bereft of all reason.

The first to fall was the standard-bearer, Sir William Brandon, his head cleaved from his shoulders. Henry dismounted along with most of the rest of his meagre bodyguard, but kept hold of his horse by its bridle, as if there might still be some means of escape. He watched, sickened and terrified, as John Cheyne was unhorsed by a berserk demon wearing a coronet, who hacked him into silence before rearing up only two men away from Henry, screaming 'Treason! Treason!'

Earl Stanley had been watching from his vantage point, and could see for himself that his stepson was only minutes from death. He turned to his second-in-command.

'Order the men to horse. We fight for Lancaster.'

'My lord,' the man reminded him, 'you have a son...'

'I also have a stepson,' Stanley replied, 'and I fear his mother more than I do Richard of Gloucester. To horse! For Lancaster!'

The cry was taken up by a thousand other voices, as Stanley's warriors swept down on Richard's small force from both sides. Henry had stood, frozen to the spot by his old malady of lack of breath when in sudden crisis, and he closed his eyes to await a messy death that he hoped would be short in the execution. Then he heard horsemen smashing through the escort that

Richard had brought with him, and opened his eyes again. Suddenly he could see the rolling landscape beyond as Richard's escort began to fall to the ground.

Richard himself turned with a snarl, and began swinging his axe in all directions, until felled by a mace blow to the head that pierced his helm. The mounted soldier who had struck the blow leapt from his horse, and was joined by four others, who between them rained so many blows down on the prostrate form of the fallen Gloucester that blood and brains began to seep from his battle helm, and the coronet was lost under the hooves of milling horses. Eventually Richard stopped twitching, and one of those who had brought his life to an end pulled Henry to his feet as he gasped desperately for his next breath.

He was aware of Jasper hugging him and crying tears of relief through the blood that splattered his face where he had lifted his visor to gain a better aim at the enemy soldier whose throat he had slashed with his sword. Then the crowd parted, and there stood Earl Stanley, his horse being held by a squire, as he walked towards Henry carrying the coronet that had so recently been on the head of the vanquished Richard of Gloucester.

'One of my men found this,' he said to Henry with a grin, 'which I believe is rightfully yours. May I be permitted to place it on your head?'

Henry began to kneel, until Stanley held him up by the arm.

'A king does not kneel to a subject.'

Henry gently shrugged off the restraining arm, and knelt.

'I am no king until my coronation,' he replied. 'I kneel as a son to a father.'

The coronet was placed on his head, and a deafening cheer went up all around him.

PART II

I

Henry gazed forlornly round at the human wreckage that surrounded him and tried to block out the groans and whimpers of the dying. Up above, the crows were already circling in hope of a good feed, and carrion of another sort began to drift in from nearby villages to rob the dead. By English standards it had been a relatively minor affair, with less than a thousand corpses, but Henry had never seen so many dead bodies in one place or left in such a sickening state. He leaned on Jasper's proffered arm as he said what came immediately to his mind: 'This must never happen again.'

When there was no reply, he turned with tears of rage forming in his eyes.

'Did you *hear* me? Never again must good men lose their lives because cousins cannot agree, or because one brother feels himself slighted by the fortunes of another.'

Jasper stood silently watching the turmoil raging in Henry's head, and put it down to the shock of his first battle. He looked up as Oxford limped towards them, blood splattering his entire battle armour, and tried to give him a warning look, but he was too late.

'Northumberland has surrendered, Your Majesty. Do you wish him executed on the field?'

'Did he join battle?' Henry asked.

'No, Your Majesty.'

Henry's face set rigidly in anger. 'Do you take me for a butcher? Enough men have died to satisfy even *your* bloody appetites, surely? His only sin was to support the wrong side; he has a wife and family, no doubt, and today we lost half the nobles in the land. I would not be the cause of losing one more.'

'You mean to *release* him, that he may plot against you in the future?' Jasper asked, aghast at the sickness of mind that seemed to have overtaken his nephew.

'Did I *say* that?' Henry spat back. 'You may convey him to the Tower, if it makes your mind any easier, but he is not to be harmed in any way. Is that understood?'

'Yes, Your Majesty,' Jasper replied humbly, and gestured to the Earl of Oxford, with a slight jerk of the head, that it might perhaps be best to withdraw. Oxford bowed and walked away, shaking his head in disbelief, and Jasper ventured to take Henry's arm.

'Your Majesty, let us withdraw to Leicester, where we may refresh ourselves. This charnel house is no place for a gentle soul such as yours.'

Henry was weeping silently as he was helped onto his horse and escorted to Leicester Castle, where he spent his first night kneeling in prayer for the souls of the slain.

Early the next day, Jasper found him seated at one of the lesser tables in the Great Hall, staring into a cup of wine; it was already half-empty, even though the sun had not yet made its appearance.

'Richard may not have destroyed you, but that poison will. They tell me that Gloucester drank all the passable wine in the cellars; perhaps they put into casks what he later pissed into his garderobe.'

Henry looked up with the best smile he could manage, although it was a thin one, from a face that looked to have aged ten years.

'Uncle, I owe you a deep and heartfelt apology for my manner after the battle, but in truth it was the worst thing I have ever had to endure. I would sooner pluck out my eyes than witness anything like it again.'

'God willing, you will not. But neither will your reign be a peaceful one if you show such weakness as you did toward Northumberland.'

'You did not harm him?'

'No, Your Majesty, as I must now remember to call you. He bides in the dungeons beneath us, and I gave instruction that he be fed.'

'I will forfeit his estates, but not his life, and if I am to be King, this is the way that the nation must be governed. What I witnessed yesterday was the whirlwind that a monarch reaps when he allows his leading nobles to become too strong and ambitious. We must adopt policies that prevent such men becoming all-powerful in the future.'

While he was speaking, Stanley had entered the room.

'I hope that does not include me,' he said with a grin.

Henry looked across at him. 'If I begin to make exceptions on my very first day at the head of the nation's affairs, how firm will my policies be adjudged to be? But no, I cannot bite the hand that delivered me that power. Your estates are safe.'

'Talking of which, I hope I do not need a king's permission to withdraw from the royal presence in order to be reunited with my wife?'

Henry smiled properly for the first time since Atherstone. 'Indeed not. I am not yet a king, and you are my father. By all means withdraw and advise my mother that we are both safe.'

'Messengers have already been sent ahead with those glad tidings, but I would most joyfully confirm them with my own presence. The only remaining resistance to your victory is likely to be from the north anyway, and as a true Lancastrian I would be more than happy to cross the Pennines to suppress any rumblings in Yorkshire, so I am as well sent forth in your name for that purpose.'

'Before you go, my lord,' Henry said, 'I would have your counsel regarding what should be my first actions. The Earl of Pembroke here — who, incidentally will also be confirmed in his estates ere long — can only advise me regarding the quality of the wine, it would seem.'

'You must first send out heralds to proclaim your victory, and to claim the throne. Then you must closely confine those who might be minded to challenge that right. Since Gloucester's son, the Prince of Wales, died some months ago, the only remaining Yorkist heir is the young boy of the late Clarence. He is Edward, Earl of Warwick, but he is only ten years old, and no doubt playing with his toy soldiers at Sheriff Hutton.'

'Sheriff Hutton?' Henry mused. 'Is that not also where Gloucester sent Princess Elizabeth of York, that she might be safely out of my way?'

'Indeed, Majesty. It might be convenient to have them both brought south under the same escort. You must be eager to be reunited with your future Queen.'

'In truth, we have never met,' Henry admitted, 'nor do I intend that we shall while I am in this humour. Is there ought else I must consider?'

'None that I can bring to mind. I would, however, counsel that you halt your progress towards London until I can return with a strong company of my own men. The London mob can be fickle, and we know not what poison may be tipped into their ears ere we can reassure them that you mean their city no harm.'

'Wise counsel,' Henry replied with a smile. 'It shall be as you advise, and since you are up so early, I divine that you wish to return to your estates without delay. You may leave us, and remember to mind me to my mother.'

Stanley gave a slight bow and left the hall.

Jasper turned to Henry. 'I have been giving some thought to what Earl Stanley said. You intend only to deprive Northumberland of his estates, as I recall?'

'Yes, why?'

'Upon what charge?'

'Treason, clearly.'

'And yet, when he took to the field of battle, he was merely performing knight service for his lawful king.'

'Richard was a usurper of the throne.'

'Yet he was lawfully crowned. When the crown of England is placed upon *your* head, may it not be said of *you* also, that you are a mere usurper?'

'You clearly have some device in mind to prevent this — what do you suggest?'

'If you declare yourself King *before* Northumberland, and others like him, took to the field, and then if your claim to the throne be upheld by Parliament and confirmed by God through the hand of the Archbishop at your coronation, those who stood against you at Sutton Cheney could be adjudged traitors, could they not?'

Henry thought for a moment, and a smile lit up his face. 'As ever, your mind races ahead of mine.'

'By this means, you also remain innocent of the lives that were lost on the field, but may add their estates to your own.'

'Excellent! Proclaim that I became the lawful King of England on whatever day it was that we rode from Atherstone.'

'It shall be done. May I now withdraw?'

'You may, but send me someone suitable to lead an escort to Sheriff Hutton.'

Jasper bowed out.

A few moments later there was a heavy thump on the door, and Robert Willoughby strode in, dressed as if for hunting. He looked hungrily at the side table, and Henry invited him to help himself, then take a seat across the table from him.

'The Earl of Pembroke bid you attend me?' Henry asked.

'Indeed, Your Majesty. I believe you wish me to journey to Yorkshire?'

'That is correct. You will bring back from Sheriff Hutton two persons who are to be conveyed separately once you reach Newark. The young Earl of Warwick is to be conveyed to the Tower directly, under great show of arms. Then the Princess Elizabeth of York may be escorted with all due courtesy to Eltham Palace, where she is to be reunited with her mother, the Queen Dowager Elizabeth. Should the last-named not be at Eltham, but still in sanctuary at Westminster, give her my best regards and advise her that she is once again a free woman.'

Willoughby looked doubtful. 'It shall be done as you command, but wish you not to have your future queen lodged here at Leicester?'

'No, this is a royal fortress which currently has within it men upon whom the blood of others may still be smelt. It is not fitting for a royal princess to be in such company, nor do I wish her to meet her future husband before he has been shriven of his sin in that regard. Those are my orders, and once you have satisfied your hunger and thirst, I would that you leave for Yorkshire without further delay.'

Willoughby bowed from the royal presence carrying a chicken leg and a cup of wine, leaving Henry to walk to the window and look down over the narrow streets of Leicester, deep in thought, before sending for Reginald Bray.

The stocky little Gloucestershire scribe finished off the remains of the pork when invited to help himself, and belched quietly before looking up to apologise, and asking if he might take a cup of wine in order to wash down the meat still left on his knife, which had begun to curl up at the sides.

'You may, but pray tell me why your name has changed from "Reynold" to "Reginald" as the years have passed.'

'It was because the name by which I was christened made me sound too much like a fox, Your Majesty.'

'Yet it is your fox-like qualities that I would employ,' Henry replied with a reassuring smile. 'You will not have forgotten those dark days in London, when you revealed to me how Warwick had been lining his pockets at the Treasury's expense? I would employ your skills in that regard once more.'

'You have some accounts you wish me to review?'

'Indeed I do. The accounts of the Duchy of Lancaster, no less. They are now mine.'

'And you will provide me with a note of authority that I may hand to the Chancellor?'

'There will be no need, since *you* will be my Chancellor, should you accept. You will of course be knighted for that purpose at my coronation, which is why I enquired regarding your preferred name. Your service to the young Henry of Richmond that dreary night all those years ago, when you were "Reynold Bray, Comptroller of the Accounts of the Earl of Stafford" has earned you the new title of "Sir Reginald Bray, Chancellor of the Duchy of Lancaster". Do you accept?'

'With all my heart, my lord. Oh, my apologies — "Your Majesty".'

'Excellent. Take up the position without delay, since it is my intention to combine the Crown revenues with those of the royal household, which shall also fall under your husbandry in due course, in my dispensation as the head of the Duchy.'

Bray bowed out with the facial expression of a man who had just been handed a bag of gold coins, and Henry sighed with satisfaction. There was a man he could trust, he assured himself, and once there were others such as he in positions in which such trust would be essential, the security of his throne would be all the greater.

On the fifth day of their residence at Leicester, word came by fast horse that Earl Stanley was expected late the following day, and Henry ordered that a banquet be organised to celebrate both his return and the long-delayed progress back to London. As the sun's rays began to sink in the west on the sixth day, adding a golden glow to the flag of St. George that was flying from the main flagpole at the top of the ancient tower, Henry sat grumpily in a corner of the Withdrawing Chamber next to the Great Hall, from which came the sounds of pages laying the trestles and serving girls giggling as they went about the task of putting out the trenchers. He was hungry and anxious to complete the main business of the evening, which would be to bestow further titles and honours on the man who had handed him the crown of England, but who was now keeping him from his supper.

An usher knocked respectfully on the chamber door, entered, and bowed.

'Earl Stanley has returned, Your Majesty, and seeks your presence in his chambers.'

'In future,' Henry responded testily, 'it shall be *his* place to answer to *my* summons, but tell him that I shall attend upon him shortly.'

Henry checked his dress in the long mirror, took a final swig of wine, and strode purposefully down the hallway that gave rear access to the guest apartments. He hammered impatiently on the chamber door and walked in. Stanley stood up as Henry walked in, a sly smile on his face.

'It would seem,' Henry muttered, 'that Earl Stanley has a habit of being late for everything. He arrives late on the field of battle, and now late for a banquet held in his own honour. May we now eat?'

'Mind you do so slowly, that your stomach be not discomforted,' came a voice from the adjoining room that he had not heard for fourteen years, and there stood his mother in the doorway. They raced towards each other and embraced warmly, before Margaret stood back to take a better look at him, a tear forming in each eye.

'When last I saw you, it was in the company of your uncle, and you were running for France, a fresh-faced youth who had not then begun to grow a beard. Now you are a man, a king, and you need a barber to your face.'

'I am King thanks to you, and my father here. You are forgiven your lateness, Earl Stanley, since you bring me such company. Were I not a king, I would have tears of joy rolling down my face.'

'I shall, with your leave, withdraw,' Stanley said with a beaming smile, 'that the mother and child reunion may be more private.' He bowed, but before leaving the room he looked back with a mischievous grin. 'Do not delay too long, Your Majesty — I also am hungry.'

Henry hugged his mother to him again, and kissed her on both cheeks.

'Dearest mother, how can I thank you? Through all the years that have passed so fretfully, you have ever worked for this moment, and now it has arrived. No longer Dowager Countess of Richmond, nor even simply Countess of Derby, but Royal Mother. Is that how you wish to be styled?'

'"My Lady the King's Mother" would seem to have the appropriate ring to it,' Margaret replied with determination. 'And if you would truly reward me for all that I have done, might you make it a royal order that I live separately from Earl Stanley?'

Henry's face fell. 'You love him not?'

'Love is one thing,' his mother replied, 'but wifely body service is another. Since your uncle assures me that you go not to your marriage bed a virgin — although thank God he spared me the detail — you will perhaps be able to imagine how such activities might weigh heavily on a woman of my age, with my slightness of body, and given the long service that my womb has performed for England. Were I to live separately, his lordship might feel more free to take a mistress, lusty old goat that he seems to have become in his later years.'

Henry was embarrassed by all this confidence, but managed a smile.

'It shall be as you wish, if it be possible. Leave it with me, and let me escort you to supper.'

Over an hour later, fortified by several goblets of wine, Henry rose to his feet at the high table, and a herald called for silence. Henry cast his eyes slowly around the assembled company, and summoned up the words he had been practising for several days.

'My lords, ladies, and most esteemed Mother. We are here this evening because God has smiled upon our enterprise. Thanks to you all, I will tomorrow progress to London to claim my rightful crown.'

He paused for a few moments, then raised his hands to quell the loyal cheers that had greeted his opening words. As the noise subsided, he picked up his theme again.

'I would not be in that happy position without all of you. I cannot take the time to do full honour to you all, else there would be insufficient time for you to drink yourselves into a stupor, but there are some whose faithful service I must acknowledge, if I am to be accounted a grateful monarch. First, there is my most beloved mother, who has spent the best years of her life working for the moment when Lancaster and Tudor combine together with York to rule England in peaceful perpetuity. She has chosen as her title "My Lady the King's Mother", and it would be deemed a courtesy were you all to commence using it even before the tables have been cleared this evening.

'Secondly, my uncle, Jasper Tudor, who is confirmed in his Pembroke estates, and further created Duke of Bedford. He was my constant guide and protector during my years in exile, and taught me all that I require to know in order to rule the nation, in addition to certain matters of which my mother disapproves.'

He paused for the chortles, then continued.

'Finally, Earl Stanley of Derby, who is confirmed in all his lands and titles. Likewise, his brother Sir William Stanley. Their forces were the ones that drove Gloucester and his men from the field, and saved me from almost certain death at the hands of a devil wielding an axe with the same bloodlust with which he attempted to rule this nation. Those days have now been consigned to history, and I would ask you all to stand and toast Earl Stanley, Lord High Constable of England, and Sir William Stanley, Royal Chamberlain.'

II

Late on the afternoon of 3rd September it was the newly-created Constable of England who led the massive procession through the streets that formed the northern approaches to London. It proceeded with great pomp, with an entire company of heralds blowing their hearts out, all the way down to the Western Postern of the Tower of London, where Henry was to take up residence until his coronation, provisionally planned for six weeks time, on 30th October.

There were two more senior appointments to be made, and Henry had decided to combine them in the one person, since that was the tradition. Bishop John Morton had been continuing his duties as Bishop of Flanders since the day after the battle, when he had returned to tend his Flemish flock, and he was now summoned back across the water to attend Henry in the royal apartments in the Tower.

Henry welcomed him warmly into his reception chamber.

'Now, there are two things I must ask of you.'

'Certainly, Your Majesty.'

'The first is whether, in keeping with all such men as yourself, learned in religious matters, you also have skill in the law.'

'Some, certainly, Your Majesty. I studied Civil Law at Oxford, and I also have familiarity with the canon law of the Church that I serve.'

'My question is whether it is the law of the land that a woman must give her estates over to a man upon matrimony, or whether, instead, she may hold her own property in her own right.'

'The so-called law that you cite is custom only,' the clergyman replied. 'Custom may be overridden by royal decree, or by Act of Parliament. It is so across the Channel, where such fortunate women are said to be '*femmes sole*', and are held in great esteem.'

'Thank you,' Henry replied, greatly reassured, 'and now to my second question. Would you accept office as Archbishop of Canterbury when the seat next becomes vacant?'

The prelate's mouth fell open in sheer surprise, then formed into a smile of gratitude. 'Your Majesty does me great honour, of which I am not worthy. Were Your Majesty to be so gracious as to imbue me with such an honourable office, I would swear before God to serve you always with total fidelity.'

'I would expect nothing less of you,' Henry replied, 'but with that position has traditionally been coupled another, that of Lord Chancellor. I would also wish you to accept that, although the day-to-day financial work of the office would be carried out by a Treasurer who I have yet to appoint. However, it would be in matters of high diplomacy where I would be relying upon you, most notably in negotiations with foreign monarchs, of which you have had ample experience already.'

'Your Highness surely does me too much honour,' Morton replied, his head bowed in humility.

'We shall see whether or not it be *too* much,' Henry replied with a smile. 'Now prepare yourself for a journey to Rome immediately after the coronation, since I will have need of your services in order to obtain a papal dispensation for my marriage. However, this will need to wait until after the crown is finally on my head.'

The following day Henry was quietly studying his bible when a shadow fell across the door to his chamber, and there, unannounced, was his mother. He jumped up in surprise and walked over to embrace her. Before he could do so, she thrust a bunch of flowers into his hand.

'These are from the princess to whom you are spoken in marriage, who is in no small manner put out that you do not summon her to your presence, since you have yet to meet.'

'You would have me summon her to the *Tower*?' Henry asked, grinning. His mother's frosty glare did not melt.

'And why not? It is secure, is it not? Although, given the ease with which I gained access to this chamber without so much as a challenge, I might equally well have been an assassin.'

'I must apologise for the lack of courtesy in announcing your arrival,' Henry replied submissively, 'and the matter of security shall be dealt with immediately following your departure.' He looked down at the flowers in his hand, adding, 'These are beautiful — please thank the princess for her kindness.'

Margaret tutted. 'I can only conclude that the days of chivalric romance are over. In my youth, it was the man who sent flowers and other tokens of affection to the lady. Your father wooed me with such gestures, and — as I hope you would agree — no harm came of it.'

'Red roses with white roses — symbolic indeed,' Henry observed.

'Do not seek to evade the issue,' Margaret replied in her sternest motherly tone. 'Why do you not receive your bride-to-be?'

'Do please sit down, Mother, and I will explain my reasons. It is important that there be no challenge to my throne. The first challenge — that of military might — has been done away with. The second comes from possible rival claimants, and if

101

the royal princes truly be dead — in this very place, if rumour be correct — then that leaves, apart from Elizabeth of York, only Edward of Warwick, who now takes his meals in the White Tower. But how strong is my claim in my own right? It comes in two lines from Edward III, both of them from the wrong side of the marital bed. One of those lines comes through you, and, dear mother that you are, you are still a woman, and this counts for little in our world.

'My only other claim would be through my wife, should she be my wife at my coronation. Am I to receive the crown of England on my head amid whispers that I only became entitled to it through my mother and my wife? Far better, surely, that I become King first, *then* take a wife? Nor can I risk rumour that the daughter of Elizabeth Woodville inherited her mother's fabled power to seduce men in high positions, and by this means so bedazzled a young man so innocent of the ways of the world that it may be doubted whether he has the wit to rule a nation.'

'A pretty set of excuses to cover your shyness with the opposite sex,' Margaret replied, unconvinced by any of this.

'I have found you a house in which to live,' Henry blurted out, in order to stem Margaret's indignant wrath before it had time to gather any further momentum.

'Indeed? That at least is some comfort,' Margaret conceded somewhat huffily. 'Where is it, pray?'

'Thames Street, just down the road from here. In fact, you may almost see it from the outer wall. Until last week it housed the Garter King of Arms, who has now been ordered to Westminster, along with his tribe of scribblers. The house is already a burden on the royal accounts, and is called "Coldharbour". Hopefully it will provide a warm harbour for you against the "sweaty fumblings" of the brother of my recently appointed Chamberlain, who is, by his office, responsible for the security within the Tower of which you so recently complained.'

'If the drains be sour, you shall hear more from me,' Margaret warned him with the suggestion of a renewed smile.

'If the drains be sour, have resort to Uncle Jasper,' Henry replied cheekily, 'since he was the one who chose the house.'

'In the belief that I will be farewelled with the same ceremony with which I was admitted,' Margaret said as she rose to leave, 'I will leave you now. But you are required at Eltham a week today to meet with the Princess Elizabeth.'

A week later Henry dressed in his favourite blue and silver surcoat, donned a new feather bonnet and joined Jasper for the ride out to Eltham, accompanied by half a dozen mounted men from the new royal bodyguard, still wearing Stanley livery. He had insisted that his uncle accompany him and had jokingly threatened to exile him if he did not, but Jasper could sense that his nephew was as nervous as he had been before his first experience of the battlefield, but for different reasons.

Henry and Jasper were shown into the reception room, where they stood edgily awaiting their hosts. Henry had just announced in a whisper that 'I need a piss' when there was a rustle of movement in the doorway, and in walked Margaret with a vision of loveliness on her arm.

'May I introduce my god-daughter, the Princess Elizabeth of York?'

Henry stood, transfixed, as he took in the long pure white gown with gold filigree from head to foot, and a matching gold gorget from which her long hair, the colour of burnished gold, flowed promiscuously to cascade onto her shoulders. Instantly forgetting all the Courtly compliments that Uncle Jasper had been teaching him, Henry opened his mouth in astonishment and blurted out, 'But you are *beautiful*.'

Elizabeth blushed, almost giggled, but dropped her eyes to the floor, before replying, 'Is it not meet that a future Queen of England be comely?'

'If you were the daughter of the Palace fishmonger, you would still be beautiful.'

'Hopefully I do not smell of fish,' Elizabeth fired back from under her eyelids. At this point Margaret decided that this conversation was proceeding in entirely the wrong direction, and coughed loudly.

'I believe that His Majesty has something of yours.'

Jasper dug him sharply in the ribs, and Henry remembered the pouch in his surcoat pocket, which he hastily withdrew as he walked towards Elizabeth with an outstretched hand.

'I return the ring you sent me during my exile in Brittany. As a simple token of my deep regard for your act of kindness, I have had it encrusted with diamonds by a royal jeweller. Please accept it as a token of my troth.'

'Gladly, my lord. I shall wear it on our wedding day.'

Shortly afterwards, as Henry and Elizabeth stood, their heads bowed closely together, at the chamber window that overlooked the ornamental garden beyond, the pages began laying the single table, while the serving girls followed behind them with the trenchers, occasionally looking up furtively at the handsome young man who was their new King, and secretly envying Elizabeth both her looks and her future marriage partner.

As they took their seats at the table, Jasper pulled Henry grumpily to one side.

'Your mother is not pleased by your forward behaviour towards the Princess Elizabeth. She has chosen to blame me for that, and as penance has insisted that I sit at table alongside yon spider in green.'

Henry looked across towards his mother, who was engaged in conversation with a somewhat gaunt-looking, but still attractive, lady in her late twenties who so closely resembled the young Elizabeth in her facial structure that Henry had little difficulty in identifying her as Katherine Woodville well before his mother effected the introductions. Then, as a delicious aroma of roast suckling pig permeated the room, the kitchen servers entered in a line with dishes of cooked meats, pots of salmon soup and a selection of fruits, while several young girls stood by with pitchers of wine.

Jasper had been seated to Margaret's right, with Katherine at the far end of the line, to Jasper's right. Henry was seated with his mother to his right and Elizabeth to his left, and to Jasper's consternation, and Margaret's barely concealed delight, Henry and Elizabeth behaved, throughout the meal, like long-lost childhood friends on an adventure without benefit of parental supervision. They laughed and giggled in conversations that Margaret feared might be bordering on the lewd, and Elizabeth found several excuses to let her cool, ringed hand rest on Henry's for longer than was either necessary or accidental.

After a while, Margaret was sufficiently convinced that the young couple would need no further encouragement to lay joint claim to a marriage bed, and concentrated instead on occasionally reviving the stilted conversation that was taking place to her right. Jasper was striving manfully to display interest in the inevitably limited tittle-tattle of which Katherine was capable, given her long period of enforced absence from the Court since the execution of her late husband for treason.

'That was one of the most tedious women I have ever had the misfortune to encounter,' Jasper complained to Henry as they cantered over Peckham Common with the lowering sun in their eyes.

'But she was comely enough, surely?' Henry suggested.

'Comely enough for *what*?' Jasper asked. 'And what did your mother say as we were leaving?'

'She wishes me to order you to make her the Duchess of Bedford,' Henry grinned.

Jasper was thunderstruck. 'You would sully the image of your throne by ordering me to tup an old crow like her?'

'You need not tup her — simply marry her. And she is *not* an old crow. While your tastes might run to young serving girls who have barely reached the age of their monthly leaking, some would say that she has retained a certain amount of her youthful beauty, albeit that the cares of recent years have begun to leave their lines. But examine the matter this way; the uncle of the King marries an aunt of the Queen, thus completing the family circle, and — as an additional benefit — drawing the Woodvilles further into the royal camp.'

'So it is now a matter of State that I must share my bed with Methuselah's mother?'

'If you see it that way. I will decree it if I must, but my mother insists.'

Jasper spat to the side of the track. 'The great and noble King Henry makes state policy under dictation from his mother — how well *that* will go down when you call your first Parliament!'

'The mere suggestion of that, and I truly *will* have you exiled,' Henry joked, but the humour seemed to be lost on Jasper.

Later that evening, Henry sat in his private chamber, thanking God for his good fortune, and fantasising about his wedding night with the beautiful, spirited young girl who had taken his emotions hostage. His gaze wandered towards the vase in which one of the valets had placed the red and white roses a week earlier. Henry was in the process of praying that their marriage did not wilt as quickly as the flowers had done when his attention was gripped by the way in which the petals had fallen. An entire flower head from a red rose lay on the cabinet on which the vase had been placed, and several petals from a white rose had landed on top of it.

He got up and took a closer look. Then he reached up to the plants that had not yet completely wilted, and removed more white petals, which he arranged around the centre of the red rose. He laughed out loud in sheer delight, and summoned a page, who stood uncertainly in the doorway after answering the loud call.

'Yes, Your Majesty?'

'Have the Garter King of Arms attend me tomorrow. He lodges now at Westminster Palace, and I would speak with him as a matter of urgency. I have an idea for a new coat of arms for my coronation. It shall be called "the Tudor Rose".'

III

Early on 30th October of that year, the entire city seemed to be stirring long before the sun appeared over distant Gravesend. Grooms of the Household were preparing baths in various noble houses, including the Tower and Coldharbour, where Elizabeth was now residing in a suite of chambers all of her own, while her generous godmother Margaret confined herself to the ground floor. Grooms of the Stable were ensuring that pedigree mounts were rubbed down and gleaming, pages were dabbing last-minute stains off liveried tunics, while other pages were entering withdrawing rooms with trays of sustenance while their lords and ladies dressed, in the bedchambers beyond, in the clothes that seamstresses and ladies-in-waiting had carefully laid out.

The crowds were ten deep along Thames Street, Blackfriars and Whitehall long before the procession formed up on Tower Green and commenced its stately procession with the Lord High Constable of England at its head, carrying his mace of office, while the royal orb and sceptre were held by lesser officials, each mounted on a royal grey charger that was draped with cloths bearing the royal standard. Behind, in the order of seniority of their ancient titles, rode the dukes, earls and other nobles of the houses of England, and behind them those senior clergy who were not required for the service itself. There was then a noticeable gap before Henry rode into sight on a huge warhorse, dressed in his robes of State, and followed immediately by the newly created royal bodyguard, resplendent in their hastily commissioned tunics featuring the Tudor Rose for the first time that it would be seen in public.

There were hundreds of ordinary foot soldiers with halberds holding back the massive crowd outside Westminster Abbey, most of whom cheered at their first sight of Henry, who smiled as they called out 'God Bless Your Majesty!' 'Long Life and Happiness to Your Highness!' and 'God Speed King Henry!' The procession dismounted some hundred yards back from the open cathedral doors, and wound its way, on foot, into the cool of the Abbey stonework, down the long nave towards the raised platform that had been specially erected for the occasion behind the main altar.

The senior nobles, including Jasper, Duke of Bedford, took their seats among the choir stalls behind the altar, while Henry sat in the ornate chair in front of Archbishop Thomas Bourchier, to whom, by tradition, fell the solemn task of anointing a new king. Henry gazed down at the crowded ranks of those who sat in the nave, smiling up at him. On the front row was his mother, looking as solemn as she was able while fighting back tears of joy; next to her sat Elizabeth, smiling back at him proudly with a look of profound love in her eyes. He looked beyond them, to the men who had risked their lives for this moment, some of them bearing the healing scars of the encounter that they would carry for the rest of their lives.

The ceremony began with a High Mass, everyone except Henry moving to the altar in strictly prescribed order to take the sacrament. Then the Archbishop presented Henry to the assembled company, which with a united voice yelled back the traditional response of 'So be it King Henry!' The Archbishop then beckoned Henry forward to the altar, where he prostrated himself while the Bishops of Exeter and Ely moved silently to their places on either side of the senior prelate of the realm.

The rest of the ceremony was conducted in accordance with the *Liber Regalis* that had governed previous coronations. Henry was anxious that it should be so, since he had broken with that tradition in not having ridden, bare-headed, through the streets of London from the Tower to Westminster Palace the previous day, but had elected to commence the procession at the Tower. This was on the strong urging of Sir William Stanley, who was anxious about Henry's personal security at a time when it was believed that his accession was still resented by a few remaining Yorkist hotheads.

Henry was raised to his knees by the Archbishop, who extracted from him the promises to 'grant and keep the laws and customs' of the realm, to respect the Church, and to grant 'equal and rightful justice' to all, regardless of rank. He was then given the sacrament, and anointed with holy oil while the choir moved discreetly in from a side chapel and sang '*Veni Creator Spiritus*' before withdrawing. The Archbishop then took the crown from the Bishop of London, who had been holding it as he stood at Henry's side, and placed it reverently on Henry's bowed head. Then with a broad smile he turned to face the congregation, made the sign of the cross high in the air, and pronounced that Henry of Richmond had now become '*Henry, by the Grace of God, King of England, France and Lord of Ireland.*'

Almost as important to Henry as the coronation itself was the swearing of fealty to him by as many nobles of the land as could be persuaded, under pain of attainder or imprisonment, to declare their allegiance to the young man upon whose head the Archbishop had placed the crown of England. Henry was just as interested in their revenues as he was in the loyalty of those who enjoyed them, particularly after Reginald Bray (now

Sir Reginald Bray) had taken one look at the royal accounts and advised Henry that he was nearly bankrupt.

It was therefore of considerable satisfaction to Henry that the vast majority of the leading nobles attended one or other of several ceremonies in the weeks following his coronation, in order to bend the knee and swear the oath that went back centuries. Perhaps one of the most reassuring heads he saw bowed before him was that of John de la Pole, Earl of Lincoln, nephew of the former Richard III, and the man who had been all but declared his successor following the death of Edward of Middleham, Prince of Wales and Richard's natural heir, the year before the battle. With the only other remaining potential Yorkist heir, Edward, Earl of Warwick, safely installed in the Tower, and the Earl of Lincoln a popular and influential figure among those at Court who might still retain fond memories of the halcyon days of Edward IV, it was as well to have him on one's side.

There were also two other matters that required his urgent attention. The first was ensuring that Uncle Jasper did what was required of him in the matter of his marriage to Katherine Woodville. Jasper would marry Katherine in Wales only a week before the first Parliamentary session, and Henry wanted him back in time for that. However, Jasper in his mid-fifties was no longer the dashing young spark who could ride through the night from one adventure to another, and he would be returning with his bride after only the briefest of wedding celebrations, while the new Duchess of Bedford, although not yet thirty years of age, could hardly be expected to thunder across England like some highway robber escaping the law. Henry had therefore ordered an entire royal progress, in order to ensure that the newlyweds would travel with both comfort and speed, and had underlined it by placing himself and his mother at the head of the guest list.

There was also the urgent matter of a papal dispensation. The entanglement of families that had led to the dynastic strife between York and Lancaster that Henry hoped to have suppressed for good had resulted in Henry and Elizabeth being related, by marriage, in the fourth degree. Given the strict provisions of the 'canons of consanguinity' by which marriage was governed under the law of Rome, it was necessary to obtain Papal dispensation before their union would be recognised as lawful throughout the Christian world.

Margaret Beaufort and Elizabeth Woodville had already obtained one — secretly — during the final year of Richard's reign, but the need for secrecy had resulted in a degree of anonymity in the resulting document, which referred only to 'Henry Richmond' and 'Elizabeth Plantagenet'. However, Henry wished to leave not the remotest possibility that the validity of his impending marriage might be challenged at a later date, and any heirs to the throne thereby bastardised, so he sent John Morton on a mission to Rome for something more specific, and while he awaited Morton's return, Henry did nothing towards the planning of his own wedding other than commissioning the ring.

This did not mean that he hid from his bride-to-be, however. Henry and Elizabeth spent many happy afternoons, suitably chaperoned, listening to musicians, playing cards, planning the royal apartments and dreaming up names for the many children that they hoped to have between them. Elizabeth was aware that they were awaiting Papal dispensation before they could tie the knot, and Henry had also promised that before that happened he would arrange for Elizabeth's official bastardy to be revoked. Those late autumn and winter afternoons spent holding Elizabeth's hand by the roaring fire in her suite of rooms would remain among Henry's favourite memories as the storm clouds gathered round the throne in later years.

IV

Henry faced his first Parliament — a joint sitting of the Lords and Commons — in the White Chamber

'Gentlemen,' Henry began, 'you need have no fear that you have been summoned here in order to approve new taxes. As your new monarch, it is my wish to live within the means that fall naturally to me from my estates, and I will only seek to levy new taxes in times of urgent need, such as the invasion of our realm by a foreign power.'

The collective sigh of relief was clearly audible, as Henry continued with the most endearing smile he could summon.

'First, on a matter touching and concerning the rights of this assembly, the Commons is currently without a Speaker. It is my wish that your new Speaker, the man I have already appointed as my Chancellor of the Exchequer, be Thomas Lovell, but he is currently under an attainder imposed by the late usurper of the throne, Richard of Gloucester. To avoid any further such injustice, and in view of Lovell's valiant actions on my behalf when we defeated Gloucester in battle, I hereby formally remove that attainder, and ask that you now elect Thomas Lovell as your Speaker.'

Given the unpopularity of the position anyway, and the gracious reward for loyalty that Henry was granting to one of the most popular members of the Commons, there was a hasty response of 'aye' and 'so be it' from almost every member of it who was present. Having now in effect ensured that 'his man' was in nominal control of the entire Commons half of the Parliament, while the nobles in the Lords stood to lose the most by antagonising the new King, Henry moved on to the next items of business with renewed confidence.

'As your first item of business, I seek confirmation from you that Parliament recognises my title to the throne of England, as symbolised by the placing of the crown on my head by the Archbishop of Canterbury. Not only that, but that this right came by conquest on the twenty-first day of August past. Bearing in mind my undertaking to raise no new tax immediately, are there any among you who would wish to debate this simple matter?'

Given that many of those present had already pledged their fealty to him, and stood to lose their estates if they said otherwise, the general muttering that followed was largely affirmative, and the newly-created Speaker, who owed his elevation to Henry anyway, simply shouted, 'You have our confirmation of both of those matters, Your Majesty.'

'Thank you, gentlemen,' Henry responded with a slight bow of his head. 'Now that my authority as your King is placed beyond all challenge, I hereby remove *all* attainders imposed during the period of supposed rule by Richard of Gloucester, other than those imposed by me on certain nobles, now in sanctuary, who escaped from the field when Gloucester was defeated by my armies. There may of course be attainders imposed by me in appropriate future cases, but hopefully that will never prove necessary.

'On the subject of Gloucester's misrule, it is my dearest wish that this Parliament repeal that most iniquitous Bill forced upon your predecessors, and known as the "Titulus Regis". Its primary purpose was to render the late King Edward and his family illegitimate, Edward because of his alleged parentage, and his children because Edward was allegedly not lawfully married to the now Queen Dowager. As you will know, it is also my wish to take, as my Queen, one of the daughters of that marriage, Elizabeth of York, and I feel sure that you would agree that it would not be good for the image of England among the crowned heads of Europe for your King to be known as someone who married a bastard.'

Again, only the briefest of muttering, accompanied by the vigorous nodding of heads, preceded the Speaker's assurance that 'It is repealed, Your Majesty.'

'I thank you for your loyal support on a matter close to my own personal happiness,' Henry responded with a beaming smile that was almost genuine. 'It is my intention, which I now declare before you, to delegate the day-to-day decision making on internal matters of State to a council of leading office-holders under the Crown who will henceforth be known as my "Privy Council". You have my undertaking that any matters that pertain to England's foreign affairs, or that are likely to result in the imposition of additional revenue burdens on the people you represent, will be referred to you as is your right and entitlement. But otherwise, routine government shall be by Council.

'Finally, you will recall my sincere undertaking to live within my private needs, and without the necessity for new taxes. Part of the traditional direct income of the Crown comes, as you will know, from customs revenues, which are within the province of this assembly to grant or withhold. Rather than trouble you annually with an item of business that may be disposed of this day, for once and all time coming, I ask that you grant these traditional customs revenues to my household for the duration of my reign.'

Given that, during the periods of office of even the longest-serving member, this right had been granted to each incoming monarch for their lifetimes as a matter of course, the members saw no reason to quibble, even had they been in the mood, and Henry had obtained from his first Parliament everything he had sought from it. There were a few private Members' Bills that were of no direct concern to Henry when they were raised, and he cheerfully waved them through before thanking the members for their attendance, and assuring them that he would not be troubling them again for the foreseeable future.

Then, as the members made their exit from the Chamber, Henry rose as a sign of respect from the throne he had been occupying, on a slightly raised dais, for the entire proceedings, and stood smiling, nodding, and occasionally bowing, to those who were heading for the massive rear doors. As he was coming to the end of this display of humility, Jasper walked onto the dais and placed a warm congratulatory hand on his shoulder.

'Well done, Henry!' he said, 'I would never have anticipated such inspired statecraft from my nephew. You had them eating out of your hand!'

'And woe betide anyone who bites that hand,' Henry muttered as he turned abruptly on his heel and left the Chamber by the private door on his way to Coldharbour.

The following morning, Henry met, by prior arrangement, with Sir Reginald Bray, Chancellor of the Duchy of Lancaster, which since the days of Henry IV had been a royal estate, with its revenues payable directly to the Crown. The information that Sir Reginald had to impart was hardly encouraging.

'It is riddled with corruption, Your Majesty, made possible by the confusion and uncertainty of the days of the usurper Gloucester. As a consequence, much revenue that should have fallen into the royal coffers has been either diverted or withheld completely — with, I am sad to say, the active connivance of those who should be upholding the laws of the realm in your name.'

'Give me an example,' Henry muttered, his face set in displeasure.

'Well, Your Majesty, take the estate of William Higham, lord of Tutbury, in Staffordshire. Being *bona vacantia*, its lands should have reverted to the Crown under the normal operation of the law when William died without heir. Instead, it seems that it was sold by Sir Geoffrey Wingate, the feudal administrator, to Richard Malvern, for seventy marks. When I made enquiry, it seems that the deed of sale was witnessed by Roger Littledale, Your Majesty's justice of the peace for the county, and — if rumour be correct — he was bribed to do so by Sir Geoffrey.'

'Disgraceful!' Henry responded. 'Take the necessary steps to have Roger Littledale relieved of the burden of his office, and replace him with someone more trustworthy.'

'Gladly, Your Majesty, but is that not something within the authority of the Justiciar?'

'Leave the Justiciar to me. If he complains, the response is surely that, as Chancellor of the Duchy, you are empowered in all matters relating to its management, and that royal estates fall outside the purview of the officers of State.'

'It shall be as you instruct, Your Majesty.'

'By how much have we been robbed, by such devious practices?'

'It is almost impossible to calculate, Your Majesty, given the corruption in public office that seems to accompany such underhand dealings. But it would seem, by reference to the rolls for the years immediately prior to your accession, that the Duchy is now worth less than half what it was — perhaps slightly less than fifteen thousand pounds in this current year.'

'If it is thus in the Duchy, which is subject to closer scrutiny than other sources of royal revenue, then it must be even worse in the Exchequer,' Henry observed. He turned to a page who was standing quietly in a corner, awaiting any royal command. 'Seek out Sir Thomas Lovell, and have him attend us.'

The page bowed out with the message. For the next hour or so, Henry became increasingly angry as he listened to the litany of malfeasance that Sir Reginald had to relate, almost fearfully, as he watched the royal ire rising. By the time that Sir Thomas was ushered into the presence, Henry was red in the face.

'Good Sir Thomas,' Henry said in a measured tone that was clearly intended to control the obvious anger betrayed by his countenance, 'how go matters in the Exchequer?'

Sir Thomas bowed uncertainly, and did his best to be tactful.

'Your Majesty, I have but recently become its Chancellor, as you know, and there are certain senior office bearers who seem determined to keep from me the true state of the Exchequer.'

'Dismiss them this very day, on my authority,' Henry spat back, 'and return tomorrow in the forenoon with more detailed intelligence of how woeful are the financial affairs of State. Make particular note of any evidence of corruption and deceit that you may discover, that I may punish those responsible.'

'It shall be done, Your Majesty,' Sir Thomas promised as he bowed out of the presence, thoroughly relieved to have escaped what threatened to be a storm of royal rage. The next morning he returned, to find Sir Reginald Bray once more in attendance, and he did his utmost to soften the blow.

'I have as yet discovered nothing of a dishonest nature, Your Majesty,' he began, 'but I am sad to report that matters are much delayed. Due to recent disruptions and uncertainties... '

'Yes, yes,' Henry replied testily, 'so much for their excuses — and spare me any of your own. When was the last completed audit of the rolls?'

'In truth, Your Majesty, there has been no audit since the year before the late usurper Gloucester fell from power. Even *that* audit was open to criticism, in that it was not initialled by the chief Receiver, but only one of his deputies. It would seem that office holding within the Exchequer has become something of an uncertain matter, open to argument and private warfare between several Deputy Keepers.'

'We clearly need to clean the stables,' Henry muttered irritably. 'I do not hold you responsible personally for what has been allowed to happen,' he assured Sir Thomas, 'but in return for the advancement and preferment that you have received at my hand, I *will* expect matters to improve. Have particular regard, in the first instance, to the receipt and transmission of customs revenues, since they remain, as you are well aware, for the benefit of the royal purse. Sir Reginald here may well be of great assistance to you in this regard, since he has, as I know from personal experience, the nose of a bloodhound when it comes to snuffling out corruption and false dealing.'

'Yes, Your Majesty,' Sir Thomas replied dutifully. 'Do you wish me to speak with the Chamberlain of your household, regarding how much has recently been consigned to his husbandry?'

'It might perhaps be wise counsel to do so. Would you, in addition to your other duties, be prepared to supervise him as "Treasurer of the Household"?'

'I would deem it yet another honour, Your Majesty.'

'Consider yourself appointed,' Henry replied with a knowing smile, 'and remember my preferment of you should you learn of any disloyalty by others. As for you, Sir Reginald, I wish you to draw up a list of all those justices of the peace and other law officers who have been malfeasant in the performance of their duties. The corridors of royal justice would also appear to be in need of a stiff broom. You may now both withdraw.'

Both men did so in no doubt that financial and legal mismanagement would soon be a thing of the past.

A month later, Sir Thomas was back to present Henry with a list of those in the Exchequer who had been dismissed, and those who had replaced them. Just as he turned to leave, he hesitated and looked back at Henry.

'Your Majesty, in my capacity as Speaker of the Commons, might I respectfully raise with you a delicate matter that has of late become of concern to the Members?'

'Which is?' Henry enquired suspiciously.

'The matter of the royal marriage, Your Majesty. It is felt that until England has heirs to the throne, it will be ever plagued with uprisings and rebellions. You have declared your intention to marry the Lady Elizabeth of York, and I have been requested to ask, with all humility and due regard to your personal dignity, when it is intended that the marriage shall take place.'

'I thank you and the Members for your concern,' Henry replied with a smile, 'and you may assure them that Lady Elizabeth and I are deeply aware of the significance to the security of the realm of our intended marriage, quite apart from the personal joy that it will bring to have such loving hearts united. But I may tell you privily that it shall not take place until Morton returns from Rome with a dispensation that he is seeking in my cause from the Pope. But, since you are so minded to jog my arm in the matter, I shall consult with the Lady Elizabeth regarding a suitable date, and send word to you all by royal proclamation.'

Henry kept his word, and the happy couple selected 18th January of the following year, hoping that this would be sufficient time for Morton's return with the all-important piece of paper, even though they were technically covered by the dispensation already granted in their natural names. No expense was spared, and much velvet was purchased from London merchants during the weeks immediately prior to Christmas, both for the royal dress (blue) and the royal bed hangings (red and blue). A new feather mattress was installed in the Painted Chamber, the most luxurious chamber in Westminster Palace, and around it was constructed a brand new four poster bed with richly embroidered coverlets encompassing all the colours of the rainbow.

The long looked-for dispensation arrived two days before the ceremony, which was conducted, as tradition demanded, by the Archbishop of Canterbury in Westminster Abbey. Her father being dead, Elizabeth was given away by a surviving Woodville uncle, while one of her aunts, Katherine, Duchess of Bedford, was her matron of honour, with the remaining daughters of York, Cecily, Anne, Katherine and Bridget, as her bridesmaids. The best man — by instant agreement between Henry and his mother — was Jasper, Duke of Bedford, and the two royal mothers — Queen Dowager Elizabeth and Margaret, the King's Mother — were allocated places of honour immediately behind the bridesmaids in the bridal procession that took place under a deafening fanfare from a dozen royal heralds, heartily blowing a piece they had composed especially for the occasion, and had been rehearsing for weeks.

The wedding feast was a fifty-course affair celebrated in the White Chamber, the only one large enough to accommodate the over one hundred guests. Minstrels played, jugglers juggled, and mummers performed a distraction especially written for one performance only, featuring prancing red dragons, and fireworks for the cannons that symbolically blew away a giant white boar. Then it was time for the wedding night, for which members of the Household had dug deep into their precedent books.

Elizabeth was slowly and carefully disrobed by her ladies-in-waiting, one of whom was Katherine Hussey, the young wife of Sir Reginald Bray, who had progressed through Margaret Beaufort's household at Coldharbour, and had formed a natural bond with her new employer while she had occupied her rooms there. This disrobing was done in a side chamber to the Painted Chamber in which the bed had been carefully made and inspected well in advance. Elizabeth was then led slowly into the Chamber in her richly embroidered nightdress, and put to bed. A few minutes later, Henry entered in a nightshirt down to his knees, on which was embossed the Tudor Rose that been so in evidence during the wedding and the feast that had followed. He was accompanied by several of his grooms and a handful of selected musicians who blew and drummed his progress towards the royal bed.

Then they all withdrew, once they had witnessed Henry sliding into bed alongside his bride, still dressed in his nightshirt. Once the room was empty, Elizabeth coyly raised her nightdress over her head and slid it to the floor, then turned and smiled at Henry.

Henry grinned back as he slid across the bed and pulled her towards him.

V

A royal wedding was one of the major occasions in the regal calendar upon which a king could create new nobles. However, Henry had already determined on a policy of breaking the power of such nobles as already existed, mindful of the role they had played in the dynastic struggles that he hoped to have put to an end. It was, therefore, hardly to be expected that Henry would create any more powerful nobles, but it caused considerable surprise, and not a little unease among his more senior advisors, when he released Henry Percy, Fourth Earl of Northumberland, from the Tower of London, as a gesture of mercy and magnanimity on the occasion of the royal wedding.

The Percys had been among the most powerful earls of the realm for as far back as anyone could remember, and there were many who counselled Henry that he was showing too much mercy to a potentially powerful enemy. Henry's response was that by his inaction on the battlefield, Percy had demonstrated an underlying loyalty to the House of Lancaster, and had, in his own way, delivered victory to Henry.

Not content with releasing him, Henry sought to play upon his anticipated gratitude by appointing him Lord Warden of the Tower from which he had so recently been released, and also Lord Warden of the East and Middle Marches, which made him responsible to Henry for holding back the Scots not only in his traditional lands of Northumberland, but also further north, all the way to the border at Berwick on Tweed. By the time that Henry had decided to test the wisdom of this decision by progressing north in order to sniff the air for whiffs of disloyalty, other matters were preoccupying his mind.

For the first few weeks after the royal wedding, the prurient tittle-tattle running through the kitchens and stables of Westminster Palace had been that the King and his bride were early to bed and late to rise, and that the new lady of the house was always smiling, and with a rosy glow around her countenance. A few weeks later, the talk among her ladies-in-waiting was of her occasional light-headed spells, and her inability to hold down even the light curds that were offered to her after rising for the day. By the end of April a royal physician, Thomas Linacre, had confirmed what hitherto had only been whispered conjecture — the Queen was with child.

It was decided that Elizabeth would retire to Eltham for her pregnancy. Henry occupied much of his time consulting genealogists and reading Geoffrey of Monmouth's writings on the legendary King Arthur, the Welsh-born hero of the now almost mythical Camelot. This ancient palace was believed to have existed at Winchester, to which Elizabeth was sent as her time grew near. Henry was further heartened by reading that according to the legend, the fabled King Arthur would return to claim England when a red pennant became joined with a white one; the imagery was too specific to be ignored, and if the queen gave birth to a son and heir, there was never any doubt in Henry's mind that he would be named Arthur.

Margaret of Beaufort took charge of the domestic arrangements for Elizabeth's 'lying in', which took place at St Swithin's Priory, Winchester, where in the early hours of the morning of 20th September 1486, Arthur was born, a month premature. Church bells were ordered to be rung around the nation to peal out the joyful tidings that the succession was secured, and that England would shortly have a new Prince of Wales.

While Henry had been absorbed in all these domestic triumphs, others had been casting a jealous eye on his initial success. Yorkist ambitions had not yet been completely suppressed. Not all of those who had taken the field against Henry south of Sutton Cheney had either died or been captured. Two in particular had escaped, and had successfully sought sanctuary in Colchester Abbey. The first of these was Francis, Lord Lovell, a die-hard Yorkist and former Lord Chamberlain to Richard III, who was not related to Sir Thomas Lovell, Henry's Chancellor of the Exchequer, but who fumed at the success that seemed to have followed Henry Tudor after the battle. Because of the danger that he still posed to Henry's throne, he was one of those attainted by his first Parliament in November 1485. Lovell's companion in sanctuary was Humphrey Stafford of Grafton in Worcestershire, also under an attainder that had not yet been acted upon. Both men believed that Henry was too soft to retain his crown, and that out in the free world there must be many resentful Yorkists who would rally to the first standard raised in rebellion.

Both men slipped out of sanctuary in early April 1486, and sought to promote an uprising that would commence at opposite ends of the country, and meet in the middle. Lovell headed north, where he remained convinced that he would find support among the traditional enemies of Lancaster, the people of Yorkshire. Stafford concentrated instead on his family connections in the West Midlands, and was initially successful in raising a small force that he intended to take north to join up with the army raised by Lovell that had failed to materialise.

When news first reached Henry that a rebellion of sorts had been launched, Henry let it be known that he was about to ride north to swat away this inconsequential fly in the royal ointment, and sent Jasper, Duke of Bedford, ahead of him with a pannier full of pardons for all those, apart from Lovell himself, who were prepared to walk away from the uprising before it began. As a result, long before Henry entered York on 20th April 1486, Lovell had considered discretion the better part of valour, and fled to Flanders.

Humphrey Stafford and his unwise brother Thomas had similarly miscalculated the strength of Lancastrian support in the western counties, and when Henry turned south-west in a show of force, they fled into sanctuary at Culham Abbey, south of Oxford.

At Kenilworth, Henry sat with John Morton, considering his options. He was anxious to make an example of Stafford, who was — at least in theory — still available for punishment other than the inevitable execution of the existing attainder that would drop his estates into Henry's pocket, and no-one could better advise him regarding the laws of sanctuary than the clergyman who was so highly regarded by the Pope, and who was an expert on canon law.

'Is it not a sin to violate sanctuary?' Henry asked.

'Not necessarily, Your Majesty. Since your accession has been blessed by the Pope himself, and since these men sought to act in violation of that blessing, would you not be merely upholding a Papal Bull by removing them from sanctuary?'

'Would the Pope not seek to excommunicate me?'

'I would seriously doubt that, Your Majesty, particularly were I again to travel to Rome and assure him that you sought only to uphold his holy will. In any case, it may be that we could hide the royal hand from such a procedure.'

Henry looked at Morton in surprise. 'You know of those who would conduct such an action?'

'I am sure that they could be found, Your Majesty. It would simply be a matter of ensuring appropriate financial reward.'

Henry thought briefly, then smiled back at Morton. 'Do it, Morton — whatever the cost.'

A few nights later, a man named John Barrowman was richly rewarded for breaking down the sanctuary door, together with an accomplice, and dragging out the loudly protesting Stafford brothers into the welcoming custody of a group of royal retainers who conveyed them to the Tower. They were placed on trial for treason, and the Justices of the King's Bench, who knew a popular ruling when they made one, found them both guilty. Humphrey Stafford was executed at Tyburn on July 8th, although his brother Thomas was pardoned. There was the predicted outcry over the violation of sanctuary, but, as anticipated by Morton, the Pope settled the matter by issuing a Bull that made the nice distinction that once a man had left sanctuary and committed more treason, he could not lawfully return to it. This fitted the Stafford case admirably, while at the same time acting as a deterrent to others who might be of like mind.

At approximately the same time, in another part of Oxfordshire, the next challenge to Henry's throne was being carefully prepared, and this was to prove more threatening. An ambitious Oxford priest named Richard Symonds had among his pupils a young man of lowly origins who bore a striking resemblance to at least one of the young Yorkist princes believed to have been murdered in the Tower. His name was Lambert Simnel, and Symonds considered that his prospects of acquiring the Archbishopric of Canterbury that was his fervent dream might be well bolstered by bringing his young pupil to the attention of those who could employ his remarkable appearance in order to place him on the throne.

There had been much speculation regarding the ultimate fate of the two royal princes, and Symonds's first thought, after he had schooled the young Simnel into Courtly manners and bearing, was to pass him off as the younger of the two, Richard, Duke of York. But then came a second rumour, regarding the escape of ten-year-old Edward of Warwick, nephew of the late King Richard, whom Henry had also cautiously imprisoned in the Tower, and Symonds set about persuading Simnel that he was that heir to the throne. He was soon to be assisted in this by an incautious, and uncharacteristically provocative, action by Henry himself.

By February of 1487, when Henry held a meeting of his Great Council at his royal palace at Richmond, he already had a well-developed network of spies and informers assembled by Morton and Bray, in order to keep themselves abreast of developments that they might report to the King in order to further justify the preferment shown them. By this means, Henry was advised that Francis Lovell, who had escaped to Flanders following his failed uprising the previous year, had the ear of the Dowager Duchess of Burgundy, the sister of the late King Edward IV, and that between them they were plotting to restore the York line to the throne of England, using a surviving member of its line as the rallying figurehead.

It was also rumoured that just such a contender had recently appeared in Ireland, claiming to be Edward of Warwick. The Earl of Kildare had fared well under Yorkist patronage, and was anxious to prevent Lancastrians overrunning his country and suppressing Irish ambitions to remain independent of the English crown. He would be just the sort of military supporter any Yorkist pretender could rely upon, and if the Irish joined with the Burgundians, Henry's crown would be in considerable peril.

Margaret and Henry were sitting alone in his withdrawing chamber at Richmond Palace, after the latest news had reached their ears.

'It is concerning, is it not, that your royal son and heir now has his inheritance put at peril by these disturbing rumours?'

'They may yet prove to be just that — rumours,' Henry sought to reassure her.

'But such wickedness — and so close to the nursery.'

Henry stopped, the goblet halfway to his lips. 'What mean you? *What* is so close to the nursery?'

'The plotting and scheming — as if she has not been honoured and rewarded enough. And she a former Queen who should know only too well how unstable one's throne can be.'

'What former Queen? You do not refer to the Queen Dowager, the mother of my royal bride?'

Margaret allowed her face to fall, as if in embarrassment. 'You did not know? Oh, please forgive me — I assumed that Sir Reginald — or perhaps John Morton — would have advised you already.'

Henry was now completely hooked, and Margaret knew it.

'Advised me of *what*?' Henry demanded, now thoroughly concerned.

'Well, obviously, given that Edward of Warwick is her nephew by marriage, and that Margaret of Burgundy was once her sister-in-law, and given that the Yorkist cause is not completely played out...'

'You are trying to tell me that the Queen Dowager plots against my own throne? And her daughter sharing the throne with me?'

'She has not yet been through her coronation,' Margaret reminded him.

'But Elizabeth Woodville is your close friend, is she not?'

'She was — once,' Margaret conceded. 'But that was when she felt threatened, first by Warwick, and then by Gloucester. I can only offer you my deepest apology if, by feigning to be my friend, she has insinuated her own daughter onto the throne, in order that you might be eased from it. It was, after all, she who said and did nothing when Gloucester showed your wife so much attention while you were still in Brittany. She clearly sees herself as a manipulator of thrones, and obviously resents my own preferment through your kindness. If the young Warwick were returned, and a Regent were required until he came of age, who would be more obvious than Elizabeth Woodville?'

'As ever, I am in your debt,' Henry said as he took her hand and kissed it. 'I must confer with Sir Reginald, to see if there be any truth in these vicious rumours.'

When confronted, Bray confirmed what Margaret had said.

At the meeting of the Great Council, Henry announced to its astonished nobles that the Queen Dowager Elizabeth Woodville was to be stripped of all her lands, and was to be allowed to retreat to the Abbey of Bermondsey, where she had accommodation rights as a widow of the House of York that had so generously endowed it over the years. The lands themselves were to be passed, in return for a relatively modest annuity, to her daughter Elizabeth, which of course meant that they would fall to Henry. The amazement and confusion with which this news was received by the nobles was nothing compared with the outburst from Elizabeth of York when she learned what Henry had done, and the grooms listening surreptitiously at the royal bedchamber door were well rewarded for their prurience by the sound of a dreadful argument in heated voices.

'You would ever listen to your mother ere taking the counsel of others.'

'It was *not* my mother who warned me of it, but one of my most trusted advisers.'

'Everyone knows that your mother is your most trusted adviser, and that she comes before your wife, whom you never even consulted before disgracing my dear mother so publicly.'

'Would I put my mother before my Queen?'

'Your *bed partner*, you mean! I am no more Queen than that bedpost! You delay to have me crowned, for reasons that escape me. Have I not already produced a royal heir? Have I not freely and lovingly given of my body? Am I not worthy of having a crown placed on my head?'

Henry promised to take urgent steps towards a coronation for 'Queen Elizabeth', but before that could happen he was advised that the Earl of Lincoln, to whom he had in many ways been more generous than Elizabeth Woodville, had fled from court and taken ship for Flanders. Before leaving, Lincoln had cunningly confided to close friends that he was in fear of his life, since if the King could do what he had just done to the Queen Dowager, who had evinced no threat to him, what would he be likely to do, in his increasing paranoia, to someone whose very continued existence was the greatest threat to his throne?

It was soon brought to the royal ear that Lincoln had joined the escaped Lord Lovell in Burgundy, where they both had the ear of the Dowager Duchess of Burgundy, the aunt of the young boy who was being proclaimed as the lawful King Edward VI of England. She was also the aunt of the Earl of Lincoln, and a disturbing Yorkist power-base was rapidly being assembled.

Henry's reactions to the situation that he now faced were two-fold. First of all, once it became clear that this new treason was based on the assertion that the young boy now being paraded around the streets of Dublin was Edward of Warwick, Henry ordered that the real Edward be taken from the Tower and led through the streets of London. He also put all the sea approaches from Flanders under constant watch, with beacons ready to be lit at the first sign of an invading naval force and commissioned two land armies — one under Uncle Jasper, and the other under his victorious commander-in-chief of two years previously in Leicestershire, the Earl of Oxford. For good measure he imprisoned in the Tower the Marquis of Dorset, Elizabeth Woodville's son by her first marriage, who Henry suspected of being part of the widespread plotting that his fevered brain was imagining.

Next, he renewed his insurance policy with God by visiting the Shrine at Walsingham on Easter Monday, before renewing his contract with St. George on his feast day at Coventry. During the same ceremony, he had Morton, in his Archbishop's robes, read out to the congregation the Papal Bulls that confirmed Henry's right to the throne, along with that of his lawfully wedded wife, and add some additional drama to the proceedings by cursing 'with bell, book and candle' anyone who sought to oppose the Pope's will.

On 5th May it was confirmed that a force of some 2000 German mercenaries hired by Margaret of Burgundy had accompanied the Earl of Lincoln and Lord Lovell to Dublin, where later that month Lambert Simnel was crowned as King Edward VI. Henry moved behind the walls of Kenilworth Castle and sent for his wife and mother to join him, before convening a council of war upon receipt of news of the long-expected landing in Lancashire. The Earl of Oxford was given, at his own request, overall command of the royal army that proceeded north once it was learned that the invaders had crossed the Pennines and were heading for York.

The foreigners were even less welcome in York than Lovell's forces had been the previous year, and therefore turned south, intent on seizing Newark Castle, while Henry entered Nottingham, where he was joined by a sizeable force donated by his stepbrother Lord Strange. The two armies raced towards each other across rural Nottinghamshire, and the rebels set the battle agenda by encamping on a hill outside the village of East Stoke.

Both Henry and the Earl of Oxford had recent experience of fighting an enemy with high ground advantage, and while Henry hung back with his bodyguard, Oxford repeated his triumph of two years previously, checking the downhill charge of the enemy, then countering it with his own attack. This battle was considerably longer than the one at Sutton Cheney, lasting for a brutal three hours, at the end of which half the enemy force lay dead, and among the fallen were most of the rebel leaders, including the Earl of Lincoln. Lord Lovell was last seen urging his horse in retreat across the Trent, and was never heard of again. If Henry recalled his own words on the previous battlefield that 'This must never happen again', he had clearly not chosen to honour them.

Henry rejoined his family at Lincoln, where prayers of thanksgiving were offered, before the royal caravan turned north once more and progressed through Yorkshire and the Scottish Borders, if only to demonstrate that the rebellion had been unsuccessful.

Elizabeth's coronation followed in November. Henry ensured that the splendour of this ceremony more than made up for its delay. The celebrations and pomp occupied, in total, four days, beginning with a stately river procession by barge from Greenwich to the Tower, where Elizabeth was formally welcomed by Henry. Symbolically, the barge in which she was carried was decorated as a giant Welsh dragon that belched fire ahead of it into the Thames as it glided sedately downriver.

Two days later, the people lining the streets to Westminster Abbey gasped in awe at the sheer beauty of the woman who was about to be crowned by the Archbishop. She was dressed from head to foot in a long, damasked, cloth of gold kirtle, over which was a matching mantle edged with ermine, and with gold tassels hanging almost to her knees. Her rose-gold hair swung freely under a cluster of gems that would shortly be replaced by a crown. In attendance upon her were her half-brother the Marquis of Dorset, recently released from the Tower after he had sworn further allegiance, and her sister Cicely, three years her junior but just as beautiful and, by her recent marriage, now Viscountess Welles.

Henry and his mother had no wish to distract attention from Elizabeth and hid themselves away in a closely latticed box set high in the wall between the altar and the pulpit, from where they beamed down happily on the proceedings. But Uncle Jasper was there, as High Steward of the entire production, and handed the crown to the Archbishop, who then symbolically placed it on Elizabeth's head to cries of '*Vivat Regina!*' from the enthralled congregation. Jasper was also the co-ordinator of the two days of feasting that followed, in company with his wife, the newly crowned Queen's Aunt Katherine, Duchess of Bedford.

Once the festivities had finally come to an end, Jasper's presence was once again required in the Great Council that had been meeting on and off throughout the entire coronation distractions, since there were urgent matters of State that Henry wished to have resolved.

He had learned valuable lessons from recent events, not the least of which was that while domestic security must always be a priority, he could not ignore the possibility of rebellions against his rule being fermented and launched from abroad, most notably Ireland, Burgundy or France. Ireland was a long-standing thorn in Lancastrian flesh, since the Earl of Kildare, the most powerful noble in this outpost of nominal English rule, had for many years enjoyed *carte blanche* from Yorkist monarchs, and had grown to enjoy, and profit from, his dominance of all the lands around him. But the Council was divided on how he should be dealt with for his part in the Simnel rebellion.

'If we invade now, with half his soldiers fertilising Nottinghamshire soil,' Oxford urged Henry, 'we can add his corpse to the collection, and hang him high from Dublin Cathedral.'

Henry's face set in a stubborn frown, and Morton, who knew the King's mind better than most, offered an alternative.

'It might be better to have such a powerful landowner on our side, enforcing the King's peace at his own expense, in return for a merciful pardon.'

'Leaving him free to interfere again, whenever some harlot's offspring who resembles a royal prince chooses to tilt for the throne?' Oxford countered.

Jasper was the one who found the compromise.

'Let us send emissaries bearing a royal pardon, and confirmation that his lands remain his own unless he supports further rebellion.'

Morton could see a further advantage in this proposal.

'Let us also demand that he hand over a substantial sum of money in security of such good behaviour, to be forfeit if he renege on his oath of fealty.'

Henry's face lit up in a smile. 'And what do we do with the money if he does not prove disloyal?'

It was Morton's turn to smile. 'If he does not prove disloyal, then he will in due course die without the bond being relinquished from the royal coffers. It can be worded so that the bond is not repayable to his estate, but that our debt dies with him, in accordance with the law of the realm.

'The Pope might even be persuaded to excommunicate him in advance, for any treason he displays to the English crown,' Morton added, and the matter was settled.

This left for discussion matters across the Channel. The remaining English foothold on the continent was still the fortress at Calais, of which Jasper, Duke of Bedford, was the Lieutenant, and from which armed expeditions could be launched inland to both Burgundy and Paris, and Henry was all for expressing his displeasure at the recent meddling of Dowager Duchess Margaret of Burgundy by raising an army to invade the duchy. However, Jasper persuaded him that he could ill afford to equip an army for such a venture, and that the presence of English soldiers once again on French soil — that they would need to cross to enter Flanders from Calais — could provoke Charles VIII, whose assistance had been invaluable to Henry when he had mounted his own invasion of England two years previously.

But, reluctant as Henry and Jasper might be to fight battles outside their own still far from secure kingdom, events that were about to unfold would leave them with little option but to commit troops in lands that Henry for one had hoped never to have to revisit.

VI

'What am I to do, gentlemen?' a perplexed and sorely troubled Henry asked his Great Council at the start of a hastily-summoned meeting at Westminster in November 1487.

Henry's successful invasion of England two years previously had been down to two nations that appeared to be destined for direct conflict, and somehow he had to choose which of them to support. On the one hand was the ailing Duke Francis of Brittany, to whom Henry owed so much for his generous hospitality during his many years in exile, while on the other was the full might of France, whose Regent, Anne of Beaujeu, had willingly provided some of the troops who had given their lives at Sutton Cheney.

Only months previously, Duke Francis, aware that his days were numbered, had begun negotiations for his heiress, the Duchess Anne, to marry Maximilian of Germany, who would be likely to inherit the Holy Roman Empire upon the death of his father Frederick III. The Regent Anne of France had other ideas, however, and was insisting that the Breton heir marry her brother, the future King Charles VIII of France, and was mobilising her forces to invade Brittany in order to ensure that this occurred. Francis was anxious to call in all his debts, and had sent emissaries to the court of Henry VII to jog his memory. However, Henry now had his own throne to defend, he was short of money, and he was anxious to expand trade with various commercial powers across the Channel.

'We cannot afford to antagonise France at this time,' Morton insisted. 'And yet the Pope would wish us to side with the Holy Roman Empire.'

'But we owe so much to Duke Francis,' countered Giles Daubeney, who had been one of those sharing Henry's later years in exile after he had fled to Brittany after the disastrous Buckingham Rebellion.

'What do you think, Uncle?' Henry asked Jasper. 'You were with me all those years in Brittany, and you also recall the Duke's generosity to us for all that time — surely we cannot desert him, now that our fortunes have so improved, and it is he who now needs our help?'

Jasper looked enquiringly across at John Dynham, Lord High Treasurer. 'Would Parliament be likely to grant us the money? And can we afford it if it will not?'

Reginald Bray snorted loudly. 'After the sums the Duke of Bedford here spent on the Queen's coronation last year, the Household could not afford to send a herring boat, still less a fleet of ships.'

'The last time His Majesty and I travelled to Brittany, it was in such a vessel,' Jasper joked, looking sideways at Henry, who turned pale at the mere memory, and added another argument to the mix.

'We surely cannot let France extend its northern shores any further west, thereby acquiring ports from which it could do grievous damage to both our military ships and our trading vessels?'

Henry had only recently persuaded Parliament to enact legislation that vastly improved England's trading profits — and, coincidentally, the customs dues flowing into the Household Chamber accounts — by insisting that both imports and exports to Flanders and Brittany, two of its most important trading partners, could only be carried on English ships, at least half of whose crews must consist of English sailors. The point was well made, and it fell silent until, as was becoming customary, the diplomatic mind of Chancellor Morton came up with a workable compromise.

'Might I suggest, Your Majesty,' he said quietly, 'that you send a token force to assist the Duke, while sending me, or one of my staff, to act as mediator between the two nations?'

'That sits well with me,' Henry agreed, after a brief period deep in thought. 'The Duke and the King are the two persons in Europe to whom I am most obliged for the happy position in which I am now placed. As a common friend to both, I cannot sit by and watch while they lock horns in such a way that one of them must prevail at the expense of the other. It shall be as Morton suggests — but no more men than can be dispatched without the need to seek special taxes.'

The Council dispersed, but Henry asked Morton and Bray to remain for refreshment in a smaller chamber while they considered other weighty matters. As they helped themselves from a platter of fish, washed down with small beer, Henry asked for an account of how matters stood with regard to the ingathering of money into the royal household, via the estates, and the improvements in law and order that he had demanded.

'The matter of enforcement is much improved, Your Majesty,' Bray assured Henry, 'and yet it could be better. There is still corruption in various quarters, as those who are charged with the duty of reporting chargeable events do not always do so. I have reason to believe that, by this means, we are deprived of at least one fifth of the potential income to the Household.'

'By whom are these sums collectible?' Morton enquired.

'The feudal overlords, in the main,' Bray advised him. 'But at the very top of the collection chains of the large baronial estates are the very overlords Your Majesty sought to restrain under the recent laws against livery and maintenance. It is clearly in their interests to maintain the old ways, remain silent on matters of maintenance, and simply pocket the revenues otherwise due to the Crown, and this unfortunately provides a precedent for those at the head of the estates that have fallen into the Household.'

Henry tutted and reached for the beer jug. 'What of the new justices of the peace that we have appointed? Do they not discharge the duties with which they are charged?'

'It is too early to tell, Your Majesty,' Bray replied. 'They are but recently installed in office, and as long as they remain unremunerated for their duties it is all too tempting for them to accept bribes and other inducements.'

Morton had been listening to this exchange with mounting irritation, and could no longer withhold his opinion. 'This is surely treason, Your Majesty? They are office-bearers under the Crown, and if they decline — or even delay — to perform their office, they are denying your prerogative right and power.'

'May they be fined for such malfeasance, say you?'

'Most certainly, Your Majesty,' Morton assured him.

'See to it without delay,' Henry ordered Bray, who was looking increasingly uncomfortable, 'and as for the feudal overlords who withhold money due to the nation — if not the actual Household — then we must consider arraigning them for treason.'

'Or might we simply not fine them, or seek bonds for their future good behaviour?' Morton suggested. 'By those means you will collect more revenue for the Household, while making the same point, namely that your laws must be obeyed.'

'Can we rely on our King's Bench Justices to bring in true bills against them?' Henry asked doubtfully. 'And by what law do we have them brought to court? Is it not better that it be treated as a Chancery matter?'

'There is yet another avenue that might be explored, Your Majesty,' Morton advised him. 'Since not all the laws of this realm proceed via Parliament, and since you are the fount of all justice, there is the matter of the Royal Prerogative.'

Henry frowned. 'The people would see me as worse than Gloucester in those uncontrolled days in which he put to death whomsoever he chose, without recourse to the law,' he objected.

'No, Your Majesty,' Morton insisted, 'with respect, there is no valid parallel or comparison. The King has always possessed prerogative power in matters not reserved for Parliament. It is essential that such authority be recognised and obeyed in times of urgent national necessity, such as foreign invasion. You would simply be reminding the nation that in your hands remains a discretionary authority to uphold the peace and good order of the realm. And what could be said more to touch and concern the good order of the realm than bringing the powerful lords to heel in the matter of moneys due to the Exchequer?'

Bray spoke in support. 'The Chancellor has a valid argument, Your Majesty. What is more, armed more publicly with Your Majesty's prerogative writ, I could probably increase revenues to the Household by a considerable sum — a sum you may need if you are to send fighting men to Brittany in support of Duke Francis.'

Henry thought for a few moments, then nodded his royal approval. He looked back at Morton. 'Does this prerogative of mine have a court of law for its enforcement?'

'No, Your Majesty, but it could be introduced as we sit here. After all, it would not need the consent of either House, since it proceeds from your royal authority.'

The reference to where they were sitting set Henry's mind on another track. He looked up at the vaulted ceiling of the small chamber in which they were met, with its gold stars set in a canopy of blue, in a mirrored reflection of the floor of the larger Painted Chamber, which was still a royal bedchamber when the King and Queen were in residence.

'This very chamber would serve our purpose, would it not?' Henry suggested. 'All we would require, as I see it, would be Justices from King's Bench brought in to try those powerful nobles whose very status would be likely to overawe lesser judges, but who would hesitate to be seen to be partisan towards them with the King or Chancellor also sitting in judgment.'

'I think Your Majesty has grasped the point to perfection,' Morton concurred.

Henry continued to think aloud. 'This chamber is still known by its Latin name of *camera stellata*. My Latin was ever lacking, Morton — how does that best translate?'

'"The Chamber of Stars", Your Majesty — no doubt a reference to the magnificent ceiling above us.'

'"The Star Chamber" has a neater ring to it,' Bray added.

Henry smiled again. 'Very well — our new prerogative house of justice shall be known as "The Star Chamber". Bray, find us a suitable case to begin with, that we may show these barons that there is no hiding place from royal justice. The King shall have his rights.'

Within a week, Bray had found the Star Chamber's first victim, a minor knight who had continued to insist that his small retinue wear his colours in public during a time of peace. He was fined forty marks by a court consisting of the King, his Chancellor, and two King's Bench Justices who had been drawn aside by Morton ahead of the proceedings and left in no doubt as to where their loyalties lay. Then they successfully prosecuted a Lincolnshire duke who had failed to pay into Exchequer both the sum due upon the majority of his first-born son, and the fee payable for consent to the marriage of one of his daughters to a neighbouring earl.

Within two months, the list of those awaiting judgment was such that weeks at a time had to be set aside for hearings, all of which went in favour of the Crown. An additional bonus, for Bray, was the noticeable increase in eagerness to pay relatively small amounts into the Household for similar feudal dues payable in estates ruled directly by Henry, and by February of 1488 it was possible to fund a token expeditionary force under Lord Scales to travel to Brittany in support of Duke Francis. In the meantime, Chancellor Morton negotiated safe passage through Normandy to Paris for a group of his senior emissaries to parley with the Regent Anne, and her brother, the impending King of France, regarding their intentions towards the proposed marriage of Anne of Brittany into the House of Valois.

All came to nothing, as French forces rode virtually unopposed across the borders of Brittany in July of 1488, and defeated the mixed Breton and English forces twenty miles north-east of Rennes. Employing a strategy well learned from his stepfather Earl Stanley, Henry publicly disowned the English troops who had fallen in the battle. Within two weeks of the defeat, Duke Francis died, leaving his daughter Anne to inherit, as Duchess of Brittany. However, without support from abroad, it looked increasingly likely that Anne would be transported back under French military escort to a forced marriage to Charles VIII of France.

Henry could no longer sit on the fence, and in February of 1489 he signed the Treaty of Redon, which committed six thousand English troops, under the command of Lord Giles Daubeney, to Brittany's aid. However, the treaty was more form than substance, since the troops were to be paid for by the Duchess Anne, despite the fact that a specially called Parliament in January had granted taxation finance for the venture. Henry was content with the precedent thereby set, that his Parliament would finance armies for overseas campaigns when they could be persuaded that it was in the nation's best interests to do so, particularly since it had taxed the nobility especially for that purpose, and had agreed to continue to do so in subsequent years, should circumstances so require.

Significantly, forces were also sent by Maximilian of Germany and by the increasingly powerful force in southern Europe, Spain, which was slowly forming into a single nation as the result of inter-marriages between the royal houses of Castile and Aragon. After landing at Calais, and before marching west to Brittany, Daubeney, under special orders from Henry, had committed one-third of his force to the banner of Maximilian in order to lift the siege of Dixmunde by the Flemish, as part of the Holy Roman Empire's ongoing warfare with Burgundy, with which Henry had a score to settle after the recent meddling of its Yorkist Dowager Duchess Margaret.

In Brittany itself, the commanders of the three supporting forces never saw eye to eye on matters of military strategy, and it was with a sense of sad inevitability that Brittany prepared for annexation by France, and the marriage of Duchess Anne to King Charles.

In the meantime, Henry had matters of a personal nature to occupy his attention, since the Queen was once again expecting his child. Although the young Prince Arthur was thriving in his nursery at Farnham, and had been created Duke of Cornwall on the day of his birth, Henry and Elizabeth were hoping for another son, to reinforce the dynasty and act as a reserve heir, should anything happen to their firstborn. As she had previously, the Queen withdrew to Eltham Palace for much of her confinement, leaving Arthur to be fussed over, and competed for, by his rapidly ageing nurse, Elizabeth Darcy, and his paternal grandmother Margaret, the King's Mother. However, it was agreed that the birth itself would take place in Westminster Palace, where the royal physicians could be more swiftly assembled from their various residences in and around the city.

Within days of receiving the good news of his Queen's second pregnancy, Henry was sharply reminded that there were still pockets of Yorkist sympathisers who did not take kindly to be being ruled by a Lancastrian. The tax levied by Parliament to finance the military support for Brittany, which in the event had not been required anyway, was resisted in parts of Yorkshire, where royal taxation commissioners sent to collect the sums due were subjected to verbal abuse, sullen silence, or missiles intended to send them back south. Henry ordered Percival, Earl of Northumberland, to justify his status as maintainer of the King's justice in the north, and he was brutally done to death during a riot on 28th April.

Henry wasted no time in marching north in retribution, and entered York a month later in company with his uncle Jasper, in his role as Earl Marshall of England, and an impressive array of armed soldiers. Heads rolled, necks were suspended in nooses, and heavy fines were imposed on even minor offenders in the show trials that followed, but Henry was still minus a Northern Marcher Lord. In an inspired fit of generosity, and in order to underline the mercy he could show to the truly repentant who were prepared to bow the head and bend the knee, he replaced Northumberland with Thomas Howard, Earl of Surrey. Thomas had acted as deputy to his slain father, the Duke of Norfolk, in Richard's defeated army, but had long since been pardoned, and was now appointed as the first President of the Council of the North, in a further indication by Henry that he would brook no more nonsense from that region of his kingdom.

In a short meeting ahead of a scheduled session of the Star Chamber, Henry and Morton were congratulating themselves on how the new jurisdiction was proving so successful. Not content to rest on his laurels, Morton had another strategy in mind.

'Your Majesty, there is a young lawyer in my office called Edmund Dudley, and he has, at my request, devised a strategy that might be employed to ensure a further means of both raising revenue and holding powerful nobles in check.'

'Speak further,' Henry encouraged him.

'It was, you will recall, during our discussions following the Simnel matter that we took to considering ways of holding the Earl of Kildare to account for any future actions he might take against the security of your throne?'

'Yes, I recall some talk of a bond,' Henry reminisced, 'although in the event he foreswore to enter into one, being content only to bow his head in the face of excommunication.'

'Quite so,' Morton confirmed, 'but the thought came to me that others might be persuaded to come to heel by extracting such a bond, which could be made non-returnable should they die without forfeit thereof. You recall, Your Majesty?'

'Indeed I do,' Henry replied with a faint smile, 'but few would be so incautious as to enter into such a recognisance as would deprive their heirs of an inheritance of any size.'

'Quite so,' Morton agreed, 'and this was the task I put to my man Dudley, that he might come up with a form of words that would have that effect, but might be so devious and convoluted that its true import was not immediately obvious.'

'This would surely reek of fraud,' Henry objected, 'and would be no more worthy of your high office than it would of my honour as monarch.'

'I also share that reservation, Your Majesty,' Morton was anxious to emphasise, 'but while seeking to penetrate the conundrum, Dudley had another idea. Instead of holding the sum handed over in recognisance in some dusty box, we should employ it to generate further monies, in the manner of merchants investing in goods.'

Henry was puzzled by what was being suggested, and frowned as his brain tried to come to grips with it. 'You are suggesting that we launch some sort of trading venture?'

'No, Your Majesty, although that would be one option. My suggestion — or perhaps, more truly, Dudley's suggestion — is that we loan the money to others who seek to launch such ventures.'

'I know enough of our laws to condemn that as usury — as would many others,' Henry frowned. 'And indeed, if I am correct, previous Popes have declared it to be a sin.'

'Indeed, you are correct, Your Majesty,' Morton conceded, 'but in Flanders and other parts of the Low Countries, as indeed in Germany, there is a different religion abroad, based upon a rejection of the infallibility of the Church of Rome. Usury is not regarded by them as a sin, and in towns such as Antwerp and Bruges there are merchant houses in which money can be left securely in deposit, and returned, much enlarged, at a later date.

'For example, on my last mission into France, I diverted to Bruges, where I was assured that the sum of a thousand marks, if deposited today, could be returned within a year with one hundred marks in addition, as a fee for the use of the money. Sir Reginald advises me that he could make five thousand pounds available from the Household at a week's notice, and by my calculation, I could, by such means, return to him, in a twelve-month, five and a *half.*'

'If I understand you aright,' Henry said, 'it is your counsel that we make a separate account of money handed over by rich nobles by way of bond, employ it in the manner you suggest in order to earn for ourselves the fee for its use, then return the sum first lodged if it be not forfeit in the meantime?'

'Precisely, Your Majesty.'

Henry chuckled. 'I shall instruct Sir Reginald to make over the sum of one thousand pounds only, in order to test the wisdom of your proposal. Should it be successful, this man Dudley of yours may be brought to Court, that we might employ his fertile brain in other such schemes.'

'Gladly, Your Majesty,' Morton smiled reassuringly as he bowed out of the presence.

It was noticeable that thereafter, those nobles hauled before the Court of Star Chamber, in addition to being forced to hand over sums of money that they had sought to hide from royal eyes, were in addition 'bound over in their own recognisance' by a sum of money to be handed to the Treasurer of the Household within twenty-eight days, which would be forfeit if any further transgressions were discovered. Those who had the temerity to enquire why the money was not payable to the Exchequer were tartly advised that they had been adjudged by a court that acted in pursuance of the royal prerogative, and that it was against this that they had been found guilty, and to this that they must give recognisance.

The royal child was born on 28th November 1489, and it was a girl. She was named Margaret, after her paternal grandmother, and the following day, amid much ceremony, her older brother Arthur was invested as Prince of Wales. Early in the New Year, following the precedent he had set in the north, and in case his uncle felt slighted by the investiture, Henry appointed Jasper President of the Council of Wales and the Marches.

Two years later, the royal heralds were again set the task of announcing to the excited crowds gathered outside Greenwich Palace on 28th June 1491 that the country had a new male prince, a second heir to the throne named after his father Henry. He was consigned to the royal nursery with his older siblings, four-year-old Arthur and their sister Margaret, now in her second year.

In what some might have regarded as indecent haste, Elizabeth again fell pregnant within months of Henry's birth, and she was heavy with child when Henry was urgently required to turn his attention once more to events across the Channel.

Another pretender had emerged from the shadowy legend of the Princes in the Tower, and this one was to prove more of a threat than Lambert Simnel had done, given Henry's meddling in foreign affairs.

VII

Charles VIII of France might still be a youth of twenty, but his sister Anne, still acting as his Regent, was far from impressed by Henry's interference in Brittany, particularly after she had given him troops to support his invasion of England, from which only a precious few had returned. Also with a slow-burning angry fuse pointing in his direction was Margaret, Dowager Duchess of Burgundy, the last of the York dynasty, who had so enthusiastically sought to destabilise the Lancastrian English monarchy with the aid of Lambert Simnel. Henry had added to his sins, in Margaret's eyes, by allowing his troops to be employed by Maximilian of Germany in his long feud with Burgundy, and she was the very person to approach when it looked as if there might be a more valid claimant to the throne of England, in the person of a son of the late Edward IV.

Rumours were still abounding regarding the ultimate fate of the two royal princes in the Tower, Edward, Prince of Wales and his younger brother Richard, Duke of York. The one certain fact was that they were no longer in the Tower, and the most popular theory was that they had been conveniently murdered. But for whose convenience? Richard of Gloucester clearly possessed the earliest reason for disposing of rival claimants to the crown, and most people at the time were disposed to believe that he had ordered their murder, if he had not carried it out by his own hand. But had their disappearance not also benefitted the incoming Henry of Richmond, who was rapidly becoming the unpopular King Henry VII?

And who was to know for certain that both boys were dead, and that one of them had not escaped abroad until he was old enough to return and point an accusing finger at his usurper? If he had, what would he look like now? Would he resemble his late father King Edward IV, or would the eight years that had intervened since he had last been seen — and even then only by Tower guards — have altered his appearance so much that it would be impossible to tell? These — and other conjectures — bubbled back to the surface in late 1491 when rumours reached England that a young man called Perkin Warbeck was being hailed in Ireland as Richard, Duke of York, long ago mourned as lost forever.

Warbeck's earlier years were shrouded in mystery, but it was beyond contest that having been brought up in Antwerp, he had entered the service of a silk merchant who took him, as part of his household, to Cork, in Ireland, where those who saw him, richly dressed as befitted his office, took him for a high-born scion of the House of Plantagenet. Although he tried to deny it, this was all the incentive required by the Earl of Kildare to stir up more trouble for the English monarch who had called in the Pope to threaten him with excommunication, and following discreet enquiry abroad, the young man was presented at the court of Charles VIII of France by an Irish noble in the pay of Kildare. English spies across the Channel picked up the rumours, and relayed them back to the English Court, which was soon abuzz with the news.

Late one evening, Henry sat alone in his robing chamber to the side of the royal bedchamber, head bent over the Household accounts that he had taken to initialling personally on a weekly basis, after they had been meticulously scrutinised by Reginald Bray. Queen Elizabeth had been prepared for bed by her ladies-in-waiting, but instead of slipping behind the rich hangings that shrouded the four poster feather bolster, she walked through the main chamber into the one in which Henry sat, in front of a candle burning brightly on the small desk he had installed there.

'Is it true?'

'Is *what* true?' Henry asked, half distracted from the task in hand.

'That my brother Richard is still alive, and received at the court of France?'

Henry sighed. 'You should not listen to the tittle-tattle of your Ladies. It is a rumour only — or, if not a rumour, then the boy must be another imposter like the one who is currently sweating out his days in the kitchens.'

'How can you be so certain that Richard is dead?'

'Your uncle murdered him — it is generally known.'

'But,' Elizabeth persisted, 'that too is surely only a rumour. How can you truly know that this boy in Paris is not Richard unless…' she continued falteringly, 'unless it was *you* who had him murdered?'

Henry looked up from his accounts, and glared back at his wife. 'You would accuse *me* of such a thing? What ails your senses, woman?'

Elizabeth advanced slowly towards him, carrying her bible, which she held out for him to take. 'I wish you to swear on this holy book that you had nothing to do with the death of either of my brothers, as is now being rumoured around the city.'

The colour slowly drained from Henry's face as he took the book from her.

'It has come to a sorry pass,' he muttered, 'when idle rumour can cause such distrust between those joined together in matrimony. However, since it would seem that my word alone is not sufficient, I will grant your request.' He placed both hands around the bible, looked her firmly in the eye and intoned, in a voice flat with distaste, and devoid of any emotion, 'I swear upon my immortal soul, and on the immortal souls of my mother, my wife and my two children, that I am innocent of the blood of either of the royal princes consigned to the Tower by Richard of Gloucester.' He handed back the bible, then looked back down at the rolls on the table. 'I shall be some time with these important accounts. You may take yourself to bed. Do not trouble yourself to remain awake.'

Elizabeth hesitated for a moment, her teeth over her bottom lip in a sign of regret. She began to hold out her hand towards him, in the hope that he would enfold her in his arms and reassure her that something important had not just been lost, but realising that the figures he was studying on the rolls were momentarily of more interest to him than she was, she stepped slowly backwards towards the chamber door and withdrew.

Long before the rest of the Great Council assembled, Henry had been deep in conversation with his Lord Privy Seal, the gifted clergyman Richard Foxe, recently consecrated Bishop of Bath and Wells. He was valuable to Henry in two main ways; first of all, he cost nothing, since his ecclesiastical stipend ensured him all the material comforts to which he was accustomed, but secondly he was a superb diplomat who maintained a network of spies all over mainland Europe, from whom Henry gathered most of his intelligence.

Henry had first made his acquaintance in Paris during his last year in exile, where Foxe had also been in hiding from Richard III. Since then, he had repaid Henry's protection and preferment by acting as Morton's deputy in diplomatic matters, requiring retainers posing as part of his household to obtain as much intimate information as possible regarding those with whom he had been sent to negotiate. Foxe had often returned from such expeditions with fewer staff than he had set out with, leaving his own men in positions from which they could, through Foxe and sometimes Morton, continue to pass information back to Henry's ears.

Henry was in urgent need of more information regarding the young man who was now recognised — and feted — at the French Court as Richard of York, and potentially Richard IV of England. It was May 1492, another royal child was expected within weeks, and Henry was impatient to learn all he could about the young man at the court of Charles VIII who was causing such unrest among Henry's courtiers, and fanning the smouldering embers of Yorkist resentment up and down the nation.

'The story he tells, Your Majesty,' Foxe advised Henry in the lowered voice that came so naturally to him when he was not in the pulpit, 'is that one night two men came to the chamber in the Tower where he was lodged with his older brother, Edward, and took the brother into an adjoining chamber from which could be heard the dreadful sound of the boy being smothered or choked. Then, according to the boy's account, the man who was holding him took pity on him, and smuggled him out of the Tower, and from thence to a boat moored lower down the river, from where he was spirited away to Flanders, to live with a wealthy merchant. He claims to have forgotten much of his early life apart from that fateful night in the Tower, and to have learned to speak Flemish with such fluency that he now has to be coached in his English.'

'A convenient fiction,' Henry muttered. 'Does he say aught of who sent the men to carry out the murders?'

'Nothing that has been reported to me, Your Majesty. But it seems that Charles of France sees him as a means of unsettling your grip upon the English throne.'

'Unless I first loosen *his* grip upon his own,' Henry growled. 'What is Charles's current weakness, would you say?'

'It is known that he wishes to wage war on his southern neighbour, Italy,' Foxe replied. 'There are disputes regarding trade routes across the Alps, and the mountain people have been enlisted by certain Dukes in Italy's northern kingdoms to harass Charles's caravans. In order to make the mountain passes safe for his own traders, Charles seeks to occupy Italy's northern border regions.'

'So the last thing he will wish is for harassment in his own northern realms,' Henry thought out loud, before enquiring, 'What about the Burgundy witch?'

'They say she is much taken up with negotiating a marriage between her grandson Philip, the heir apparent to the Duchy, with a young princess of Castile and Aragon, to further protect her nation against the ever-present threat of Charles of France. But since, as I have already said, the King's attention is directed to the south of his lands, Duchess Margaret is free to meddle, and it is said that she has expressed an interest in receiving the young man believed to be her nephew.'

Most of the Council having drifted in while they were talking, Henry called them to order and announced his main reason for convening the meeting. There was a sharp intake of breath when he announced, 'It is my wish to invade France with as large an army as I can muster.'

As the assembled nobles absorbed this startling piece of information, Henry turned to Lovell.

'I shall of course require more taxation, in addition to the sums presumably lying to my credit, unspent, after the Breton

156

venture that was paid for by Anne of Brittany. Since she seems resigned to marriage with Charles of France, there is some irony in the fact that we shall be using all the money we might have expended in her interest in order to lay siege to her new dwelling in Paris.'

'You intend to lay siege to *Paris*, Your Majesty?' Daubeney asked breathlessly.

'I wish to wage war against the King of France,' Henry reminded him sarcastically. 'Would you counsel that I do so by occupying Lisbon?'

As the laughter subsided, Daubeney sought to recover his credibility.

'My point was simply this, Your Majesty, that it will be late in the campaign season ere we can amass the necessary forces in Calais, and King Charles will hardly expect an invasion in, say, October. However, that will also be the time at which they are ingathering their harvest, and if we lay waste to Normandy, we can both ensure provisions for our own fighting men, and deprive France of its much-needed crops. By this means Charles might be brought to heel without the need to go deeper into France, which would be required if we were to advance on Paris.'

'Wise counsel. How many men can you raise, assuming that they can be paid for?'

'Perhaps, at most, twenty-five thousand, Your Majesty — although that would leave England poorly defended.'

'And how soon might they be assembled?'

'Not before October, to be on the side of caution. There would need to be several fleets, and given the inclement weather at that time of year, I would recommend that they be sent from Deptford, and thence down the Thames, to reduce our exposure to the westerlies.'

'This is well,' Henry nodded. 'I wish to remain in England for the birth of the royal child, but then I wish to lose no time in leading my own force into France. I may tell you privily that I have no wish to conquer the nation, or win back those lands lost during the reign of the late King Henry VI. What I seek is to tweak Charles's nose so severely that he signs a peace treaty that will include the handing over of this new scullion pretender who would have us believe that he is Richard of York. That will end the current mutterings around the nation, and will restore the prestige to my throne, which is put in doubt when others may scoff at my rightful occupation of it with such impunity.'

'Touching the matter of mutterings around the nation,' Bray chimed in, 'the imposition of another tax will not sit well with the nobles.'

'They can afford it, if they live in such pomp and finery,' Morton observed sourly, 'and if they live poorly, then they must surely have much coin stored under their beds for just such a purpose as we have in mind.'

'Oh for a devious lawyer's mind like yours, Morton,' Henry chuckled. 'Now I must depart to Eltham, where my wife and mother are even now supervising the installation of a new nursery to accommodate my growing brood of offspring. We meet again a week today.'

VIII

The fourth royal child — a daughter — was born on the second of July at Richmond Palace, and was named Elizabeth after her mother.

As Prince of Wales and heir apparent, Arthur was becoming a major bargaining counter in his father's slowly awakening foreign policy, and he was already spoken for in marriage to Katherine, the infant daughter of Ferdinand II of Aragon and Isabella of Castile. This had been negotiated with characteristic guile by Richard Foxe, two years previously, in the Treaty of Medina del Campo, which also gave Henry a potential ally against France, and enhanced trading potential between the two nations that Henry had been anxious to preserve for his ships when Charles of France had been harassing Brittany.

While the nation celebrated the birth of a second royal princess, leading nobles were sending their finest warriors to the royal standard, with their home liveries tactfully hidden in their saddlebags, while shipwrights hammered away in a newly-created royal dockyard at Portsmouth, and merchants were haggling with the Exchequer over the charter fees for the larger of their vessels that might transport men and horses across the Channel. No doubt French spies were urgently reporting back to Charles VIII that he might be required to turn his eyes back north, but by the middle of October he could, had he been free to do so, have stood on the cliffs of *Cap Gris Nez* and watched for himself the first of many ships tacking against the westerlies as they heaved and creaked out of the Thames Estuary and steered carefully around the Goodwin Sands on their way to Calais. By the time that Henry himself arrived, the total number of fighting men he would be riding at the head of was no less than twenty-six thousand, financed by a grumbling populace.

Henry was wise enough to leave the actual military strategy to others, and at the urging of Daubeney he led his troops southward along the enemy coastline towards Boulogne, the most important sea port still left in French hands. The very sight of so many English knights in siege formation around the ancient walls was enough to bring emissaries from Paris suing for peace terms, and Foxe was sent in to negotiate the Treaty of Étaples. Henry had left him in no doubt that Perkin Warbeck was high on the agenda, and that if possible he was to be handed over. The negotiations almost faltered on that point, until Charles promised to banish Perkin from his court, and pay Henry five thousand pounds a year for the rest of his days on the throne. Henry took the money, and Perkin Warbeck was free to take up a generous invitation from the Dowager Duchess Margaret of Burgundy.

Henry had successfully blocked one line of support for the impudent youth who was claiming his throne, by negotiation with Charles of France. He also took comfort in the fact that Isabella of Spain, when approached by Margaret of Burgundy to recognise Warbeck, in what Margaret no doubt intended as a means of destabilising the treaty that Henry had with her for the marriage between her daughter and Prince Arthur, held firm to her opinion that the boy was simply an imposter who was the tool of others. But the support being given to Warbeck in Flanders could not be ignored, and it was beginning to cause trouble behind Henry's back in England.

It was therefore an irritable, and deeply troubled, Henry who summoned his Lord Chamberlain, Sir William Stanley, to an urgent audience late one afternoon at Westminster Palace several months after his triumphant return from Boulogne. Henry owed a considerable debt to the man who had guided him, unchallenged, through those parts of the country that Stanley should, in 1485, have been guarding for Richard of Gloucester, but somehow they had never shared any natural warmth, and on occasions Henry had been critical of the manner in which Sir William performed his duties, notably in matters pertaining to the security of the royal residences.

'What measures have you taken to guard against this invasion from Flanders which seems to be the talk of the Palace kitchens, not to speak of the city alleyways, the dockside ale-houses and the merchant houses?' Henry demanded. Invasion fever seemed to have infected everyone, from the highest-born courtier down to the meanest street beggar, and those walking the narrow alleyways of the overcrowded city, or the country lanes of adjoining counties such as Middlesex, Surrey and Kent, were openly carrying arms which, when occasionally challenged, they claimed to require for their own protection should 'King Richard' emerge from the Channel mists with hordes of Flemish warriors in order to claim his usurped throne.

Stanley adopted a dismissive tone that did not sit well with his troubled patron. 'Since they are merely rumours, Your Majesty, I have not sought to embroider them with the vestige of truth by posting extra guards. At any event, should there be an invasion, our spies and fast messengers will bring the news to Westminster in abundant time for a fitting response.'

'Might I remind you, *Uncle*,' Henry snarled back, 'that there was once a time when the late usurper of the throne, Richard of Gloucester, was also relying on you to warn him of the progress through his realm of *another* invader who was claiming *his* throne. As you are well aware, the man entrusted with this solemn duty was, instead, guiding that invader through the Welsh Marches and carrying messages between him and the second most powerful man in the realm, Earl Stanley.'

Stanley's face flushed with anger. 'You do me no kindness to cast my loyalty to you in my face, Your Majesty. I will ever work to maintain your grip upon the throne, as I hope I have demonstrated.'

Sir William bowed out of the presence, and an usher closed the chamber door behind him. As he stormed down the corridor, he let fly a stream of muted invective that contained words such as 'ungrateful' and 'spoiled brat'.

The next to have cause to step cautiously around the royal paranoia was John Morton, summoned from his London townhouse, where he had been preparing a suitable peroration for the impending investiture of the young Prince Henry as Duke of York, the date for which was not yet fixed.

'I wish to suspend all trade with Flanders,' Henry advised him sternly. 'It is intended as a punishment for Duke Philip, or rather his mad father Maximilian, who is acting as his Regent, and who is affording such honour to this peasant spawn who claims to be of the House of York. My question of you is this — should I do so, will it harm England more than it harms Burgundy?'

Morton took time to consider his answer. 'In terms of the trade itself, it will fall heaviest on the cloth merchants of both nations, Your Majesty, although clearly it will be resented by a significant portion of your subjects here in London. But Your Majesty must also bear in mind the reduction in customs revenue that this will involve for the Household, and of course the possible reduction in income from our loan activities in towns such as Bruges and Antwerp.'

'But it will bear equally hard on the Duchy?' Henry persisted.

'Indeed, Your Majesty,' Morton reassured him. 'If anything it will hit Flanders harder, since it is their leading source of revenue.'

'Excellent!' Henry grinned. 'See to it without delay. There is, however, another matter, and one which requires your utmost discretion, and the employment of certain of Foxe's ferrets. Draw closer.'

As Morton leaned in closer to Henry, the latter lowered his voice in a conspiratorial tone.

'I wish Foxe to select suitable persons to work in various parts of my Household, to report back to him — and thence to me — regarding ought they may hear touching the subject of rebellion or conspiracy against the throne. If he can let me know what skills they already possess, I will arrange for suitable positions to be created in which they may employ a vigilant and ever-open ear. They will be remunerated as befits their notional duties, but I will also authorise additional reward in return for their services as speaking tubes for what is being talked about around the kitchens, the stables, the chambers and so on. May I entrust you with this matter?'

'As ever, Your Majesty,' Morton assured him.

On 29th October 1494, it was time to put Morton's long-prepared sermon to good use, and to make a public point to the pretended Duke of York across the water. Three-year-old Henry Tudor astonished the lines of onlookers when he rode, unaided, on a small horse through the narrow streets, surrounded on all sides by royal bodyguards, to Westminster Palace. There, he was greeted by his father and shown, for the first time, the chamber he would occupy instead of the nursery to which he was more accustomed. He would be reunited with his older brother Arthur, who, in accordance with tradition, had also been transferred to live with his father two years previously, leaving the royal princesses to be educated in the nursery.

The following day — the Feast of All Hallows — Henry was invested with the regalia of the Duke of York, following which Archbishop Morton, surrounded by no less than eight English bishops, all in full mitred splendour, preached a Mass to the echoing of a *benedicat vos* from the Chapel Royal choir. The splendour of the procession that followed, with much purple and red in glittering evidence under the flickering light of the torches that had been specially lit, and were burning incense, was in no way diminished by the fact that the tired little prince had to be carried by his great uncle the Duke of Bedford, who was himself beginning to show signs of the diminished mobility that was to increase shortly before his death just over a year later. However, nothing could mute the loud message that was being broadcast to all the crowned heads of Europe — that whoever the young man at the Burgundian Court really was, he was no longer recognised in England as the Duke of York. That title had been passed to a young, and somewhat overawed, prince who would grow up to become one of the most powerful monarchs that England would ever know.

In the second week of January 1495, the news broke that Earl William Stanley had been arrested and was languishing in the Tower.

'By what right am I brought here?' Stanley demanded as he stood, shackled at the wrists, before a row of inquisitors who sat on a raised bench, and included the King, beside whom sat Chancellor Morton.

'By the prerogative right that I possess to suppress treason in my own realm,' Henry advised him from a mouth that seemed to have thinned since Stanley last saw it. 'This, as you well know, since you oversaw its equipage, is the Court of Star Chamber. The two other gentlemen with whom you may not be acquainted are Justices Coleridge and Denby, of the King's Bench. We are here to try you for treason.'

'On what evidence?' Stanley demanded indignantly.

'The best evidence there could be,' Morton replied. 'That from your own words and actions, as disclosed to us by various persons working in and around both your personal household, and the very royal Household in which you sought to influence others.'

'Produce these persons!' Stanley demanded. There was a hasty consultation between Morton and the two King's Bench Justices, the latter nodding to a question put to them by Morton, who looked back triumphantly at Stanley.

'We are not required, in this court, to produce the witnesses, since their testimonies have already been secured by sworn affidavit. We may begin with that of your head groom, one William Featherstone.'

'He was dismissed for the theft of horse brasses some two months since,' Stanley objected.

'Which is why he was no doubt so eager to give certain intelligence regarding your frequent trips by horse to a certain house in Sandwich, close to the Kent coast.'

'It is my *own* house,' Stanley replied with a confident smile.

'Within which,' Henry added, 'resides a lady named Katherine Broadley, of whose existence, I have no doubt, your wife is completely unaware.'

'She is my mistress, certainly,' Stanley replied, 'and what of it?'

'She was also lately the mistress of Sir Edward Brampton, a treasonous Yorkist who is rumoured to have been the one who carried the pretender Perkin Warbeck to safety in Flanders,' Henry replied. 'You do not choose your fucks wisely it would seem, Uncle.'

'This is pure chance,' Stanley objected.

Morton decided to move the matter on. 'We have also an affidavit from one Gervais Montsorrel, a member of the King's own Yeoman Guard, who swears that on diverse dates around the time of the investiture of Prince Henry of York, you ordered the Yeomen to step down from their duties in connection with the King's own personal safety, and replaced them with men of your own, one of whom, whilst supposedly on duty, was found in the Palace cellars, insensible after consuming wine breached from a stored barrel. It would seem that this matter was not reported.'

'The man was dismissed,' Stanley explained. 'As for my not reporting the matter, His Majesty had already expressed his displeasure regarding what he perceived to be my slackness in matters of Palace security, and I was not anxious to repeat my experience of the rough edge of the royal tongue.'

'This I can well understand,' Henry replied with a self-satisfied sneer, 'but what is less easy to understand is that the man in question was allocated duties immediately outside the royal chambers, but was so easily seduced into the cellars by a person in the employment of Sir Richard Foxe, posing as a Groom of the Chamber, who told him where he might find the open cask.'

'Slackness I will confess to, Your Majesty — but *treason*?'

'Would you agree,' Morton asked him in measured tones, 'that it would be treason to state openly that you would not raise a hand to resist were the Duke of York to invade?'

Stanley began to look like a cornered beast in a royal hunt as he searched his memory for some careless word he might have uttered in the recent past in the hearing of some other paid spy of one of the royal officers of State.

'In the way in which you express it, yes it would indeed be treason,' Stanley conceded,' 'but I never said same.'

Morton smiled triumphantly before continuing. 'I read from the affidavit of Simon Henshaw, your newly-appointed Groom of the Chamber, who, you will not perhaps be surprised to learn, is also in the employ of Sir Richard, "On the fourteenth day of October last, I heard my Lord Stanley say, to the lady I know as Mistress Broadley, on the occasion of his retirement to her bedchamber, and while the door was still not yet fully closed, that I would not raise a hand were the Duke of York to assert his rightful place on the throne. I mind those words well, because when my Lord became aware that the door was still ajar, he placed a single mark in my hand, and bid me say nothing of what had occurred." Now then, sir, on your own admission, would you not account those words treasonous?'

'I spoke of the Prince Henry,' Stanley objected, 'who is now Duke of York. My exact words, as I can best recall them, were that were he to become King, I would not raise a hand to prevent it.'

'Dissemblance!' Henry shouted. 'He was *not* the Duke of York when you spoke those words, a clear fortnight before his investiture!'

'But he was popularly referred to as same around the Court, Your Majesty,' Stanley argued.

'But spoken in a certain house in Kent, in the company of someone intimate with the man who had allegedly spirited Richard Plantagenet from the Tower, the reference to "The Duke of York" could only have been a reference to the pretender to that title across the Channel,' Morton cut in with a finely honed legal distinction. 'And why seek to bribe the boy into silence?'

'Not for my *words*,' Stanley insisted, 'but because of my actions. He had seen me embrace the lady in her nightdress, and I was anxious that no word of it should get back to my wife. If I might have access to a bible, I will swear to these facts.'

'Under the rules of procedure of this court,' said Justice Coleridge in his first words of the day, 'a prisoner is not allowed to give testimony on his own account, merely to answer to the accusations brought against him.'

'What manner of justice is that?' Stanley shouted, red in the face.

'Royal justice,' Henry replied quietly.

Stanley went to the scaffold protesting his innocence, and declaring his undying loyalty to the man who, because of Stanley's high birth, and a sneaking feeling that he might have got it wrong, insisted that his uncle — the man who had all but handed him his crown — should meet his end by means of a single clean blow of the axe. Any residual doubt Henry might have been experiencing was no doubt dissipated when his men arrived to take possession of Stanley's estates, which had fallen to the Crown, and would fetch a handsome sum on their resale to some carefully vetted nonentity. Among his possessions was found a collar richly studded with white York roses worked in diamonds, plus a sum of money that would have put an entire army into the field for a sustained period of time.

Stanley's execution had a profound effect on what had once been a cheerful and optimistic Court. The security of the Household was consigned on a temporary basis to Sir Reginald Bray, and those reporting for duty in even the humblest corner of Westminster Palace were daily required to prove their identity to Richard Foxe's men armed with rolls of names and physical descriptions. The corridors closest to the royal apartments were thick with Yeomen of the Royal Guard, a food taster was employed to forestall any possibility of poison, and the only ones allowed near the King were members of the Great Council.

As predicted, Henry was also the subject of treasonous words spoken under the breath by those whose livelihoods had all been wrecked by his embargo on trade with Flanders. It was not just the merchants who were in the front line of trade, but those who earned their living indirectly from it, such as carriers, boat owners and captains, clerks, lawyers and innkeepers. The wharves at Rotherhithe were almost silent for several months, while the merchants whose warehouses fringed them cursed roundly at the sight of so much English textile output being stored because it could not be traded. The ban on exports to Flanders had not only closed down their most lucrative market, but had allowed their great trade rivals, the Hanseatic League, to take over their markets for woven woollen goods, and the framework knitters were also beginning to feel the financial pinch, since no-one wanted to buy their product simply in order to store it in a rat-infested riverbank warehouse.

Henry was kept ignorant of most of this by Morton, who was responsible for the seething atmosphere that was building up within yards of the Tower, in the mean streets bordering the wealthier establishments in Thames Street itself. Morton cheerfully reported that the English merchants who had previously been expanding their businesses in Bruges and Antwerp, using largely royal money at ten per cent interest, had nailed up their shutters and moved to Calais. When riots broke out in the dockside areas in mid-1495, Morton was able to convince Henry that it was directed solely at foreign ships that were docking without taking on English crews, or paying English customs dues, and Henry believed it because he wanted to.

The man most welcome in the royal apartment in which Henry spent most of his time, alone and brooding, while the Queen preferred the more genial atmosphere among her daughters in the royal nursery up-river, was Richard Foxe, who was now openly in overall control of the largest spy network that the nation had ever known. His eyes and ears were concentrated in those home counties south of London that provided the most convenient coastal landing sites for any force from Flanders, bearing in mind the information supposedly sent to the pretender Warbeck by Stanley. Then shortly before sunset one afternoon in late June of 1495, Lord Daubeney urgently sought audience with Henry.

'It is happening, Your Majesty! The Pretender has sailed with a small army, and is expected on our shores within the day!'

Henry breathed out a long sigh of relief. One way or another, it would soon be over.

IX

Perkin Warbeck ordered the first three of his vessels, containing one hundred and fifty of his soldiers, to land on the beach ahead of them through the breaking surf, but there was a commanding shout from the high ground above the beach, and out of the sand dunes rose lines of archers in the livery of England, firing volley after volley as the Flemish troops began dropping by the dozen. Confusion and chaos reigned, while Warbeck watched in horror as his spearhead army was decimated before his eyes. The men on horseback raced down through the dunes to finish off the few surviving Flemings who had waded back through the surf in retreat, hoping to scramble back on board the vessels that had brought them, before they could be cut down by an English axe or broadsword. Only a handful succeeded, and Warbeck ordered his own vessel back out into the Channel, paralysed with shock as he dumbly gave instruction to plot a course to Ireland.

Richard Foxe had once again triumphed at his own game. Warbeck had been lured out into the open by a series of letters, supposedly from an English knight named Sir Roland Melton, who did not exist. The letters had been penned by Foxe himself, had promised Warbeck that England would rise in his name against King Henry, and had been slipped to their victim by Foxe's men posing as emissaries from the fictitious Sir Roland. It had then been a simple matter of posting English forces along the south coast until the invading vessels came into sight, and hiding men in the dunes before those approaching from the Channel could get close enough to see them, being preoccupied in looking for the mounted men on shore who, Warbeck had been promised, would convey him to safety while his army gathered in revolt.

Foxe was not, however, smiling when he conveyed the news to Henry.

'I regret, Your Majesty, that the usurper was not lured onto the shore, and therefore remains free. My information is that he is back in Ireland, where he hopes to be crowned as Richard IV by the Earl of Desmond.'

'There will be no reprisals against the Irish, since I rely on the more sensible of them to maintain my peace. As for those who support Warbeck, who are no doubt the same that supported Simnel, they will probably crown an ape next.'

Even as they were speaking, Warbeck had failed to find the support he needed in Ireland, and was landing in Scotland, where he was well received by King James IV, who saw in this young pretender just the sort of excuse he needed to invade England.

Henry had just received news of Warbeck's arrival in Scotland when the first of two family tragedies overtook him. The young Princess Elizabeth had only recently celebrated her third birthday in the royal nursery at Eltham Palace when she began to sicken. She was put to bed, and every royal physician plied their skill in an attempt to halt the slow decline, but to no avail. Queen Elizabeth and her mother-in-law were beside themselves with worry, and Henry made an excuse of the urgency of various matters of State to keep himself at Westminster, and to conceal his own emotions, lest they be seen as a sign of weakness at a time when he needed to appear strong to the rest of the world.

The news of baby Elizabeth's death was brought to him late on the afternoon of 14th September 1495, while he was conducting a meeting of his Great Council to discuss the strategy they should adopt against the threat posed by Warbeck beyond the Tweed. Henry ordered a fast horse and a small Yeoman escort, and thundered into Eltham Palace courtyard just as a watery sun was setting over Richmond in the west. He found Elizabeth sobbing over the inert form of their daughter, surrounded by physicians who looked stunned and beaten.

The young princess was buried in the Chapel of St Edward the Confessor in Westminster Abbey, in a service conducted by John Morton, in the Cardinal robes with which the Pope had invested him two years previously. Henry made a point of spending more time at Eltham, particularly after it was confirmed, almost as an expression of consolation by God himself within days of the funeral, that the Queen was again with child.

Then, shortly before Christmas 1495, it was Jasper Tudor's turn to leave the family in mourning. He had reached sixty-four years of age, a respectable achievement for the times in which he had lived, but he had grown increasingly depressed by his inability to lead an army of men, as he had so often done in the past. He took to his bed a week before he died, summoned his confessor and a local attorney, and calmly set about dictating his will in the certain knowledge that he was not long for this world. He was proved right on 21st December, and Christmas festivities were placed in abeyance while Henry and his mother went into official mourning. Neither of them attended the funeral itself, Margaret because she was overcome by grief, and Henry because of urgent matters of State. However, Henry arranged for the Mayor of Bristol to act as proxy for him, and to meet the coffin with a suitable retinue as it approached Keynsham Abbey.

The day following the funeral, Henry was busy initialling Household accounts in his withdrawing chamber when an

173

usher announced the arrival of his mother. He looked up briefly, and saw her standing silently in front of the door that she had closed behind her, the all-too familiar look of disapproval written clearly across her face.

'I am engaged in affairs of State,' Henry advised her, to break the silence and to justify the lowering of his eyes from the almost hypnotic stare.

'You are too often involved in such matters,' Margaret replied in a determined voice, 'when you should perhaps be more concerned with matters closer to your heart — that is, if family still means aught to you.'

'Your meaning?' Henry asked casually, without lifting his eyes from the account roll, although he would have placed a large wager on what was coming next.

'You would have *no* affairs of State to concern yourself with, were it not for the uncle who was buried yesterday, and whose funeral you did not even bother to attend.'

'I have already given my reason for my absence,' Henry replied. 'We are threatened from Scotland, and if Foxe's ferrets be correct, also from Cornwall. Uncle Jasper would have been the first to advise me to guard my realm.'

'The realm he all but handed to you, along with my husband,' Margaret replied stonily. 'It seems that it is the role of your family to supply all that you require, in return for which they are ignored.'

'Did I not reward Uncle Jasper enough?' Henry countered.

'Whether you did or no,' his mother replied, 'it would have been seen as a noble gesture on your part to have taken two days aside to pay your respects to him as a nephew, rather than as a king. The same respects that are due to your wife, who this very day is laid up in her chambers at Eltham with an aching of the spine that causes her much discomfort.'

'Is there any risk to the child she is carrying?' Henry asked.

His mother's eyes narrowed into a glare. 'Is that all she is to you? A baby carrier? She is a woman — a wife — and someone who loves you dearly. She bears your children proudly, as would any loyal wife — is she somehow in a different position if she is also bearing heirs to the throne? And what of those royal children that she has already borne? Are they not entitled to loving visits from their father, rather than loyal visits from their King?'

Henry looked up sharply. 'Were I of a mind to insult the woman who gave *me* birth, I would be inclined to observe that I visit my children in Eltham more often than *my* mother visited me in Pembroke.'

The only answer was a snort, and the slamming of the chamber door. Henry was to learn at a later date that Margaret had ridden, with her retinue, to Keynsham Abbey, in order to leave money for prayers for Jasper's soul, and for the commissioning of a stained glass window in his memory.

Perkin Warbeck married Scottish noblewoman Catherine Gordon in January 1496, and Catherine immediately awarded herself the title 'Duchess of York', giving birth to their first child in September of that year, almost nine months to the day after their marriage. Foxe had his spies in the Scottish court in Edinburgh, who shared information with the Spanish ambassador to Scotland, from whom he learned that James IV was seeking to undermine the Treaty of Medina del Campo.

Foxe was also able to confirm what Henry had already guessed — that James intended to use Warbeck as a figurehead for an invasion of England. Henry wasted no time in instructing the Earl of Surrey to ensure that his border territories were constantly patrolled by armed troops, who would be supplied by the Crown, and in order to pay for this he persuaded Parliament to grant him yet more taxes.

This was far from popular in the city, where cloth merchants were still reeling from the impact of the trade embargo with Flanders, and in Cornwall, where taxes were being imposed in breach of a charter granted over a century earlier that had given the region's tin extractors an exemption from tax. The mutterings in Cornwall began to translate into physical action, after a local blacksmith named Michael Joseph commenced plotting with a lawyer from Bodmin named Thomas Flamank to raise an army to march on London, and received unexpected support from a member of the old nobility, Baron Audley, who regarded recent events in England as some sort of dynastic plague. In the belief that men of the south-east would rise up once they had arrived in London, the three men began to assemble an army, which had soon risen to fifteen thousand in strength, although it was poorly armed and even more poorly commanded.

As ever, it was Chancellor Morton who brought Henry the good news and the bad news.

'It is feared, Your Majesty, that if the Cornishmen receive the support of the city merchants, they could fund an army to march on London.'

'And as ever, Morton, I assume that you have brought me the solution to the problem before announcing the problem itself?'

'Indeed, Your Majesty. Foxe advises me that the Flemish are at breaking point with the trade embargo that is also causing such unrest among the city merchants. This might be a good opportunity to negotiate with Philip of Burgundy for favourable terms upon which to lift that embargo. It is now unnecessary anyway, since the Dowager Duchess can offer no new aid to the pretender Warbeck, and is in any case deprived of many of her dowager estates since her meddling in the Warbeck matter has cost the Duchy so much in financial terms.'

'And the Cornish matter?' Henry enquired.

Morton shook his head. 'I must leave military affairs in your hands, Your Majesty. I merely suggest that an end to the trade embargo with Burgundy would silence the London mob, and make them less inclined to support any uprising in Cornwall. They would be too busy, in any case, making up for lost time and revenue by reviving their business interests.'

'Who would you propose that we send to negotiate with Duke Philip?'

'Who else but Foxe, Your Majesty? He knows men's weaknesses more than most, and I feel sure that if there are favourable terms to be wrenched from Duke Philip while he is at his weakest, Foxe will secure them.'

'I have no doubt that he will,' Henry replied with a grimace, 'and I only pray to God that the day does not dawn when I am at that man's mercy. Instruct him to proceed with the negotiations.'

Within a fortnight, the deal had been brokered, and the final document was signed in February 1496. It was officially known as the *Intercursus Magnus*, and unofficially recognised as a humiliating climb-down by the Duke of Burgundy, and a slap in the face for his meddling grandmother Margaret, who realised that she had played her last card, and retired ungracefully to what few estates she had left. The reciprocal customs duties imposed on imports and exports between England and Flanders were so favourable to England that merchants who had recently been cursing Henry so roundly were now heard raising their wine goblets to propose toasts to his long life and good fortune.

There was further toasting of long life and good fortune on 18th March, with the birth of another royal princess — named Mary — at Richmond Palace. Elizabeth had moved the royal nursery upstream by a few miles, away from Eltham, which was believed to attract unhealthy miasmas from the Port of London, and which in any case held sad memories of the loss of Princess Elizabeth. Henry had forced himself away from affairs at Westminster to be in an adjoining chamber, and when the wet-nurse brought the bawling child out of the laying-in chamber in a shawl to be presented to her royal father, Henry was seen to have tears rolling down his face that he was doing his utmost to hide. A hand came to rest on his shoulder, and he turned to see his mother gazing at the child in his arms with a lingering look of unveiled love and affection.

'No doubt you are already considering which of the princes of Europe she shall be married off to?' she said, wryly.

'You do me wrong, Mother,' Henry choked back, 'as ever. These are the tears of a father, not a king. As for the matter of my ingratitude towards those who assisted me to the crown, was it not you yourself who strove for all those years to persuade me to tilt for it? Why should you be so critical, now that I have achieved your ambition?'

Margaret leaned forward over Henry's shoulder, and as he lifted the child towards her, she kissed it on the forehead. 'See that you also fulfil the ambitions of your wife and children.'

Henry was back at Westminster the following week, when he had much to occupy his attention, thanks again to the agents of Richard Foxe who were busily monitoring events in Edinburgh. After a year of financing the rich lifestyle of the young couple residing at his Court, who were now expecting their second child, James IV of Scotland decided that the time was ripe to test England's northern borders. Throughout the Summer of 1496, it was obvious to anyone who kept their eyes and ears open along the Lawnmarket, at the foot of the Castle, or on the greens before Holyrood Abbey, in the shade of Salisbury Crags, that an army of some size was being assembled. When it marched south with banners flying on 15th September, Foxe's advisers assured him that it would not even reach Newcastle with the supplies it had. They were proved right shortly after Warbeck's army crossed the Tweed at Coldstream to discover that the only ones waiting for them were soldiers commanded by Lord Neville, sent north from Newcastle by the Earl of Surrey. The intended Scottish invasion troops marched back into Edinburgh with more speed than they had left it, and James IV was sufficiently embarrassed to finance a journey across the Irish Sea for his former guest, while seeking humiliating peace terms with his English neighbours.

Foxe realised that James IV would be seeking to save face for having backed the wrong horse, and that he would lose a good deal of this if he negotiated directly with England in order to buy off the troops that were straining at their leash at his southern border, awaiting the order to settle some very old scores with their noisome northern neighbours. Foxe therefore engaged the good offices of the Spanish ambassador Don Pedro de Ayala, who was also an accredited ambassador at the English Court, and could travel backwards and forwards between the two nations' capitals without attracting any undue attention, at the same time reporting back to his masters Ferdinand of Aragon and Isabella of Castile. On this occasion, Foxe was able to employ, as his hidden go-between, the young and ambitious confessor to the Governor of Calais, Father Thomas Wolsey, who was eager for royal preferment.

Don Pedro had already proved invaluable in brokering the marriage contract between the Infanta Katarina de Aragon, now aged eleven, and Arthur, Prince of Wales, who had just celebrated his tenth birthday when Don Pedro succeeded in persuading James IV to sign the Treaty of Ayton, promising perpetual peace between England and Scotland, cemented with a marriage contract between the Scots king himself and the young English Princess Margaret, who was approaching seven years of age. Her mother and grandmother were appalled, and protested strongly at the arranged marriage of such a young girl to a supposed barbarian who was already in his mid-twenties, but Henry pacified them with assurances that she would not be handed over until she was of an age at which she could safely bear children.

It was a relatively joyous Christmas in 1496, with all the traditional feasting, pageantry and exchanges of gifts that had been severely banned by 'Her Lady the King's Mother' the previous year, when in mourning for the passing of Jasper Tudor. In consequence, the merrymaking was enjoyed with even more enthusiasm than before, and it was early in January 1497 before anyone was in either the mood, or the bodily condition, to get back to the business of running the nation. At the head of the agenda for every Great Council meeting for the first half of the following year was the mounting threat from Cornwall.

Henry, through Foxe, had been kept well abreast of the plotting and planning that had been taking place in small tin-mining communities such as St. Keverne, but thought nothing of any of it, since the Londoners to whom the Cornishmen had looked for support were now too busy refilling their warehouses and commissioning vessels to cross to the Low Countries. However, when it was reported that over fifteen thousand Cornishmen had marched into neighbouring Devon, gathering support like a crudely armed snowball as they rolled east, action was clearly called for. Since the Scots had come to heel the previous year, the massive army that Giles Daubeney had been granted, at public expense, was instructed to turn its eyes to the west and watch for insurgents on the march.

While they were looking westwards, the rebels sneaked past them to the south, convinced that the men of Kent — the birthplace of uprisings such as those of Wat Tyler and Jack Cade over a century in the past — would honour their treasonous traditions and join the tax protesters. When they not only failed to do so, but actually formed local militias to drive them back, the Cornish freedom fighters fell back on Guildford, while the royal family took their Archbishop of Canterbury with them behind the walls of the Tower, which were ringed with Yeomen of the Royal Bodyguard for several weeks. Elsewhere in the city itself, those who the previous year might have welcomed the treasonous tin-miners now boarded up their houses and fled for safety to relatives in the countryside to the east, while those of their neighbours who had nowhere to run to spoke in terms of manning the western city walls and making a last stand of it.

The royal army under Daubeney gathered around their various battle banners on Hounslow Heath, to the west of the city, where their catering needs were met by a grateful Mayor and Corporation of the City of London, who sent wagonloads of food and wine to sustain them while they awaited the expected onslaught.

When it failed to materialise, Daubeney sent out a scouting party of some five hundred mounted spearmen, who routed a force estimated as four times greater than theirs so badly that it opted to move around the north of the city, and leer down at it from Blackheath. Yet again the advantage of a hilltop position proved illusory, and on 17th June a royal army of some twenty-five thousand succeeded in surrounding the poorly commanded Cornish rebels and cutting them to pieces.

The leaders of the rebellion were either killed in the battle, or hanged at Tyburn ten days later, while Henry's subsequent taxation policies left the residents of Cornwall in little doubt of what he thought of their misplaced loyalties. Cornwall remained an under-privileged area of the country for several generations, the royal coffers swelled considerably from the forced sale of more than one forfeited estate, and several well-remembered heads remained on spikes along London Bridge until the crows had picked them clean.

At this point the ever-optimistic — and poorly advised — Perkin Warbeck grew tired of skulking in Ireland, and answered the call of a few remaining diehard Cornish dissidents who had added the slaughter of many of their friends and relatives to the original taxation grievance. Warbeck landed at Land's End on 7th September 1497, and promised immediate tax reform once he was King. He led some six thousand noisy supporters into Exeter, before marching on Taunton. When Warbeck learned that Daubeney's royal army was at Glastonbury, heading in his direction, he concluded that discretion was the better form of kingship, and deserted his men in order to seek sanctuary in Beaulieu Abbey. He was headed off before he could reach it, and it was a jubilant Henry in person who learned of his capture, and accepted the formal surrender of Warbeck's deserted army at Taunton.

After a few weeks cooling his heels in the Tower, Warbeck indicated that he was prepared to make a full confession to being an imposter. Anxious that his Queen should also hear it, Henry commanded that Warbeck be brought into Westminster Palace under armed guard, hooted and derided during his horseback procession through the mean streets of the city that had only months previously been deserted at the prospect of a Cornish incursion. Warbeck was led into the White Chamber, where Henry sat with Elizabeth at his side on a double raised throne dais to receive his formal confession.

As Warbeck was led in, manacled at the wrists and ankles, Henry sensed Elizabeth stiffening in shock. He could well understand her reaction as he looked down at the most convincing piece of Plantagenet youth he had beheld in years. His mind went back to the day of his face-to-face encounter with Richard of Gloucester, and once again it was like looking into a mirror. Whoever this youth was, he was obviously a scion of Plantagenet from somewhere in its murky past.

'You may unchain the boy, and give him a seat before us,' Henry commanded, adding, 'but if he makes any move to leave that seat, you have my order to run him through. Now then, young man, tell us your story. The *real* story, that is.'

'I am not knowing it,' the youth replied in broken English with a heavy Flemish accent. 'I remember a castle somewhere, but that was many years ago, and in a dream of the night, perhaps? I am living in a house in Tournai, in Flanders, where a man I am told is my father is always working with books. Then the lady my mother is taking me to Antwerp, and then I am working for a merchant in Brittany, who takes me to Ireland, where they say I am the King of England. The rest is known to you, I think.'

'They tell me you are married, and you have two children. Is this correct?'

'Yes,' Warbeck replied. 'They say she will be here to see me today,' he added as he turned round to survey those standing around the walls. A tall lady with luxuriantly long auburn hair and enormous blue eyes stepped forward to address the throne.

'I am she, Your Majesty. Catherine Warbeck, formerly Lady Catherine Gordon, daughter of the Earl of Huntly.'

'And your children?' Elizabeth enquired.

'A boy and a girl, my lady. The boy is nearly two, and the girl still a babe in arms. They are lodged at Deptford, with friends of my father.'

'And yet you risked coming to this Court, simply in order to see your husband, when there was a risk that you also would be arrested?' Elizabeth asked.

'I love him, my lady,' Catherine replied, as a tear rolled down her cheek.

Elizabeth whispered to Henry, 'I must have her in my household, with her children, whatever you do to her husband.'

'Do not take me for the tyrant that others accuse me of being,' Henry whispered back. 'He has obviously been the dupe of others, and I have already killed the only Yorkist who deserved it.' He raised his voice as he looked back at Warbeck. 'I will not have it said of me around the courts of Europe that I am without mercy. You — whoever you are — will be received at this Court as befits your birth, and your wife will become one of my dear Queen's Ladies. However, you must live separate lives.'

There was an agonised squeal from Catherine Gordon, and Warbeck looked back up at Henry.

'I would rather that you take me back to the Tower and have me executed before I will live freely, but be separated from the woman I love.'

'That is my decision,' Henry replied. 'And I am bound to observe that your English has suddenly improved. Take him away, and let us have some music to darken the gloom of this Autumn afternoon,' he ordered the guard, who began re-securing Warbeck's wrists and ankles while the stifled sobs of Catherine Gordon could be heard above the rattling of the chains.

For the next year and a half, Warbeck was supplied with a 'secure chamber' in Westminster Palace, in which he was well treated, and occasionally allowed to attend royal banquets, in order to publicly demonstrate Henry's mercy. Among the few hardships that the former pretender suffered were the daily visits from Richard Foxe and one of his clerks, a young lawyer in the employ of John Morton called Thomas More, to whom he dictated a full confession of how he had been cruelly misled by others, ending with the line 'I hereby, on my solemn oath, disclaim any right to the throne of England on behalf of myself, my heirs and assigns for all time coming.' Henry smiled when he was shown it, and he advised Morton that he would do well to promote the career of the bright young lawyer who had drafted it.

Warbeck's other hardship was being separated from his wife and children, a joint punishment also constantly bemoaned by Catherine Gordon in her many conversations with Queen Elizabeth, as they grew closer, particularly when Catherine remained in the lying-in chamber, holding Elizabeth's hand and wiping her brow, during the birth of the next royal prince,

185

Edmund, created Duke of Somerset on his birth in February 1499.

To avoid any chance contact between Catherine and her husband, and to Elizabeth's obvious distress, Catherine was not allowed to accompany the Queen while she was at Westminster, but became her Senior Lady at Richmond, where her children were occasionally allowed into the royal nursery in order to play with the Princess Mary, under the superior gaze of her older sister Margaret, who was being groomed to be a queen herself, albeit a Scottish one.

This somewhat strained arrangement might have continued indefinitely, had Warbeck not sought to escape in order to leave the country with his wife and children. Letters were discovered in his chamber from a minor Scottish noble with connections to the Huntly family in Aberdeen, who promised to arrange for a vessel to moor in Rotherhithe, in which Warbeck could be reunited with his family and then sail up the east coast back to Leith, near Edinburgh. Henry's reaction was to have Warbeck committed to the Tower, 'for the safety of the realm', as he justified it to Elizabeth, although he gave in to her pleas that Catherine be allowed to retain her position at Richmond after being convinced that she had played no part in the plot.

Initially Warbeck was held in solitary confinement, then Foxe suggested that he be placed in the same cell as Edward, Earl of Warwick, now aged in his mid-twenties, who had spent his formative years, since the age of ten, in the Tower to which he had been consigned by Henry upon his accession, since the young earl, as the son of Clarence of York, was a potential claimant to the English throne. However, he was no longer in any mental condition to be any threat to Henry other than a symbolic one, and a potential icon to others who might seek to use him as a figurehead in any future rebellion against what was rapidly becoming Henry's miserly grip on the nation's finances.

Years later, it would occur to Henry that Foxe had probably contrived, not only the joint incarceration of the two young men of approximately the same age in the same cell, but also the promise given to them by Tower guards that they would assist their joint escape. Contrived or not, their attempt failed dismally before they had even managed to cross Tower Green, and on 23rd November 1499, they were taken to Tyburn to be hanged alongside each other, after Warbeck had been obliged, under promise that his wife and children would be kindly treated, to read out loud the renunciation he had dictated to Thomas More.

Queen Elizabeth took to her private chamber at Richmond, and refused to share a bed with Henry for a whole month, such was her outrage and genuine remorse over the public execution of the husband of her heartbroken Lady who now had to bring up two fatherless young children. But there were no more pretenders to the throne of England.

X

As the bells welcomed in 1500, Henry was entering his fifteenth year on the throne of England. During that time he had learned many valuable lessons. The first was that maintaining a royal army was an expensive business for which he required taxation from Parliament that was increasingly unpopular with the people. As the recent uprising in Cornwall had demonstrated beyond doubt, a heavily taxed populace could rise in rebellion, even if there were no Yorkist figurehead left to use as an excuse. It was therefore necessary to obtain royal finance from other sources than by taxing the people, and expensive armies would not be needed if foreign affairs could be conducted by way of treaty.

The net result of all this was the need to have men about him who could generate finance, negotiate treaties, and demonstrate unswerving loyalty. And the final lesson that Henry had learned was that such loyalty was not to be found among the nobility, but from men who Henry had raised up personally from humble positions — men who had skills in matters financial and legal. His great officers of State had all been rescued by him from potential obscurity after they had fallen from favour under Richard III, or had been in exile with Henry in Flanders or France. But the years of experience that they had been able to bring to the service of the young Henry Tudor meant that they were much older than the man they served, and would not live forever.

The first confirmation of this was the death of John Morton in September 1500. Henry was then in urgent need of both a Chancellor and an Archbishop of Canterbury, and someone who could guide his hand in the meetings of the Great Council. In his final year or two, Morton's had been the still small voice of calm whenever Henry was in danger of excess, whether in the raising of more royal revenue or international policies that might require an army of invasion to cross the Channel at public expense.

It proved easier to find another Archbishop of Canterbury, although even in this Henry experienced some frustration. His first choice was the Bishop of Winchester, Thomas Langton, but in what might have been taken as a sign from God that Henry's judgment was failing, Langton died of the Plague five days after being advised of his appointment. Henry appointed his second choice, Henry Deane.

The death, at the tender age of fifteen months, of the third royal prince, Edmund, in June 1500, forced Henry, the following year, to divert his attention from the state of the royal finances to dynastic matters. It was time to cash in on the Treaty of Medina del Campo. The heir to the throne, fourteen-year-old Arthur, Prince of Wales, was now a prepossesing young man of above average height, slim, with reddish hair that betrayed his Angevin ancestry, his father's small eyes and a high-bridged nose that suggested high intellect and gentle breeding. He had been raised like a delicate hothouse bloom with his own household inside Westminster Palace, with tutors of the quality of John Rede, formerly headmaster of Winchester College, and Thomas Linacre, a former royal physician. In addition to his intellectual accomplishments he was, like his younger brother Henry, a good dancer and a sturdy archer.

A Papal dispensation had been acquired in order to allow Arthur and Katherine of Aragon to be formally betrothed at eleven and twelve years old respectively, below the canonical age of consent, in 1497. A marriage by proxy had been conducted in 1499, and now it was time for the fifteen-year-old Infanta to travel to England and claim her fourteen-year-old bridegroom. She was met at Plymouth by a royal delegation headed by Arthur's younger brother Henry, and she and her retinue were escorted first to a mansion in Hampshire where bride and groom met for the first time. Then it was a breath-taking entry into London across the ancient London Bridge, with massive crowds craning their necks for a first view of the young girl who was to become their Queen in due course.

Less than a week later, the bride and groom both wore white satin for the marriage ceremony in St. Paul's Cathedral conducted by the Archbishops of Canterbury and London, and then it was on to a sumptuous wedding feast at nearby Baynard's Castle, followed by a formal bedding ceremony stage-managed by the royal grandmother Margaret Beaufort.

Arthur had been granted many vast estates in Wales and the Welsh Marches, and the royal couple established their Court at Ludlow Castle, overlooking the River Teme in Shropshire. However, even before they reached it, Arthur was beginning to exhibit symptoms of the 'the sweating sickness'.

By the time they were due to set off for Ludlow, Arthur had become so weak, and so dreadfully afflicted by what was popularly regarded as a new form of Plague, that Katherine was in two minds whether or not to hang back, and remain at Tickenhill Manor in Worcestershire, where they had resided for the first month of their marriage. She was sternly instructed by Henry that her wifely duty required that she remain by her husband's side.

Henry, at Westminster, awoke from a fitful sleep in which he had dreamed of crowds of enraged subjects dressed in full battle armour and hacking at him with battle-axes, to find his confessor shaking him gently by the shoulder.

'You must brace yourself for bad news, Your Majesty, for inasmuch as God giveth, God also taketh away.'

'Meaning?' Henry demanded sleepily, as he rubbed his eyes.

'Meaning, Your Majesty, that your dearest and most precious of sons has been taken from us.'

'Arthur? What of Arthur?'

'Your Majesty, he died of the sweating sickness yesterday evening.'

Henry sat up fully, temporarily stunned. His first thought was of what this meant to the succession, then an image floated before his eyes of his radiant wife beaming up at him from her childbed, snuggling a red-faced bundle lovingly to her breast. His emotions as a father broke through his concerns as a monarch, and the first warning signs reached him of what was about to follow.

'It is in these greatest moments of personal loss that we turn to God for comfort, and the strength to continue,' his confessor suggested hopefully, but there was no stemming the tide of genuine grief that was about to breach the royal dam wall. Henry choked as he tried to prevent the flow of tears, then reminded himself that his confessor had seen him in worse states, and gave in to the unstoppable wave of emotion. He howled like an animal in pain, flung himself face down on the crumpled bedding and began beating his fists on the pillows.

A few minutes later, a loose robe over her nightdress, Elizabeth placed a cool hand on Henry's forehead, red with the energy of expended grief, then leaned forward and kissed his tear-ravaged cheek.

'My sweet,' she urged him, 'do not take on so — you will make yourself ill.'

'You do not yet know *why* I grieve,' Henry spluttered.

'Arthur is dead,' she confirmed calmly. 'The tidings are all over the Palace.'

Henry forced himself up on one elbow and looked at Elizabeth disbelievingly.

'Do you not grieve?' he asked.

'The time for motherly grief is not yet. My first duty is to my husband, and my King.'

'How shall we survive this?' Henry croaked.

'God will ease our burden, as ever,' Elizabeth reassured him in a voice that was beginning to waver. 'Now, if you will permit, I must dress appropriately before the members of the Court come calling with their pretended sympathies.'

'Yes, of course, my sweet. I shall join you once I am a sight fit to behold.'

Elizabeth slipped quietly from the bedchamber, and Henry forced himself out of bed. In his closet he found a suitable tunic edged in black, with matching black hose, and waved away the Groom of the Chamber who had sidled in to perform his morning duties.

'I would be left in peace,' he ordered.

He was silently coming to gloomy terms with the terrible news, his head on his chest while seated on a chair at the side of the bed, when from under lowered eyelids he saw the chamber door open again.

'I said leave me in peace!' he bellowed.

When the door did not close on his command, he looked up, and in the open doorway stood Katherine Hussey, wife of Reginald Bray and one of Elizabeth's Ladies.

'You must come to the Queen's chamber immediately, Your Majesty,' she urged him. 'Her Majesty has had some sort of seizure.'

Henry raced down the staircase, rushed past the guards who barely had time to uncross their halberds, and scurried into the Queen's Bedchamber, where Elizabeth was sobbing hysterically, and being held upright by Catherine Gordon. Henry gestured with his head that Catherine was to stand aside, and he enfolded Elizabeth in the fullest embrace they had shared for some weeks, as he repeatedly kissed the top of her head and uttered the most soothing words he could think of.

Eventually she regained control, and pushed him gently away as she rose to her feet.

'Forgive me, Your Majesty,' she said.

'Do not call me "Your Majesty",' Henry replied as the tears began to flow down his cheeks. 'Today I am Henry, your husband, and I am here to comfort a grieving mother.'

Henry gave orders that the Council meeting scheduled for that day was cancelled, and that he and the Queen would sit in the White Chamber in the late afternoon in order to receive the formal condolences of all those who cared to attend. He also sent messengers to Ludlow, to order that Arthur be buried in Worcester Cathedral, with the Earl of Surrey as chief mourner, representing the King. By tradition Katherine his widow would not attend the burial, but would hear a private Mass for Arthur's soul in the parish church of Ludlow, prior to his body being removed from there down river to Worcester. Dirges were ordered to be sung in St. Paul's Cathedral, and every parish church in the city, and Arthur's body was to be embalmed and sprinkled with holy water before its internment. Then, after a brief midday meal of cold meats and fruits, Henry sent for Reginald Bray, now a Knight of the Garter.

The man was now into his early sixties, and was somewhat stooped and frail, in contrast to his sturdiness in previous years. Henry's mind had dwelt on human mortality for the entire morning, and he first urged Bray to lose no time in commencing the planning of a new chapel at Westminster in which Henry himself hoped to be buried, before turning to a topic of more immediate concern.

'The death of Prince Arthur...' Henry began.

Sir Reginald bowed his head and interrupted, 'If I might be permitted to offer my condolences on your sad loss, Your Majesty? My wife tells me that the Queen is greatly affected.'

'She is a mother first, and a queen second,' Henry replied. 'But I am a king first, and I did not summon you here to receive your condolences. We need to consider what is to be done in the matter of the succession.'

'Surely, the Prince Henry?' Bray suggested.

'Of *course* the Prince Henry,' Henry responded testily, 'since he is the only royal prince left. But what of the Infanta Katherine, widowed at fifteen?'

'There are two issues there, as I see it,' Bray observed, 'and indeed they are closely related. The first is whether or not she is to be returned to Spain, along with her dowry, and the second is whether or not a suitable replacement husband may be found.'

'Which brings us back to Prince Henry,' Henry observed. 'Would we need a Papal dispensation, were he to marry Katherine?'

'But surely, Your Majesty, since he is not yet ten years of age...'

'His brother was little older, when we first concluded the treaty with Ferdinand,' Henry pointed out, 'and we would surely only need a betrothal in order to be allowed to retain the first instalment of her dowry, which I have little doubt you have already spent.'

'Some of it, certainly,' Bray conceded, 'but only on the marriage celebrations. The larger part of it remains in the Chamber accounts, which currently display a healthy credit balance, as you will have observed from the latest roll that was sent to your chamber but yesterday.'

'It lies there still, the seal unbroken,' Henry observed sadly, 'since the death of Arthur has somewhat disrupted my normal routine. But you evade my question — shall we need a Papal dispensation?'

Bray's reply was so immediate that Henry made a mental note that he must have been considering it already. As ever, Bray's mind had been working ahead of events.

'If the marriage was not consummated, Your Majesty, then we would need only the general impedimentary dispensation. But if there was congress...'

'You seriously suggest that one could put two lusty fifteen-year-olds in bed together *without* congress?' Henry grinned for the first time that day. 'Assuming that there *was* congress, then what?'

'Then we would need Papal dispensation for Prince Henry to marry the widow of his older brother, Your Majesty, since the impediment would be classed as one of "affinity". I am advised that the Bible forbids a man to have congress with his brother's wife.'

'And his *widow*?'

'Likewise, Your Majesty. We would also need to involve the Spanish Ambassador in the matter, or so I am advised. Then, of course, we would need to persuade Henry himself.'

'He will be the next through that door,' Henry replied, nodding towards the chamber entrance. 'In the meantime, take you to the Spanish Ambassador, to seek his counsel on the matter.'

Prince Henry entered at the summons from the usher, dressed as if for horse-riding. He was still only nine years old, but with the height of a thirteen-year-old, and his ruddy cheeks and generally athletic bearing were the result of not having been confined, like his older brother, indoors studying to be a king. Nevertheless, his sweeping bow was that of an experienced courtier as he stood before his father, awaiting paternal orders.

'You will know, of course, that Arthur has died,' Henry said sadly. 'Have you considered the many ways in which that unhappy event has turned your life upside down, young Hal? It makes you the next King of England.'

'I was planning on going hunting this afternoon,' Prince Henry replied as his face fell. 'There is a splendid lodge at Egham, and Sir Manvers always keeps a fine table.'

'Silence!' Henry bellowed. 'I was not proposing to make you King this afternoon, you poltroon! Apart from aught else, I intend to live until your brain is capable of absorbing matters other than the condition of the royal deer. You are already Constable of Dover Castle and Lord Warden of the Cinque Ports. You have been Earl Marshall of England since you were three years old, at which age you also became Lord Lieutenant of Ireland. Fortunately, those tasks are performed in your name by men who know what they are doing. In addition to all this, you are Duke of York and Warden of the Scottish Marches. To your existing Order of the Garter I intend to add the Order of the Bath, and you will shortly discover that you are also Duke of Cornwall and Prince of Wales, titles you must inherit from your poor dead brother as a sign that you are my heir apparent.'

'Thank you, Father,' Prince Henry replied dutifully.

'But with rank comes responsibility,' Henry reminded him, 'and the greater the rank, the greater the responsibility. You must learn all the arts of statecraft, and all the secrets of finance. The Crown is much richer than it was when I won it from Richard of Gloucester, but it is still not so wealthy that I can summon an army without either begging Parliament for money, or relying on nobles to bring out retainers that they are not supposed to have anyway. And you must, of course, marry, since a long succession line cannot be constructed using only bastards for bricks.'

'There are many comely Ladies at court from whom I might choose,' Prince Henry replied.

'That is something *else* that a king soon learns to his cost,' Henry advised him. 'We cannot marry whomsoever we wish, but must take, for a queenly bride, someone whose position in the world enhances the throne, whether by wealth, or — for preference — by virtue of connection with another royal house.'

'And you chose that Spanish pudding for Arthur because she will inherit Spain one day?'

'You do not find the Infanta comely?' Henry enquired.

'She has a face like one of those lamprey dumplings that are served from the kitchens on holy days.'

Henry was inclined to agree with him, but this was hardly the time. 'You would not wish, therefore, to marry her?' he enquired.

The young prince's face screwed up in distaste. 'I would rather marry my horse,' he replied, 'and if inheriting your crown means that I must share a bed with her, as you do sometimes with mother, then I would rather continue with my hunting, and let someone else be King.'

Henry sighed, and waved for his fool of a son to leave him, after one final piece of advice. 'You must therefore pray for another brother. And pray that your father lives long enough to sire another boy who can become King in your place while you slaughter the game in the royal parks. Take yourself off, but give serious thought to what we have discussed.'

Something at least came out of the dreadful events of that month. In accordance with strict protocol, one of Elizabeth's Ladies informed Henry's official Groom of the Chamber that it was the Queen's wish to resume sleeping with her husband in the royal bedchamber, and it was a sweet reunion in which the couple cried in each other's arms, renewed their intimate embraces, and rekindled a fire that had almost dwindled to embers in the cold douche of national politics.

One night several months later, as they sank back on the feather bolster, breathless with spent passion, Elizabeth reminded Henry that she was still of child-bearing age, and that there was every prospect of another son and royal heir, should God choose to bless them.

'God grant us that at least,' Henry muttered up at the ceiling. 'Hal is fit only for hunting and roistering with those wild youths who cling to him like oysters in a shell because they believe that he will be King, when in truth he could not run a nunnery, given his dismal Latin and other book-learning. Would that he could acquire someone like Bray to advise him, as I was fortunate to do. Now that Bray has taken to his bed, I fear that even I am without a rudder to steer the ship of State.'

'What say the physicians regarding his prospects?' Elizabeth enquired.

Henry sighed. 'It depends which leech jockey you enquire of, but all say with one voice that he will not make another year, such is the state of his innards. He is in much pain, so his passing would be a blessing for him and those who gather dolefully around his sick bed. But I am in sore need of his wise counsel. It is not like the days when Morton would be at my elbow, guiding my every action, and now that Foxe is taking his clerical duties more seriously since he smells death swirling around his cassock, I must make my decisions alone. We must press on with the Scottish alliance before another year is out.'

There was a sharp intake of breath from the pillow next to his, and Elizabeth reached out to grab his arm. 'You do not intend to give little Margaret to him so soon, surely? She is yet but twelve years old, and has not yet commenced her monthly flow. And James of Scotland is a lusty man of thirty-two.'

'My mother bore me when she was only a year older than that, and she was married at twelve, when my father was twice her age,' Henry countered.

Elizabeth snorted quietly. 'Believe me, she never tires of reminding me of what an ordeal your birth was to her, which is one of the reasons why I implore you, as Margaret's father, not to hand her over to be violated by a fully grown man before her maidenly parts are fully developed to take the strain.'

'As I told Hal only recently,' Henry replied, 'when one is of royal lineage, duty comes before either comfort or pleasure.'

'Talking of both,' Elizabeth replied quietly, 'unless my flow comes as it ought to next month, you may look forward to another of royal lineage. *Our* joint pleasure, *my* duty, as usual, but I missed last month. Pray God, if I am right in this, that it is another boy.'

'Amen to that,' Henry whispered as he grasped her hand in grateful thanks for some good news for once. 'This nation is in dire need of an heir to the throne who knows what he is about.'

XI

Henry stood to one side with Bishop Richard Foxe while architect Robert Janyns waved an expressive hand upwards in order to explain the concept of a pendant fan vault ceiling. Reginald Bray had, a few minutes earlier, laid the foundation stone of the new 'Henry VII Lady Chapel' that he had commissioned, and financed from the Chamber account. Although he bravely claimed to be in remission from his recurrent stomach ailment, he was still clearly not well, and immediately after the ceremony he had been excused further presence and had been carried home on a litter.

It was going to be a busy few days, a busy month, and what already promised to be a busy year. Today was 24th January, and on the morrow Henry's oldest surviving child, daughter Margaret, was to be formally married to James IV of Scotland in a proxy ceremony at Richmond Palace with the Earl of Bothwell standing in for the bridegroom. There would be two days of jousting, and Margaret, aged just thirteen, would be Queen of Scotland. Then in the following month, Elizabeth was expected to be delivered of her seventh royal child.

'Foxe here tells me that by building such a magnificent edifice to God, I shall be more assured of a seat in Heaven, but I would that my mortal bones be laid here anyway,' Henry advised Janyns.

The architect smiled cynically. 'As His Majesty is well aware, it will not be cheap,' Janyns confirmed, 'but when completed it will be the most splendid house of God built in the past thirty years. It will have three aisles, instead of the usual two, and five side chapels, with room behind the altar for more than one royal tomb. But, as his Grace has no doubt already advised Your Majesty, one cannot build a staircase to Heaven itself. Were that possible, mere designers such as myself would no doubt reap even more earthly reward for so doing.'

'I must take the royal barge to Richmond ere the sun begins to sink this afternoon, so perhaps you would show us the first sketches of what the completed chapel will look like, Master Janyns?'

The next day, his new chapel was still on Henry's mind as he watched, from the front row, the ceremony that would make his daughter a queen. It was taking place in the Queen's Great Chamber, and Henry looked lovingly down at the bulging stomach of his wife as she leaned backwards slightly to ease the pressure on her spine, and her over-gown slipped back from her shoulder.

Next to his Queen was their younger surviving daughter, Mary, approaching her ninth birthday, and so excited to be wearing a new gown of cloth of gold for the occasion. Henry allowed his mind to wander from the solemn ceremony taking place at the altar that had been temporarily constructed, and began to explore his memory for any recollection of the existence of a prince of Spain who might be married to her, should it be necessary to send Katherine back to her parents, along with the dowry that Henry had already committed to his chapel.

On the other side of Mary stood her older brother Henry, some six inches taller than her, so that his peacock-feathered bonnet was clearly distinguishable above Mary's more sober white hood. It might all come down to whether or not the young buck could be persuaded to take 'the Spanish pudding' as his wife, and currently the omens were not propitious.

Henry frowned disapprovingly at his son's choice of clothing for this solemn State occasion, and idly wondered if there was any colour of the rainbow that he had not managed to incorporate into his cote-hardie and cloak, and how much the royal tailor had charged for them.

Then, at the end of the family line, the stern face of his mother, the royal grandmother who had made even more protest at the early marriage of her namesake than Elizabeth had, accompanied by her usual stomach-churning descriptions of the agonising labour that had brought Henry into the world, torn her open all the way to her anus, and rendered her incapable of bearing any more children. Perhaps that was why she still made so much effort to control the life of her only one, Henry mused. It was a pity that Elizabeth did not maintain the same stern motherly regime over Hal, since the young devil seemed determined to spend his life roistering with his young companions in the hunt and the tiltyards. If the child that was due to be born in a few weeks was another boy, there might still be hope for the kingdom, but if not, Henry would have to work with what he already had.

A week later, Henry and Elizabeth travelled in solemn procession to the Tower, where it had been decided that the Queen would have her lying-in, within convenient distance of the large contingent of royal physicians who could be assembled at a moment's notice, if required, since at thirty-six she was giving birth for the seventh time, and the received medical wisdom was that there was a heightened risk of infection or stillbirth.

Henry left her surrounded by her fussing Ladies, until a few days later when he was summoned to her chamber. Down at the Tower, it was all fuss and activity, as the royal physicians jostled for position around Elizabeth's bed. They stepped aside dutifully as Henry's entry was announced, and watched unobtrusively as the King sat on the side of the bed and took Elizabeth's hand. She was sweating profusely, but smiled as Henry kissed her forehead lovingly.

'Another boy, perhaps?' she suggested. 'Did I not say that I was still of an age to bear you more children?'

'Another boy would indeed be a further sign from Heaven,' Henry agreed, 'although it is *your* continued life that must come first. Your physicians tell me that there is a greater risk with greater age.'

'*What* greater age?' Elizabeth countered. 'It will be my thirty-seventh birthday once I rise from this bed, hopefully with another son in my arms, and the House of Tudor twice secured.'

'Even so,' Henry said out loud, 'there must come an end to all this child-bearing.'

'But I would not yet cease what leads to child-bearing,' Elizabeth whispered back with a coy smile, before raising her voice so that she could be more easily heard by those around the bed. 'Now you must leave me, my sweet. Do you wait for news in the outer chamber, that you may be the first to hold your child when one of my Ladies brings it through to you.'

Henry kissed her on the lips, and looked round at the physicians as he stood up.

'Mind that you use all your skills to good effect, and do not waste your time arguing among yourselves. And no leeches — the Queen abhors leeches.'

The physicians bowed in unison, and Henry took a seat in the outer chamber.

By the third day, no-one had slept, and the physicians who came and went displayed increasingly worried countenances. Henry demanded to know what was causing the delay, since the other royal babies had been born within a day or so of the breaking of the waters. All he received in return were defeated-looking shakes of the head, although the boldest of them advised him that Elizabeth appeared to be suffering from some sort of fever.

At the end of the third day, there was a flurry of activity, and a physician pushed a sweating head through the dividing door for long enough to call for two midwives who had been seated in the outer chamber for as long as Henry had. There came a series of agonised shrieks from behind the closed door, several loud shouts from the physicians, and then — silence. After what seemed like an eternity, a midwife stuck her head around the bedchamber door and called for 'Lady Catherine Gordon'. With a half-fearful glance at Henry, Catherine scurried into the bedchamber, and emerged shortly after with a bundle wrapped in white silk. She approached Henry as he stood up in anticipation, and bowed slightly, and somewhat formally, as she held out the bundle towards him.

'Another royal princess, Your Majesty.'

Henry swallowed his disappointment and looked down at the wrinkled red face that stared back at him, almost in accusation. He carefully placed a finger on the end of its tiny nose, and whispered an endearment. The child closed both eyes and began blowing bubbles through the mucus that still covered its face.

'It is weakly, Your Majesty,' said a voice to the side of him, and he looked round into the face of one of the physicians, who was tentatively reaching out to take the child back from him.

'And the Queen?' Henry asked.

'She is sleeping, Your Majesty. She herself is very weak, for it was a difficult birth. Perhaps there should be no more,' he added tentatively, almost as if terrified for his life to be making such an impudent suggestion, but anxious to give the best advice consistent with his profession.

'Let me know when Her Majesty is awake again,' Henry instructed him, and resumed his seat, to one side of the excited, chattering Queen's Ladies, as he tried to think of a name for the latest arrival. They had so convinced themselves that it would be a boy that no thought had been given to a name for a girl.

By the time he was readmitted into the bedchamber, he had a name ready. It was the second day after the birth, and the inner chamber stunk disgustingly. The physicians all but slunk from his gaze as he walked past them and sat on the bed, from where Elizabeth smiled up weakly at him.

'I fear that I let you down, husband — it is a girl, they tell me.'

'Have they not let you hold her yet?'

Elizabeth shook her head sadly. 'They say I have the childbed fever, and that I must not pass it to our daughter, but she has a wet nurse. What shall we call her?'

'Kathryn,' Henry replied confidently. 'That was my great great grandmother's name, and she was the start of the Beauforts, from whom my mother is descended.'

'It is a good name,' Elizabeth smiled, then winced as another spasm of pain passed through her womb. She grasped Henry firmly by the wrist, and did her best to smile again. 'If it should come to pass that I do not survive this fever, there is a great favour that I would ask of you, as a father rather than as a king.'

'Ask,' Henry invited her, a worried frown on his face.

'The Lady Catherine Gordon. She has served me well, and has grown close to Margaret, who will soon be travelling to

Scotland. Please grant that Catherine return to her own land as Margaret's companion. It is her country, where her heart lies, and she would be good for our daughter, who will be in a strange land, with strange speech. Margaret will also soon enough be bearing children, as Lady Catherine has done. Please, Henry, grant me this wish.'

'It is already granted,' Henry smiled down at her, 'but no more talk of your not surviving. It will be your birthday a week today, and I shall arrange a feast and fireworks on the river bank at Richmond.'

Elizabeth had closed her eyes, and one of the physicians sidled close to Henry's side and almost whispered as he advised him, 'She will sleep again for some time, Your Majesty. It is the way of this fever — she has lost a great deal of blood, and more besides, and it may be that her innards have become diseased with the exposure to infection. Her best hope is to sleep it off.'

'Very well,' Henry sighed as he rose from the bed. 'I shall be at Richmond. Bring me news by the hour.'

The physician bowed respectfully, and Henry left the chamber. In the outer room he saw Catherine Gordon seated in a corner, weeping quietly to herself, her head bowed. Henry walked over, and she began to rise hurriedly as she became aware of his approach. He beckoned her to remain seated, and smiled.

'Your mistress has a fever, and will no doubt have need of your comfort when she awakes. I know that you regard me as one whose heart is black to its very roots, but you should know that your mistress has persuaded me that you should accompany the Princess Margaret when she travels north to claim her crown.'

Tears of gratitude rolled down Catherine's face as she reached out and kissed Henry's hand. 'God bless you, Your Majesty — and grant a speedy return to full health to my Queen.'

Henry spent the next week withdrawn in his chambers, reading the Bible, sending out instructions for the celebration ceremony of the Queen's birthday, and praying. He appeared unmoved when they brought him the news that the infant Kathryn had died, and when eventually a nervous Bishop Foxe brought him the tidings that Elizabeth had died the following day — her thirty-seventh birthday — without even knowing that the infant whose birth had caused her infection had not survived, Henry seemed to have prepared himself for the tragic news. A man in shock, he gazed at the pouring rain through the mullioned side window.

'The fireworks would have been useless anyway, in this weather,' he commented almost casually.

In the belief that Henry required a little time to absorb the terrible tidings, and compose himself once they sank in, Foxe bowed to withdraw, but was held back by Henry's raised hand.

'My new chapel — is it yet roofed?'

'I believe not, Your Majesty, although in the past week I have been much preoccupied with — with more urgent matters.'

'Indeed, as has the entire Court. But take yourself to Westminster without delay, find the master builder, and advise him that he shall have three hundred marks as a personal gift if he can roof it by the end of the month. Do you also supervise in person the construction of the altar as soon as the roof is on. Elizabeth shall lie in the crypt of the Abbey until that much of the work is completed, then I wish her transferred behind the altar of the new chapel. I would join her there when my time comes.'

The roof was completed as required. Once Foxe had supervised the installation of the altar, he was instructed by Henry to conduct Elizabeth's funeral ceremony in his capacity as Bishop of Winchester, given the vacancy in the office of Archbishop of Canterbury created by the death of Henry Deane only five days after Elizabeth.

Due to Henry's insistence that the funeral should go ahead in the incomplete new chapel, most of the nobles and other leading worthies who had been instructed to attend felt as if they were attending a Requiem Mass on a building site, as the casket was laid ceremonially on the platform that would be lowered into the hole in the ground behind the altar, prior to the memorial plinth being built over it in subsequent days.

As Foxe began reciting the words of the *Pie Jesu Domine*, Henry was seen to walk forward carrying in his hands a white rose and a red rose. He knelt at the side of the casket, laid the roses ceremonially on its lid, and bowed his head. Foxe saw his shoulders shaking in what he took as a sign of Henry's grief finally breaking through the stern surface he had maintained for a month. When it seemed to be taking a while, he glanced back again at the bowing monarch, and saw that his face was turning purple, and that he seemed to be having trouble breathing.

Suddenly alarmed, Foxe looked down into the body of the congregation standing in the nave among the piles of dressed stones, and recognised Thomas Linacre, now tutor to the young Prince Henry, but a physician by profession, and a former personal physician to Henry. Foxe gestured with his head at the shaking shoulders of his monarch, and Linacre looked more closely. Recognising the symptoms, he raced behind the altar and called for royal grooms to attend him, while Foxe broke off his recitation, and the choir drew uncertainly to a halt.

'It is His Majesty's customary ailment when greatly overcome with emotion,' Linacre explained to the grooms. 'He must be taken back to the Palace in a litter. I will accompany you, and see to his immediate comfort, but the King's current physicians must also be called. Lose no time!'

By the time that Henry regained partial consciousness, he found himself back in his bedchamber at Richmond, to which he had been conveyed by royal barge during his insensibility. There were physicians all around him, and the ceiling seemed to him to be slowly rotating. Matthew Primrose smiled as he saw Henry's eyes partially open.

'Your Majesty has been gravely ill, and must even yet rest, if you are to survive. It was your usual malady of the chest when overcome by sudden shock or strong feelings, but it has now developed into a fever of sorts. I cannot be answerable for your condition if you do not rest as advised.'

Henry smiled back weakly. 'Thank those who brought me here. Now I would rest, as advised. Send only my mother to attend me.'

Margaret Beaufort had been in attendance at Elizabeth's funeral, and had nearly died of apoplexy herself when she saw Henry being carried out of the chapel, seemingly gasping his last. She had taken up temporary residence at Richmond, and had plagued the royal physicians by constantly stalking them in corridors, demanding news of her son's condition.

During his subsequent delirium, many sights floated before Henry's eyes. Once, he fancied himself back in Brittany, with the beautiful Eloise de Arradon slipping a green gown to the

209

floor to reveal her nakedness, and the physician sitting by his bed was startled to hear Henry mutter 'You had better put your gown back on, for my wife would not approve.' On another, less enjoyable, occasion, he was once again on the battlefield, hiding behind his horse, while Richard of Gloucester sharpened his axe in between rolling dice with Earl Stanley. He cried out in his dream, and his mother placed another cold towel on his forehead.

Finally, it seemed to him that a tall figure stood at the foot of his sick bed, and as his eyes focused he realised that he was looking at the ghost of his Uncle Jasper, who was shaking his head.

'You cannot allow yourself the peace of death yet, Henry,' Jasper said. 'You have but one son to succeed you, and he is not yet twelve years of age. When you were twelve, you were held a prisoner in Pembroke Castle by Sir William Herbert. If I had come to you at that time, and informed you that you had just become the King of England, how well could you have handled the reins of government? You have been lax in the boy's upbringing, but there is still time, if he is given the right tutors, and restrained from the headstrong lifestyle he seems to prefer. You do England no favours by delaying the education of your only surviving son in the duties for which he must be prepared. In short, get well, get up off your arse and get on with it!'

The figure faded, and Henry chuckled. His eyes opened, and there sat Richard Foxe, liturgy in hand and spouting something unintelligible in Latin.

'I am not dead yet, priest,' Henry announced. 'And if you have come to hear my confession, tell your household that you will be gone a week at least.'

'God be praised,' Foxe smiled down at him, 'your sense of humour is restored. I shall summon your physician at once.'

Instead of his physician, it was his mother who bustled into the chamber, carrying a jug of something that was steaming, and smelt of old horses.

'Drink this,' she commanded. When Henry wrinkled his nose at it, she tutted. 'I have not spent the last week sitting at your bedside, mopping your brow, for you to disobey me now. This is the finest beef tea, and you need to build up your strength.'

'She is correct, Your Majesty,' added a physician, who had crept into the chamber behind her. 'Then, when you have regained your strength, we may begin to extract the bad humours.'

'You place a single leech on my arm, and I will have your head,' Henry promised him with a weak smirk. His mother looked behind her and ordered the physician from the bedchamber in a tone of voice that Henry knew only too well, and he chuckled as the bundle of medical robes scuttled out through the chamber doors like a crow disturbed by a bowshot. 'Since you are here anyway, Mother, and in return for my drinking this dead cow like a good little boy, I have a great favour to ask of you.'

'That will rather depend upon what it is,' Margaret replied guardedly, 'although may I say how I have prayed hard for your recovery, and how joyously this will be greeted by your subjects?'

'Not those who pay taxes,' Henry grinned. 'But what I would ask of you is that you take over the upbringing of Prince Henry.'

Margaret's face set into a stony frown. 'I must admit that he was ever my favourite, but thanks to your slackness he seems not to have what it takes to become King. Unlike his father, who learned quickly.'

'Learned quickly to do what he was told, you mean?' Henry teased his mother, then gave her the benefit of one of those beaming smiles that she always found hard to withstand. 'Now that Elizabeth has gone, I must be both mother and father to the children who remain. But I must also attend to matters of State. I am asking you — as the royal grandmother — to do for another young Henry what you did for me. Without your guidance, I would never have become King — you and Uncle Jasper, that is. Hal must be kept closely confined to the Palace, he must be given the best tutors in the land, and he must be politely but firmly shown that kingship is not all about hunting and attempting to climb onto warhorses that are twice his height from the ground.'

Margaret frowned. 'Now that you are back to your old self, I had rather hoped to retire again to Collyweston. I am also much engaged, but for me it is my university college endowments.'

'Which is precisely why I wish you to engage the best tutors that may be found within the realm, and possibly from Europe,' Henry explained. 'Hal must be prepared in all aspects of kingship, and particularly those which pertain to learning and the written arts. I hear much from Foxe of scholars such as John Colet and Erasmus of Rotterdam, for example.'

Margaret's nose wrinkled in distaste. 'I, too, have heard of Erasmus, but there are those at Cambridge who think his writings heretical. Would it be wise to expose young Hal to such thought?'

'Why not?' Henry argued. 'If he is to be King, he must learn to distinguish good advice from bad advice. I would also have you seek out a young man named Thomas More, who was formerly in the employ of Bishop Morton, but who may now, they tell me, have taken holy orders. His was ever sound advice, which Morton sometimes sought to pretend was his own. I would have Hal exposed to minds such as his.'

'It shall be as you wish,' Margaret conceded, 'and I must admit that it will be nice to have the care of a grandson, to replace the son who now seems capable of ruling a nation without his mother's assistance.'

'Without your assistance when I most needed it, Mother, I would not now be ruling a nation, and it is precisely that service that I would wish you to render to your grandson.'

'So I must delay my return to Collyweston?'

'Not at all. In fact, when we progress Margaret north to take up her new crown, I would wish to spend the night there. It is only a day's ride from Westminster, and it may be that this is as far as I may venture. If so, then I shall arrange for Surrey to accompany her to the border, where King James has agreed to meet her train. There should perhaps be a banquet to commemorate her departure north — a State occasion in a palace other than Westminster — and it would do Henry good to act as your joint host on that occasion. He may also learn much from you on how such occasions are best organised. May I leave all these things with you?'

'Of course you may,' Margaret assured him. 'There is life in the old she-devil yet, and much that I can do to bring an errant grandson to heel, as I once brought his father.'

'Have a care, Mother,' Henry smiled as he leaned up to kiss her goodbye, 'or you may be thought to speak treason.'

'The only treason lies in disobeying one's mother — or one's grandmother,' Margaret smiled back.

As if being closely supervised by one's grandmother were not bad enough, Prince Henry also suffered the indignity of being advised by his father, in the middle of June, that he was now formally betrothed to Katherine of Aragon, by virtue of a new treaty between England and Spain. 'It could have been worse,' Henry told him. 'If Scotland were not ruled by a young king to whom I was able to marry off your sister, you might have been spoken for north of the border — they tell me that Scottish ladies have as much hair on their legs as their menfolk.'

At the end of June, the royal progress set out with much blowing of herald trumpets and many rich hangings around the litter that carried the young Queen Margaret out of London along the old Roman road north. At the head of the stately procession rode King Henry, with Bishop Foxe by his side, and a sizeable contingent of liveried men at arms from the Yeomen of the Royal Guard. Then came Margaret's litter, with Catherine Gordon riding alongside it on a grey palfrey, chatting away constantly to her mistress, all the baggage for her long-awaited return to her native land stowed with the rich gowns and other accoutrements that befitted a queen, and with which Margaret had been gifted by her indulgent father.

That night, young Prince Henry took great delight in acting as master of ceremonies for the farewell banquet, showing off his prowess as a dancer, and joining the musicians to demonstrate his skills with the lute. He also drank a little more than his father would have liked, and as they stood beside each other at the entrance gate to Collyweston Palace with grandmother Margaret and a handful of armed attendants, waving until Princess Margaret's litter moved out of sight around a corner of tall yew hedge, Prince Henry was looking a little paler than normal. He was already as tall as his father, but had taken more of his mother's colouring, and as he removed his bonnet to wipe the sweat from his brow in the late June sun, revealing his red-gold hair, Henry looked sideways with disapproval.

'That rich French wine is best taken with an equal part of water.'

'I am sure that was already done by that rogue who Grandmother employs as a Steward,' the young prince replied with a grimace, 'but I fear that the roast pig was underdone. I shot it myself, did you know?'

'Your grandmother *did* advise me of the pride with which you cantered back to the kitchen door and cast an entire wild boar in front of a startled cook, certainly.'

Young Henry looked ahead, to where the last of the royal progress was disappearing behind the hedge line. 'When Margaret is Queen of Scotland, and I am King of England, the nation will finally be at peace, will it not? Then I can spend more time in the hunt.'

Henry sighed. 'If my reign is anything to judge by, there will *never* be peace, and your hunting will be confined to ferreting out traitors to your throne.'

XII

Henry sat alone in his privy chamber at Richmond, thinking about death. Not his own — although that was surely not long away — but the deaths of others upon whose wise counsel he had depended for so long, or who had played such a large part in his plans for the future. First had been Morton, whom he had never known to give bad counsel, or to display the slightest disloyalty. Then the death of Arthur, the heir-apparent whose marriage to Katherine would almost certainly have ensured the survival of the Tudor family on the throne.

This was followed by the saddest death of all — his own dear Queen, the love of his life, his distraction and relief from the tense affairs of State, the mother of his children, the companion of his bed, the only one who could lighten his blow upon those who displeased him. Shortly after her death, Bray had finally succumbed to the ailment that had laid him low for his final year, and now Henry could not be entirely confident that the King's financial affairs were being conducted solely for the benefit of the King.

If he had ever needed the comfort and wisdom of those who had departed this world, it was now. Yesterday, during one of his rare Council meetings, someone — it may have been Foxe, or was it Daubeney? — had pointed out that as matters stood, the only immediate prospect of an heir from an English royal lay north of the border, from where every day they expected news that Queen Margaret of Scotland was with child. When that happened, and if Prince Henry did not produce legitimate issue, or if he perished in one of those dangerous sports in which he seemed to take such strange delight, despite his grandmother's rule of iron, then what? Would the heir to the Scottish throne then become the heir to the English Crown? Would England be tied in a ghastly family union with those barbarians with whom they had been skirmishing for centuries? As Henry had curtly pointed out to his Council, if he had not intended peace to prevail between the two centuries-old enemies, he would not have sent his oldest daughter north to seal that peace with her own body.

But it had set him thinking. It was only a matter of time before Prince Henry began siring bastards, that was obvious. But would he also buckle down and sire a future King of England? And what if Hal were to die? He was much more healthy and robust than Arthur had been at his age, but it was as if he diced with his own demise every day, riding, hunting — and now jousting. Hal's death would leave only his young sister Mary, and any husband that might be chosen for her would obviously, by his own seed, sire the next English King, who would be only half a Tudor — and the wrong half at that. Henry himself had been obliged to argue his right to the throne through the female line, and he would not wish that on any grandson. And if Mary were to outlive any such husband, leaving an heir too young to ascend to the throne, would she be recognised as the sole monarch, or would she become a mere Queen Dowager, acting as Regent for that heir? If she were to marry into a powerful house such as France or Spain, would England become simply one of its outlying possessions, as Normandy, Anjou, Aquitaine, Brittany and Blois had once been to England?

He took another mouthful of wine, and considered his options. Prince Henry had grudgingly agreed to marry Katherine once he came of age, and the Pope had granted a dispensation after receiving sworn testimonies from Katherine and her *Duenna* that Katherine's marriage to Arthur had never been consummated. In the meantime, there was already a dispute regarding her dowry.

The original agreement had been that half of the money would be paid upon her marriage to Arthur, and this had duly been handed over and converted into the new chapel at Westminster. The balance of the money was to be paid in two instalments, the second of which was in the form of plate and jewels that had travelled with Katherine, and was being held by the Spanish Ambassador in order to prevent the extravagant young princess spending it on herself and her entourage. Not only was the Ambassador — on strict instructions from King Ferdinand — refusing to part with a single gem or piece of plate, but he was now making repeated demands for the return of the money that Henry had already spent.

In the midst of all this sat Katherine herself, in a suite of rooms at Richmond rather than at the castle at Ludlow that contained such unhappy memories for her. She was entitled to 'jointure' payments as the Dowager Princess of Wales, which Henry had immediately diverted into his own Chamber account in order to reimburse himself the cost of the food, heating and other necessities of life that Katherine and her Spanish entourage consumed. As a result, she had no income of her own with which to clothe herself and her Ladies, whose increasingly threadbare clothing was becoming the scandal of Court on those rare occasions when Katherine and her ladies deigned to dine in the full Court — which she was reluctant to do, given the very public slights that she was given by Prince Henry, her rumoured next husband, who seemed to prefer the company of his favourite grooms further down the Great Hall.

In what seemed, in retrospect, to have been a madcap scheme, Henry had floated the idea that he himself might marry the young Spanish princess. The reaction had been predictable, his mother employing phrases such as 'appalling', 'sickening', 'disgusting' and 'inappropriate'. But her reaction had been nothing to that of Katherine's mother, the pious old Queen Isabella of Aquitaine, who had almost swooned at the suggestion, and had given stern instructions to her Ambassador to convey her opinion back to Henry word for word. The wily old diplomat had toned it down somewhat, so that it translated into English as 'an abomination in the sight of God', but the sentiment had not been lost, and the plan had been abandoned, even after Isabella herself had died, perhaps of apoplexy.

Henry was well aware that Katherine was urging her father Ferdinand to demand her return to Spain. Her letters were routinely opened, copied and resealed by spies within her rooms, as indeed was incoming correspondence intended for the Spanish Ambassador. The same was happening to English correspondence, and both sides of the intelligence war were well aware of what was going on; in consequence, the only written correspondence contained information that was intended for the other side to read, while genuinely secret instructions were carried by word of mouth.

'My Lord Bishop, Your Majesty,' the usher announced, and Foxe entered. Henry studied his face carefully for the tell-tale signs. On days when Foxe's countenance lived up to his name, he was the bringer of good tidings — usually of his own achievements — but if he resembled a sick cow, it was bad news, and today the facial expression was pure bovine.

'Disturbing news, Your Majesty,' Foxe confirmed. He shook his head when Henry gestured towards the wine jug, and instead strode as purposefully as his ageing legs would permit to the chair that was reserved for favoured visitors to the Privy

Chamber, and these days seemed only to be occupied by him. 'Ferdinand of Aragon is seeking a bride at the French Court.'

'To strengthen his grasp on Castile, presumably?'

'Presumably, Your Majesty.'

The situation was complex, but Henry did not require any prompting to assess the implications. The growing power of Spain that had made Katherine of Aragon such a valuable marriage pawn was entirely dependent upon the uniting of the kingdoms of Aragon and Castile through the marriage of Ferdinand of Aragon and Isabella of Castile, who had recently died. That union had produced three daughters, of whom Katherine was the second-born. Her older sister Joanna was married to Archduke Philip of Burgundy, heir to the Holy Roman Empire, and Joanna had become heir-apparent to Castile upon the death of her mother. Ferdinand was well known to be resistant to the prospect of half his kingdom falling to Burgundy, and was clearly seeking an alliance with Burgundy's old enemy, France. The death of Queen Isabella had also rendered Katherine of Aragon less of a dynastic bargain, and, given Hal's reluctance to marry her anyway, perhaps a new set of alliances would be more appropriate.

'If Burgundy threatens to acquire half of Spain, Ferdinand will clearly need allies among Burgundy's enemies,' Henry observed, as he swirled his wine-cup, deep in thought. 'England is clearly one of those allies, but given that our relationship is currently somewhat soured, it makes sense for him to be making overtures to France.'

'Ferdinand certainly appears to have a gift for statecraft,' Foxe observed unenthusiastically.

'But not as great as mine,' Henry announced with a smile. 'Ferdinand is not the only King in Europe who is minus a wife, and we too have our reasons for wishing to oppose Burgundy.'

'You are not proposing that you also bid for a French princess in marriage, Your Majesty?'

Henry shook his head. 'There are none of whose existence I am aware, but they tell me that the Italian city states grow more powerful by the year. Perhaps we should think of outflanking both France and Burgundy at their southern borders.'

'There is another good reason for opposing Burgundy, of course, Your Majesty,' Foxe pointed out.

Henry frowned. As usual, Foxe was right, but he didn't need reminding.

The death of the Earl of Lincoln in support of Lambert Simnel at Stoke Field had not entirely suppressed the remaining Yorkist sentiments in England. If anything, the attainder of the de la Pole estates by Henry in retaliation had hardened the resolve of the remaining member of the family, Edmund de la Pole, Duke of Suffolk, who had been harbouring an ambition to claim the crown through the line of his long-dead father, who had been a brother-in-law of Edward IV. Like Perkin Warbeck, Suffolk had found support at the court of Emperor Maximilian, who was the father of Philip of Burgundy, and was always ready to stir up rebellion in England.

Suffolk presented no immediate threat to Henry, but Henry was eager to demonstrate that he would tolerate no more support for Yorkist pretenders from Burgundy, or anyone associated with it. If Ferdinand of Spain became allied by marriage to France against Burgundy, while Henry could secure an allegiance with an Italian state, before becoming joined at the hip with Ferdinand through the marriage of Katherine to Prince Henry, then between them they would form a power block against the Holy Roman Empire itself. The irony was that it would be an alliance of Catholic states supported by the

Pope against the very Empire that was originally created in order to protect Rome.

Henry looked at Foxe enquiringly. 'Do you have, among your retainers, a man of the cloth — a man ordained, but with diplomatic skill or simply wise learning — who might pose as one sent on a diplomatic mission to Rome, but who takes the time, while across the Channel, to make pilgrimage to some Spanish holy site, in order to ascertain the current strength of Ferdinand's grip on Castile?'

Foxe smiled. 'You must have been listening at the keyhole of my chambers, Your Majesty, for only yesterday I received a letter from a young man who was formerly a chaplain to the late Archbishop Deane, and who is seeking some preferment. He is currently employed in Calais, as confessor to its Governor, but finds the work tedious, and is anxious for something more challenging. His name is Thomas Wolsey, and I feel sure that he would welcome the opportunity, not only to visit Rome, but also the shrine at Santiago de Compostela, where it is said that the remains of St James the Apostle are buried in the cathedral. It is a popular pilgrimage for English Christians, and to get there by land one must cross Castile.'

'Excellent!' Henry murmured. He thought a little longer, then lowered his voice. 'His instructions are to discover all he can regarding Ferdinand's popularity within his own kingdom, and the strength of those within his realm who would welcome Philip of Burgundy to Castile. He is to do that first and foremost, then he may visit Rome. While travelling through Italy, he is instructed to take note of any unmarried royal lady who may be found within its kingdoms. Preferably one young enough to bear children, and one who as closely resembles my own dear late Queen as is possible. If I am to marry such a woman, it would be tedious for an old man like myself to be obliged to gaze upon a new portrait; also, if she resembles Elizabeth of York it will not feel so much like some form of adultery. Can all this be achieved, say you?'

'Without doubt, Your Majesty. You may leave it with me.'

'I hope so. Have Daubeney attend me — I have work for him also.'

Daubeney appeared apprehensive when he entered the chamber, and gladly accepted a goblet of wine in the hope that this augered that the King was in a good humour.

'You were Governor of Calais for some years, as I recall,' Henry began.

'I was indeed, Your Majesty, and I handed over that office with a clear set of accounts. Is there now some problem of which I was not advised?'

'You may unclench your buttocks, Daubeney,' Henry grinned. 'I am not about to accuse you of something of which you are innocent. Instead, I seek your counsel regarding the captainship of Guines Castle.'

Guines was both a fortress and a prison, and it was located some ten miles south of Calais. It was crucial to the retention of the only remaining English foothold in France, but its Captain, by virtue of his isolation, always enjoyed a degree of independence, and was open to bribery and other forms of distraction from duty by foreign rulers. There was a supporting garrison at Hames, which also continued prison cells, and the unswerving devotion of its Captain was also a crucial factor in keeping England safe from any enemy force seeking to invade from the northern coast of France.

'Suffolk is causing trouble for us in the court of the Emperor Maximilian,' Henry explained. 'He fled there to escape trial after killing a man, and was allowed safe conduct through Calais by the man who was then, and remains, the Captain of

Guines, a man named Sir James Tyrrell. What do you know of him?'

'He was a trusted ally of Richard of Gloucester, Your Majesty, as you know well, and indeed, if the rumours be correct — but perhaps I should say no more on that score.'

'*What* rumours?' Henry demanded.

'Well, Your Majesty — and it is of course but rumour, as I said before — there are some who maintain that it was Tyrrell who was responsible for the deaths of the sons of Edward IV when they were in the Tower. He was in France when Your Majesty won the throne from Richard and, as I was led to believe, you pardoned him his Yorkist sympathies and in due course appointed him Captain of Guines. More than that I do not know, Your Majesty.'

'It is enough,' Henry replied with a smile. 'Please instruct Lovell to take a moderate force across to Guines, and bring Tyrrell back here on a charge of treason. Then see to the arrest of Sir John Wyndham, and — for good measure — Suffolk's brother William, and Lord William Courtenay. They are all to be held in the Tower for treason. Let me know when they are secure, and I will make arrangements for my interrogators to seek further knowledge from Tyrrell of the murders of the royal princes. This could well prove a double advantage.'

Daubeney was much relieved to be bowing from the presence with no accusation against himself, but shuddered when he contemplated the treatment that was to be handed out to Tyrrell. A week later, he was back in his capacity as Constable of the Tower, looking nervous and carrying a sealed document.

'Your Majesty, your Chief Interrogator bid me hand you this in person. As you can see, the seal is unbroken.'

'As it should be, Daubeney, as it should be,' Henry muttered as he broke the seal, read the contents, and allowed himself a smile. 'It would seem that in exchange for a slight increase in height, Sir James Tyrrell confesses not only to assisting Suffolk in his treasonous flight from England, but also the murder of the royal princes. Take this document to Foxe, and have one of his clerks copy its contents, that my subjects may no longer accuse me, while in their cups, of having been responsible for the deaths that cleared my path to the throne, as of course they did Gloucester's.'

'Yes, Your Majesty,' Daubeney replied, slightly pale in the face.

Henry held up a hand to delay him. 'Before you go, what of the other three?'

'Wyndham confesses to having given Suffolk a letter of safe passage addressed to Tyrrell, but claims that he was acting simply out of sympathy for a friend escaping a serious criminal charge for which he might be hanged, and had no treasonous intent. The other two claim no involvement in the matter other than their kinship with Suffolk.'

'William de la Pole and William Courtney are to be held in the Tower until I decide otherwise, and their estates are forfeit, as are Suffolk's,' Henry commanded. 'As for Tyrrell and Wyndham, they are to be placed on trial for treason before the Star Chamber, and then executed in full public view at Tyburn — when they are found guilty.'

Three months later, Henry took a careful look at the sleek face of the young priest who had been brought into the Privy Chamber by Foxe.

'Father Wolsey, I am much pleased with your work,' he announced.

The clergyman bowed his head graciously in thanks, adding, 'I am most grateful to Your Majesty for the opportunity to visit such foreign parts at so young an age. As I reported to my Lord Bishop of Winchester, Castile would seem to prefer the prospect of a change of ruler, and is happy to be welcoming back one of its own princesses.'

'She is not there yet,' Henry reminded him, 'but she would seem to have a better prospect of becoming a queen than her younger sister, the way Prince Henry carries on.'

'He is a young man, Your Majesty, but no doubt in the fullness of time he will grow to have the same Stately wisdom as his father.'

Henry smiled at the unashamed flattery, then recalled the other matter. 'And did you find me a suitable bride in Italy?'

Wolsey bowed again, and the candlelight flickered off his highly polished tonsure.

'As a man of God, I am clearly no judge of woman-flesh, Your Majesty, and there was only one who came close to the description I was given regarding Your Majesty's preference. However...'

'Who is she, and what does "however" import?' Henry demanded.

Wolsey bowed yet again. 'She is Joanna, the Dowager Queen of Naples, Your Majesty. She is most comely in appearance, is not yet forty, and is the widow of Ferdinand 2nd of that kingdom. She is also the niece of King Ferdinand of Aragon, so that marriage to her might serve to smooth Your Majesty's relationship with Spain. However, her jointure is confiscated, so there would be no dowry.'

Henry smiled. 'You were well instructed, and it is as if you can read my mind. Do you read consciences as well?'

'It has been my good fortune never to have to take confession from a man with an impenetrable conscience, Your Majesty.'

'Would you like to?'

Wolsey looked puzzled for a moment, until Henry made his meaning clear.

'I am in need of a new chaplain, Thomas. Would you be prepared to hear the confessions of an old man with *much* on his conscience?'

'It would certainly make a change, Your Majesty,' Wolsey oozed, 'and to be in Your Majesty's service would be a deep honour in itself.'

'I hope your penances are as easy to swallow as your honeyed words,' Henry laughed. 'Forget the matter of the Queen of Naples. I am not so desperate to climb on top of a woman that I would do so without a dowry. Foxe here will no doubt find some dusty priory where my current chaplain can eke out his days peering over the scriptures, and then you may take over his offices. I hear a private Mass daily, in my chambers, and I also make confession every week, on Fridays, otherwise you will only be required when I perceive my mortal soul to be in danger, which is not often. I am sure we will be able to use your silver tongue on other diplomatic missions while my soul takes a holiday.'

XIII

Early in 1505, Henry had another need for Wolsey's services. Ferdinand of Aragon had married Germaine de Foix, the niece of Louis XII of France, and rumour had it that he had done so not only in order to thwart the ambitions of his son-in-law Philip of Burgundy regarding the throne of Castile, but in order to demonstrate to Henry that Spain was capable of forming alliances with England's old enemy. The Scots King James had seen his opportunity to tighten the net by renewing the Auld Alliance with France that he had solemnly sworn not to do as part of his marriage vows with Margaret, but it came to Henry's ears that two Scottish noblemen had travelled south through England in disguise on their way to Paris, where they announced James's willingness to resume the anti-England pact. They were intercepted on their return journey and held for some time as honoured detainees in London while Wolsey convinced them of the error of their ways, then escorted them back over the border to perform the same service for King James.

Henry also sent a further public message to the world, and put Ferdinand in his place, by prevailing upon a bemused Prince Henry, now Prince of Wales, to publicly renounce his betrothal to Katherine, on the ground that he had been below the age of consent when first talked into it. If the young prince was confused, Katherine was heartbroken, and redoubled her pleas to her father to remove her from this terrible country where she was being held in virtual imprisonment. Ferdinand was insisting on the return of her entire dowry before he would accept that the marriage was off, and Henry's firm response was that Ferdinand would not get back a single escudo, but might see his daughter again when Henry had thought more about her future.

In 1506, Henry was staring grumpily out of his chamber window at the rain that was remorselessly battering the mullioned windows of Richmond Palace, his bare foot raised on a footstool while his physician prodded and poked at Henry's feet and ankles, despite his winces, howls of pain and protests at the indignities being inflicted on him. Finally the physician put down his eyeglass and pronounced his verdict.

'It is gout, Your Majesty.'

'It is certainly painful, and it does little for my comfort when you prod and poke me like a gypsy horse trader with a brood mare,' Henry complained. 'How may it be cured? Not leeches again, I hope?'

'Indeed not, Your Majesty,' the physician assured him. 'It is simply a matter of taking less wine and red meat.'

'How much less?'

'Strictly speaking, none at all,' was the nervous reply.

Henry snorted, and was about to tell the physician where he could insert one of his leeches when he became aware of a loud argument at the chamber door, which burst open to admit a breathless Daubeney.

'Forgive me for entering unannounced Your Majesty, particularly since they advised me that you were not fully dressed, but the matter is urgent.'

'It is only my foot that is naked,' Henry assured him, as he lowered it from the footstool, 'and there was a time when subjects would regard it a blessing to kiss the royal foot. What is so urgent, pray?'

'Your Majesty, the Archduke Philip of the Netherlands has landed at Weymouth.'

'He is invading England, in *this* weather?'

'No, Your Majesty — he is shipwrecked. It seems he was sailing to Castile with his wife the Queen when a storm in the Channel blew them onto rocks at Melcombe Regis. They made their plight known to the warden of the castle, and he had them conveyed to a nearby monastery. Their ship is quite destroyed, and they seek sanctuary until it may be repaired.'

Henry sat thinking for a long moment, his smile growing wider the more he thought about this gift from the gods. Eventually he gave his orders. 'Take a company of Yeomen Guards and escort our royal visitors to Windsor Palace. But before you leave, search out the Prince Henry, and have him attend me. In this weather, even *he* should have remained indoors — you will no doubt find him in the tennis room.'

Daubeney bowed out, and Henry climbed back into his hose while chuckling loudly. The usher announced the entry of Prince Henry, and a tall, muscular young man with a mop of red hair plastered in sweat walked in with a sour expression.

'I was beating Melford hands down, and he is said to be the best tennis player at Court. I hope this is important.'

'It is *always* important when your King summons you into his presence,' Henry snapped back. 'Take a cup of wine to sweeten your mood, and listen carefully to my instructions. You are to take yourself and your grandmother, without delay, to Windsor Palace, and prepare it for a royal reception. Fate has landed the Archduke Philip and his wife Joanna of Castile into our hands, and they are to be royally entertained without realising that they are also our prisoners. Once at Windsor, your grandmother will be able to discern what is required, and the Steward is to acquire all he needs — inform him that there is

230

to be no expense spared. In a few days, Daubeney will arrive with our guests, and they are to be received by you — as my representative — with all due honour as befits their status. The royal couple may be given the Royal Apartments, and you will occupy the Curfew Tower, along with your grandmother. I shall follow in due course with the Lady Katherine.'

'Why are you not seeing to all these matters yourself?'

Henry sighed. 'There are several reasons for that, not the least of which is that it is well time that you demonstrated to the world that you have all the grace and status of a king, which you will be ere long, if this damned cough brought on by the foul winter does not ease. But also, it suits me greatly to make them wait upon my arrival, in order to demonstrate that they are there at my pleasure, and subject to my whim. Thirdly, these old feet of mine require that I hobble like some wounded knight from a battlefield, and it would not look good for the Archduke of the Netherlands to be greeted on arrival by some war veteran supported by sticks. In the world of statecraft appearances are everything, and I do not wish it worded around the princes of Europe that England is governed by an old man who can barely stand.'

The expenditure of breath required for all these instructions brought on a fit of coughing, and the young prince stood politely waiting for it to subside before asking his next question.

'Why the Lady Katherine?'

Henry sighed again. 'Because the Queen Consort of the Netherlands, now the Queen of Castile, is Katherine's older sister Joanna. Now that my own Queen — your mother — is dead, and you are to be the host of this meeting of crowns, it is fitting that Katherine play the part of hostess.'

'But we are no longer betrothed,' Prince Henry objected.

The colour began to rise in Henry's face, and again he gave way to a fit of coughing, before he replied. 'I am not asking you to bed her, simply let her play the genial host by your side. It will serve to remind her father that, contrary to what she insists in her letters to him, she is not my prisoner. Now, if there are no more questions, lose no time in riding to Windsor once this dreadful weather eases. You should enjoy wearing out a horse on the journey, at least.'

The young prince bowed out, and Henry hobbled over to where he had left his sticks, then lurched across to the wine decanter, pouring himself a generous measure.

'To Hell with all physicians,' he muttered, as he downed a large mouthful, only to spit most of it out as another fit of coughing overtook him.

XIV

A thousand candles fluttered in the draught as they burned brightly in the candelabras suspended from the roof of the Great Hall of Windsor Palace. Beneath them could be heard the excited murmuring of a hundred guests at the banquet to welcome the Archduke Philip and his wife Joanna to the safety of England after their perilous attempt to sail down the Channel to Castile. Prince Henry sat, as usual, at one of the lower tables with a group of young knights who were wearing the Tudor Rose livery that also marked them out as royal grooms when they were not engaged in more martial duties, and they were already becoming quite boisterous. King Henry had made a tactful, limping, entry to the top table much earlier in the proceedings, and his young son would be required to join him there once the food was carried in. In the meantime, King Henry sat with his mother, talking fitfully about her future plans for the young prince's education. On her other side sat Philip of the Netherlands, who occasionally distracted her from her conversation with her son with his hesitant attempts to converse with her in English.

Several seats further down sat Katherine of Aragon, alongside her sister Joanna, whose husband Philip was on Joanna's other side. At the centre of the table, Margaret had grown tired of attempting to maintain a conversation with Philip, and during the distraction caused by the delivery of the first meat course she turned back to Henry with a whisper.

'How long will these heathens be our guests?'

'Until I choose to release them,' Henry smirked. 'I gave orders that their vessel is to be repaired at my gracious expense in the royal dockyard at Portsmouth, where of course I can detain it for as long as I wish. I have already sent Wolsey to explain to Ferdinand of Castile — as he wishes to remain — that I have his son-in-law in luxurious captivity for as long as it suits me. This will obviously buy Ferdinand the time to strengthen his position in Castile, and he will remain indebted to me. By three hundred thousand Spanish Escudos, to be precise, which is what I calculate the balance of Katherine's dowry to be worth.'

'And Katherine herself? She is a gracious hostess, and a girl of considerable piety and learning.'

'Then she is hardly a suitable match for Hal,' Henry muttered, as he leaned forward towards his wine cup, then began to cough.

'This winter chill has been upon you since well before Christmas,' Margaret observed, concern in her voice. 'Have you consulted your physician?'

'That damned fool is only fit for sticking leeches on your arm,' Henry replied between coughs. 'His only remedy for the soreness in my legs and feet is to foreswear wine and red meat,' he added, as he carved himself a generous slice from the venison in the centre of the table.

His mother tutted. 'And you clearly ignore even *that* advice, although I am bound to comment that you seem thinner of late.'

'Only because others around me are getting fat at my expense,' Henry growled, 'yourself excepted, of course.'

During the second month of their enforced stay in England, the entire Court having re-established itself back at Richmond, Philip of Burgundy requested an audience with Henry. He was received in the Privy Chamber, and was a little surprised to find a priest sitting quietly in the corner.

'May I introduce Father Thomas Wolsey, my royal chaplain?' Henry offered, as he rose uncertainly to his feet with the aid of a stick that now remained constantly at the side of any chair he was occupying. 'He is recently returned from a pilgrimage to Spain.'

'My wife's father is well?' Philip enquired coldly.

Wolsey smiled unctuously. 'Most well. He sends his best regards, and looks forward to welcoming his daughter back to her home.'

'That is why I must speak with you, Henry,' Philip said, as he turned back from addressing Wolsey. 'When is my ship ready?'

'You wish to leave us so soon?' Henry replied with a cold smile. 'In truth, the vessel will be seaworthy within a week, but we must take this opportunity to adjust our trade agreement.'

'Agreement?' Philip echoed.

'The *Intercursus Magnus*, which was signed some years ago with your father,' Henry reminded him. 'It is a treaty that has served England well, but now we find that — with conditions such as they are in Europe — it works to our disadvantage.'

'I know no treaty,' Philip insisted.

'That is why I had Wolsey attend us,' Henry explained. 'He has a copy of it with him, and being a man of the cloth he will be able to assist us through it. Thomas, if you would be so good as to hand His Majesty your copy?'

Wolsey rose from his chair in the corner, walked across the embroidered carpet that hid the wooden joists of the upper chamber, and handed Philip a large vellum roll.

Philip looked down at it disconsolately. 'It is in a language I know not.'

'Legal Latin,' Wolsey advised him with an ingratiating smile that was almost a smirk. 'I can translate if you wish.'

Philip shook his head, then looked suspiciously back at Henry. 'How is it not good for England?'

'Wolsey will explain,' Henry answered.

For the next ten minutes, Wolsey smoothly revealed the intricacies of foreign exchange rates, the fluctuating nature of customs duties according to national need, the vagaries of the European cloth market, and those aspects of the original agreement that had recently proved unfavourable to England. All of which would have been a magnificent tour de force if delivered to a class of students at Oxford, but was almost meaningless to Philip with his imperfect grasp of English. He shook his head several times, then looked helplessly at Henry.

'And if I sign a new piece of paper — one that pleases you more — you will release my ship?'

'It is not being impounded,' Henry assured him. 'But certainly, if we had no further unfinished business to delay your departure, I could have you and your party safely escorted back to Portsmouth by the end of this week.'

'When can I be given this paper to sign? It will take time to write, yes?'

Henry could barely contain the triumphant smirk that threatened to take command of his face. 'For your convenience, Wolsey has drafted a copy of our new proposal. Please hand it to him, Thomas.'

As Philip was shown out of the chamber, Henry began to laugh out loud, then a fit of coughing overtook him, and as Wolsey returned to the chamber, his own self-satisfied grin became a look of concern as he rushed to where Henry sat slumped, gasping for breath, and offered to summon a physician.

'Damn the physician, Wolsey! It will pass — and if it does not, then you may pray for my soul.'

The new agreement that Philip had been all but forced to sign — whose terms were so unfavourable to Flemish merchants that it was labelled the *Intercursus Malus* — was never formally adopted by The Netherlands, but Henry had made his point, and had bought off Ferdinand of Aragon for a few more months by humiliating Philip in the eyes of Europe. Not content with that, Wolsey had secretly made Henry aware that while Philip was pursuing his ambitions in Spain, he had left behind his sister Margaret to rule the Low Countries in his absence. The Archduchess Margaret was a woman in her mid-twenties, not unbecoming in appearance, who was twice widowed, was the daughter of Emperor Maximilian, and most recently the widow of the Duke of Savoy. Before Philip and Joanna were allowed to set sail for their much-delayed return to Castile, the opening round of negotiations had begun for a possible marriage between Margaret and Henry, which came to nothing after Philip died in September of 1506, only three months after his arrival in Castile.

Undaunted, Henry could now see another way of acquiring Castilian allies while at the same time maintaining a fruitful alliance with Ferdinand of Aragon. Although barely able to walk more than a hundred yards without being halted by either a shortage of breath or pains in his lower extremities, Henry still clearly thought of himself as an attractive bridegroom, if only because of his English crown, and he put his latest idea to Foxe and Wolsey as they sat together in his privy chamber in November of that year.

Wolsey and Foxe exchanged uncomfortable glances, and each urged the other, with eye gestures, to explain. Eventually it was Foxe who spoke.

'Thomas was most recently in Castile, Your Majesty, representing you at Philip's funeral.'

'Well, Thomas?' Henry demanded. 'Why should I not marry Joanna of Castile? From memory, she is quite pleasant on the eye.'

Wolsey coughed politely and looked down at the floor. 'She is mad, Your Majesty.'

'How — mad?' Henry shouted. 'She was here at Court not a year since, and seemed well in command of her wits.'

'Indeed, Your Majesty,' Wolsey conceded, 'but even while I was in the Low Countries, long ere she was at Court here, there were tales of her wild rages, and her fits of ungovernable temper when she believed her husband Philip to have been cavorting with other women.'

'So she is spirited, and insists on marital fidelity — what of it?'

There was another embarrassed silence, and this time Foxe broke it.

'Her husband died, as you know, Your Majesty, some two months ago, yet there are reports that she is progressing through Castile with his body still in its casket, and insists, from time to time, on opening it to kiss him goodnight.'

Henry shuddered, and dry-retched in an action that brought on more coughing. When it subsided, he looked at both men intensely.

'Is there hope that she will recover from this obsession?'

'I am no physician, Your Majesty,' Foxe replied tactfully, 'but obviously, were she given another person upon whom to shower her devotion — someone living, that is...'

'A good point,' Henry confirmed. 'And presumably, while she may have a sickness of the head, this would not affect the part between her legs, and she may still bear children?'

'I am no physician, Your Majesty,' Foxe repeated, while Wolsey suppressed a snigger, and tried to look embarrassed at the coarseness of the conversation.

The next two years were a flurry of diplomatic activity on both sides of the Channel, with every European monarch seeking to out-negotiate the others by means of marriage treaties. Henry kept up his overtures for the hand of Joanna of Castile while not having fully abandoned his marriage plans for Margaret of Savoy, to whom he made approaches via her father, the Emperor Maximilian. He also kept the pressure on Ferdinand by offering Princess Mary in marriage to Charles, son of the late Philip of Castile, and still in his minority. If it occurred to Henry that by marrying Joanna while marrying Mary off to her son, he would become Mary's father-in-law in addition to being her natural father, it did not seem to dampen his enthusiasm for such schemes, which kept Wolsey in the Channel more often than some professional fishermen.

Seemingly unfatigued, Henry also, for a brief while, toyed with the concept of marrying off Prince Henry to a princess of Angouleme, if only to show Ferdinand that he was not the only one who could arrange French marriages. He also let it be believed that Wolsey was secretly engaged in discussions with Emperor Maximilian regarding how the latter might best usurp the Castilian throne in the name of his grandson Charles. It wasn't true, but most people believed it.

When Ferdinand finally realised that it was all about the money, he buckled in and instructed his Ambassador to England to hand over the remainder of Katherine's dowry, without any further discussion regarding the repayment of the first instalment. While most monarchs would have graciously accepted this very public admission of defeat, accompanied by a very substantial financial olive branch, Henry opted to rub Ferdinand's nose in it by insisting that the whole of the balance be paid in coin, rather than plate and jewellery, and that Ferdinand ratify the treaty under which it was proposed that Princess Mary would marry Charles, heir-apparent to the very Castile that Ferdinand had been desperately trying to retain.

However, all this energetic diplomacy — that ensured that Wolsey was rarely either required or available to hear the weekly royal confession, and had long since delegated daily Mass duties to his own personal confessor, Thomas Larke — had taken its toll on a King who was almost out of control, and had little awareness of how internal matters were being handled.

XV

On the second Tuesday of March, 1509, the Grooms of the Privy Chamber were the first to notice that something was not quite right. Henry had not, as he usually did, limped from his chamber at daylight, demanding his breakfast. Of late, that breakfast had been scanty enough, since the King seemed to have lost the robust appetite of his younger years and was growing thinner by the week. But he would still appear at the door of his Privy Chamber demanding wine and a little bread, and when he failed to do so that morning, the Groom of the Stool knocked gently, and then harder, on the bedchamber door. When there was still no reply, he cautiously poked his head round the door and peered in.

Henry appeared to still be asleep, except that instead of the customary hearty snoring that was something of a joke among the Grooms of the Chamber, he sounded to be whimpering, while at the same time choking. The groom tiptoed cautiously towards the bed, then recoiled in horror when he spotted the copious amounts of blood on the white pillow. Horrified, he scuttled from the chamber and called for the Royal Physician.

Henry opened his eyes in time to see the physician fiddling in his bag. He attempted to raise himself on one elbow, then began coughing and spewing blood in all directions.

'No leeches,' he commanded in a rasping voice that sounded more like a death rattle. 'I have lost enough blood these past few weeks, and I cannot seem to stem this shivering. What ails me, for God's sake?'

The physician sat on the side of the bed, opened Henry's mouth and looked in. There was a dense white growth of some sort deep in his throat, and the physician instinctively drew back as he gave his confident diagnosis.

'Your Majesty is suffering from what we physicians call "phthysis". Some call it "scrofula", and it is easily passed from person to person. In certain countries of Europe, some monarchs are attributed with the power to cure it in others, simply by laying hands on the afflicted person.'

'So I may cure *myself* of it?'

The physician shook his head gravely. 'Unfortunately, Your Majesty, I have not heard of such a case. But we may build Your Majesty's constitution back up with suitable medications, and the shivering caused by the fever may be assuaged with more bedcovers. I will order all this immediately.'

'How many have died of this sickness?' Henry asked fearfully.

'Everyone, in my experience,' the physician answered truthfully. 'Phthysis is a common cause of death, and is no respecter of rank, rich or poor. We can only make Your Majesty more comfortable while the disease takes its course.'

Henry groaned, and sank back on the new, clean, pillow that the physician had ordered from the groom. The next time he opened his eyes, Wolsey was seated by the bed, clutching a bible and praying.

'Shall I go to Hell, Thomas?' Henry enquired fearfully.

'Most assuredly not, Your Majesty,' Wolsey advised him. 'I have never known a man who gave so much to charity, or to God. Apart from your magnificent new chapel, there is your hospital at Savoy, your alms houses in Shoreditch, your many endowments to monastic houses, the new college at Cambridge...'

'Enough,' Henry commanded with a raised hand, before breaking into a fresh bout of coughing. Wolsey turned his face with a shudder as more blood and pus soiled the royal pillow.

When he had finished coughing, Henry turned his head to look once more at his faithful cleric.

'Since I can hardly sin further while I lie here, would now be a good time for you to hear my last confession?' he asked.

Wolsey shook his head. 'It would not *be* your last, Your Majesty, since your physician assures me that your final days do not yet approach. However, you must prepare yourself for that journey that we must all one day take.'

'No-one must know that I am laid low,' Henry insisted. 'A wounded monarch is a weak monarch, and there are many princes of Europe who would seek to profit by my malady. The affairs of State must continue, and Foxe must lead the Council as if this were but a temporary late winter chill.'

'It shall be done, Your Majesty,' Wolsey assured him. 'In fact, he and I have already begun to organise matters in a way we know would be of satisfaction to you, and there is no cause for Your Majesty to concern yourself in that regard.'

'I am glad I found you, Thomas,' Henry smiled. 'No doubt my mother will insist on organising the realm when I am gone, but may I ask that you look further after the interests of the Prince Henry, as well as tutoring him in your own excellent way? He is but a youth of seventeen, and little comprehends what awaits him when he succeeds to the throne. He will be in sore need of wisdom such as yours.'

'It will be a pleasure, Your Majesty, and you may rest assured that I would wish nothing more than to serve Henry VIII as well as I hope I have served his father. Now, your physician has ordered that you do not expose yourself to any anxiety or great passion, but that you rest. I shall report to you from time to time on affairs of State.'

'Thank you, Thomas,' Henry smiled up at him, then turned his head to submit to another bout of retching and wheezing. Wolsey crossed himself as he moved swiftly towards the chamber door, and invoked a blessing from the saints. Not for Henry, but for himself.

March turned into April, and while the crocuses and daffodils in the gardens of the royal palaces gaily announced the coming of a new summer, there was an increasing winter chill in the royal bedchamber that Henry had not left for six weeks. He grew steadily weaker, despite every remedy that a team of physicians tried, sometimes arguing among themselves in their time-honoured tradition. Wolsey came and went, but by the end of the second week of April he realised that either Henry was not able to take in what he was being told, or was too weak to respond with further instructions. The King had been shriven, and it was only a matter of days. Then it became a matter of hours.

Late in the afternoon of 21st April, there were over a dozen around the royal death bed, some of them physicians, some of them senior officers of State, and some of them family. After a tearful Princess Mary had been led from the room by her stern-faced grandmother, this left only Prince Henry, who stood looking fearfully down at his father, and for the first time in his life staring mortality in the face. He looked across at Wolsey, who gestured with his eyes that they should withdraw, and as they stood together in the corridor outside, Wolsey placed a brotherly hand on Prince Henry's shoulder and muttered something in Latin that sounded to Henry like an absolution of some sort. Then Wolsey looked kindly into the young prince's eyes.

'Your father has but hours left in this world, Hal, but some time ago he earnestly requested that I look after your interests, and that of the nation that you will soon rule. I do so gladly, and with a heart humbled to have been granted such an honour and privilege.'

'You may dispense with the honeyed words, Thomas,' Prince Henry assured him. 'I am well aware of how well you served my father, and I hope — as no doubt do you — that you will continue to serve me. What would you advise at this time?'

Wolsey smiled encouragingly, and jerked his head towards the chamber door.

'When your father's soul passes, I will endeavour to persuade those in the chamber to delay news of his passing for several days. This will buy you enough time to secure your own position.'

'There are none with a better claim to the throne than mine, surely?'

'Indeed not, Hal,' Wolsey assured him, 'but of late your father's rule has proved unpopular. There is much resentment of those financial policies that have delivered you a Chamber far richer than it once was, and there is a risk of a mob uprising when one Tudor succeeds another, unless the people can be convinced that yours will be a different reign.'

'If I judge you aright, you already have a solution?'

'Indeed, Your Majesty — if I may presume by calling you that already. There is a need for others to take the blame for what in truth were your father's policies. I believe that the vulgar term for such persons is "scapegoat". At present, it is felt by those who have suffered the most that the persons responsible are Sir Edmund Dudley and Sir Richard Empson.

Your first act as King must be to have these men arrested on charges of treason and conveyed, very publicly, to the Tower. I would also respectfully suggest that you yourself take up immediate residence in the Tower, since not only may it be easily defended against any London mob, but it is also the place where tradition requires that a monarch reside prior to their coronation.'

The chamber door opened, and a groom's head appeared round it.

'The time has come, sirs,' he advised them, and the two men made their way back to the deathbed, Prince Henry thanking Wolsey profusely for his wise advice, and assuring him that his days as a royal confidante were by no means over.

Four days later, in the chapel he had created, Henry VII of England was laid to rest at the side of Elizabeth his queen. Sometime after that an inscription was carved around their memorial plinth, whose words may still be read through a narrow grille that now surrounds the joint memorial. It reads:

'Here is situated Henry VII, the glory of all the Kings who lived in his time by reason of his intellect, his riches, and the fame of his exploits, to which were added the gifts of bountiful nature, a distinguished brow, an august face, an heroic stature. Joined to him his sweet wife was very pretty, chaste and fruitful. They were parents happy in their offspring, to whom, land of England, you owe Henry VIII.'

A NOTE TO THE READER

Dear Reader,

Thank you for taking the time to read this first novel in my Tudor series, and I hope it lived up to your expectations. The Tudor era in English history has been one of the most popular with novelists over the years, and the one most familiar to those of us who remember our History classes at school. But what we were taught was very patchy, and further research rewards us with new knowledge and insights into this most significant period in our nation's history.

The drama of the reign of Henry VII is no exception. Ask the average school student what they know about the first Tudor, and they will reply along the lines that he was the father of Henry VIII, and the man who defeated Richard III at the Battle of Bosworth. The sad fact is that while those monarchs who reigned before and after him suffered from bad press ('fake news', to employ the current idiom), Henry Tudor, Earl of Richmond, suffered from no press at all. But his life was just as dramatic — romantic in places — and his twenty-four year reign marked the birth of an England that would progress to be one of the most powerful nations on earth.

Prior to Bosworth, England was at the mercy of powerful barons who were the heavily armed equivalent of our modern crime gangs. And the King was as much at their mercy as the common folk, relying on this faction or that to keep him in power. Losing the support of a noble who could put thousands of seasoned fighters onto the battlefield meant disaster, and the Wars of the Roses could not have been waged for so long without power brokers such as Richard Neville, Earl of

Warwick, who was responsible for the confusing switches between their occupations of the throne by Henry VI (Lancastrian) and Edward IV (Yorkist) that earned him the soubriquet 'Warwick the Kingmaker'.

Henry Tudor was no muscular warrior, but after almost thirty years on the touchline of Courtly life he'd come to appreciate that there were other ways of ruling a nation, and he took the crown of England with two priorities. First of all, he had to instigate stern financial measures that would rescue a Treasury that was all but bankrupt; secondly he needed to suppress the power of the warlords whose marauding depredations had left the English countryside littered with corpses.

Modern England began to take shape as he implemented strategies to achieve both ambitions. First and foremost was the need to appoint, as his closest advisers, not the latest scion of the 'old families' that had dominated Medieval life, but men with actual ability who would owe their preferment to him personally, and would serve him loyally in return for their promotion from the ranks of the lowly. During Henry's reign the warriors of steel would be replaced around the Great Council table by men with inky fingers who knew all about the balancing of account ledgers and the management of international trade.

By the end of his reign, England was a trading nation served by diplomats and ambassadors of great ability and unswerving loyalty who owed everything to Henry Tudor. When the time came to hand over the throne to his second son Henry, the nation was rich, at peace, and strong enough to negotiate treaties with its nearest potential rivals, France and Spain.

Hence why his reign should never be undervalued, even by historians. He was, at one and the same time, the last monarch of the Middle Ages, and the first ruler of modern England, a stern but able ruler who could command men of great ability from humble origins. The old order was at an end, but they took a long time to appreciate that, and bellicose warhorses like the Howard patriarchs needed constant suppression. These men who saw political power as their birth right were still causing trouble during the reign of Henry's grand-daughter Elizabeth, and they resented upstart newcomers such as Wolsey, the son of an Ipswich butcher, and Cromwell, the son of a Putney blacksmith.

It's therefore appropriate that the next novel in the series — *The King's Commoner* — has, as its central character, the butcher's son who rose spectacularly from his lowly beginnings to become Lord Chancellor of England, Archbishop of York, and Papal Legate, before crashing back to earth when he finally failed the man who had raised him so high. Cardinal Thomas Wolsey deserves his rightful place in the century-long account of this intriguing and formative period of English history.

As ever, I look forward to receiving feedback from you, whether in the form of a review on **Amazon** or **Goodreads**. Or, of course, you can try the more personal approach on my website, and my Facebook page: **DavidFieldAuthor**.

Happy reading!

David

davidfieldauthor.com

Sapere Books is an exciting new publisher of brilliant fiction and popular history.

To find out more about our latest releases and our monthly bargain books visit our website:
saperebooks.com

Printed in Great Britain
by Amazon

78035389R00144